Selling Christmas

Selling Christmas

angelina goode

Beach Blanket Publishing

1732 Aviation Blvd., Suite 423

Redondo Beach, CA 90278

www.beachblanketpublishing.com

Printed in the United States of America

Publisher's Note: This is a work of fiction. Names, characters, businesses, places, events and incidents are either the products of the author's imagination or used in a fictitious manner. Any resemblance to actual persons, living or dead, or actual events is purely coincidental.

Cover designed and formatting by Damonza

Selling Christmas/ Angelina Goode

First Edition

ISBN 978-0-9961769-2-7 (e-book)

ISBN 978-0-9961769-3-4 (paperback)

*To Mom and Dad
and their Christmas spirit*

1

Caroline

The gravel crunched under the tires as Caroline's car made its way up the long drive. As she reached the crest of the tree-topped hill, the driveway made a sharp turn to the right, then opened up to a small grassy field with an old but clean wooden house sitting squarely in the center of it. She pulled her car up to the side of the house and turned off the ignition. As she opened the door and swept her scarf around her neck, the cold air reddened her cheeks. She shivered.

The small porch that led to the front door was bare but for a pile of firewood. Caroline shook her head. Curb appeal was always important when trying to sell a home, even if the curb was a mile from the front door. First impressions count, and this curb was lacking appeal. She turned the key in the lock, and as she pushed the door open, she was hit with a gush of warm air filled with the scents of gingerbread and pine cones. She smiled. This was more like it. She made her way through the house, smoothing the bedspreads and tidying pillows on chairs.

As she straightened the table setting, there was a quiet knock at the front door. She ran her hands down her sides and put her friendliest smile on, then headed for the door.

"Come in, Dave and Sandra," she said as she swung open the door. Her clients entered. "Let me take your coats." She hung them on the hooks just inside the foyer, hoping it would help them envision living there.

"Caroline." Sandra's hands flew to her mouth. "It's adorable."

"Wait until you see the kitchen," she added, then held her hand out to the side, encouraging them to explore. Caroline followed them through the kitchen, emphasizing the retro appliances, and out the back door to a large patio overlooking an expansive yard with a peaceful brook running along the side.

When they re-entered the house and passed through the living room, Sandra cuddled her growing belly in her hands and stopped, staring at the quaint space. "The piano would fit perfectly right there." She pointed to the wall on the right.

"A Christmas tree would be really lovely over there." Caroline pointed to a corner between the fireplace and a wall with a large, picturesque window.

Dave stepped in closer to Sandra and put an arm around her. "I can see us singing carols on Christmas Eve."

She leaned in and whispered something back to Dave.

"I'm going to give you a few minutes to finish looking around and talk privately." Caroline headed to the kitchen. She took a gingerbread cookie from the table and was about to take a bite when she realized it was in the shape of an elf. She giggled, then bit off his head.

She passed the time staring out the window, appreciating the lush evergreen trees and watching the robins flit from one tree to another.

"Caroline." Dave stepped into the kitchen. "We'd like to put a bid on the house. It's exactly what we're looking for."

She smiled. "Of course. I have the paperwork in my bag."

As Dave and Sandra signed the house bid, Caroline glanced at her watch. It would only take her fifteen minutes to wind her way back down the drive, up the highway, and into town where she would meet Lauren for dinner. She waved goodbye as they drove off, then she locked up the house, heading on her way.

❊

The hostess that greeted Caroline was dressed as an elf, pointy shoes and ears and all. She led Caroline to Lauren, who sat in a dim alcove illuminated by lights muted with Santa hats. A mug in the shape of a Santa boot sat on the table in front of her. Caroline tossed her coat on the booth and rolled her eyes at Lauren. "You chose this place on purpose, didn't you?" She gestured at the decor around them.

"For someone that loves to celebrate the spirit of Christmas, you sure don't like all the decorating that comes with it." Lauren took a sip from her mug.

Caroline giggled. "You know I love Christmas. But all this is too much. It's not what Christmas is about. It's supposed to be about giving and kindness. *This* is all commercial."

"You could at least get a tree. That's not commercial."

"You know me. I don't decorate. I will provide a tree for someone else to help them feel the Christmas spirit, but—"

"No decorating. I know." Lauren rolled her eyes. "How did the house showing go?"

"Spectacular. It was right on the outskirts of town like they wanted. They put an offer on it, and I expect it to be accepted. Which is great because it will help fund my Christmas spirit. How was work for you today?"

She shrugged. "You know. It's heartbreaking to see so many

people without a place to go day after day. But I'm doing my best to change that. The police department has been very helpful this year. They've even assigned us a delegate to make sure we are helping all the people we can. Plus, the shelter's Christmas Eve dinner is going to be extra special this year."

"That's great. And that's the Christmas spirit I'm talking about."

"Speaking of that, I have just the thing you're thinking of. They are a great family that has fallen on some hard times and need a little help." Lauren pushed her curly hair behind her ears and dug in her purse. She pulled out a piece of white paper folded in half. "You know, it's really great that you do this."

Caroline took the paper from Lauren and tucked it into her purse, then plucked a menu from the end of the table. "I just want everyone to experience Christmas the way I did as a child. No one should miss out on that."

Lauren nodded. "What should we order? Should we start with an appetizer?"

❄

As Caroline drove home, passing through the neighborhoods with their lights strung and flickering in the night, she felt a tug at her heart. She slowed as she approached a home with wooden reindeer on the lawn and lit snowflakes hanging from the trees. Her dad used to love to hang snowflakes around their home. He always said he felt like it encouraged the snow on Christmas Eve.

A car behind her honked and she was brought back to the present. She waved an apology in the mirror and moved on, heading home for the night.

❄

Mary was hovering by the door when Caroline arrived at the office. Her hair was immaculately coifed, and she held a steaming mug of coffee that read *I Sell Houses—What's Your Superpower?*

"I heard the offer on the house yesterday was accepted. Good job."

Caroline's eyebrows raised. She should've checked her email before heading into the office this morning. "Thanks. I'm about to straighten out all the details now."

"Great. I also have some exciting news at the meeting this morning. Don't be late."

Caroline nodded and stopped at the coffee machine before going to her office. "Good morning, Sarah," she said to the office assistant, who was standing beside a large box with a long strand of tinsel wrapped in her arms.

"Hi, Caroline. Would you like me to decorate your office for you? You're the only one that hasn't done it yet."

"I think I'm okay."

Sarah's eyes fell. "Oh, okay."

Caroline paused. "Well, I guess you could maybe decorate the outside of my door. Would that work?"

Her eyes lit up. "Yes. I'd love to. I have just the thing." She pulled the rest of the tinsel out and found a large, bright-red bell.

Caroline took a sip of her coffee then disappeared into her office to call Sandra and Dave and tell them the good news. Sandra squealed when she heard, and Dave sounded as though he was getting choked up. "Do you think we can be in by Christmas?" he asked.

"Maybe. It's only about four weeks away, but I'll see what I can work out with the sellers."

Sarah knocked on the door just as Caroline was hanging up.

"The meeting is about to start," she said.

"Thanks." She grabbed her notebook and followed Sarah into the meeting room.

"Welcome everyone. We have a lot to discuss, so let's get started right away." Mary paced back and forth across the small room as she spoke. "This year, we have decided to partner with a local furniture store to do a fundraiser for Sweet River Children's Hospital."

Caroline turned her attention to the room. This was exactly the Christmas spirit that motivated her. Everyone looked to one another, nodding encouragement and smiling with delight. Mary stood, pleased, her hands folded in front of her, her shoulders back. Her short, straight bob swayed softly as she turned from one side of the room to the other to take in all the excitement.

"We are going to host a Christmas Tour of Homes featuring four of our properties that are currently for sale. Anderson's Furniture Store will provide the decor and we will do the decorating. I have put together a team of agents that have shown interest in decorating and have selected one person to be in charge of the team and decorating the locations."

Sarah raised her hand. "Is this the kind of tour where people buy tickets to visit the properties to see how we have decorated them for Christmas?"

"Yes," Mary said, nodding. "We get a weekend of heavy foot traffic into the homes we are selling while raising money for the children's hospital. It's a win-win deal."

Caroline gave a sigh of relief that she wouldn't have to help. It may be for a good cause, but she was clearly not the one for the job. She turned her focus to her notebook and started making a list of things she had to do for her clients.

"Caroline." Mary's voice was clear and direct.

Caroline sat up straighter in her seat.

"Caroline will be leading the decorating team. Sarah is handing each team member a packet detailing the homes that will be on the tour and the proposed rooms to decorate."

Caroline's jaw dropped. She lifted her index finger to protest, but Mary continued.

"Of course, if you find you'd like to decorate additional

rooms, that is at your discretion, Caroline. This is your project. You are in total control."

Caroline shook her head, still unable to find the words. She looked to Sarah, who had sat back down. "I'm honored to be on your team," Sarah whispered.

The rest of the meeting was a blur. Caroline tried her best to stay focused, but visions of tinsel and nutcrackers and tree ornaments the size of her head kept popping up in her mind. She tried to shake them free, but it seemed to only serve as encouragement. Her coworkers were encouraged, too. Before the meeting was over, she had already received eight emails from fellow agents and their ideas for the Home Tour.

As everyone exited the room, Caroline hung back, hopeful that she would get a moment alone with Mary. Surely, she would understand. She simply was not the one for the job.

When the last straggler had filled his plate with Santa-shaped sugar cookies from the snack table and made his way out, Caroline threw her shoulders back and approached her boss.

"Mary. I have some concerns about the Christmas Tour of Homes."

"Of course. I knew you would. But timing is not an issue. Three weeks is plenty of time to get the homes decorated."

"That's not it. I just…" She had to pick her words carefully. She didn't want her boss to think that she was refusing an important job.

No, she would do it happily, if she thought she was capable. "I'm not sure I'm the right person for this role."

"Nonsense. I spoke with Sandra and Dave this morning, and as soon as they told me they bought the house because you helped them picture what Christmas would look like there, I knew you were the one to lead the team." Mary gathered her paperwork and slid it into her briefcase. "You'd better get started. As I said, three weeks is plenty of time, but it will pass very quickly."

She gritted her teeth together, wishing she had never mentioned the Christmas tree last night. They had been so concerned about where to put a tree in the previous homes she had shown them, it seemed like the logical thing to do at the time.

Now she was in charge of decorating *four* homes? Her back stiffened at the thought of it. She swallowed hard, then nodded as she watched Mary leave the room.

Looked like she'd be decorating this Christmas after all.

2

Luke

Luke stood on the corner of the street and pulled his gloves from his pocket. It was getting colder by the minute. As he slipped them on, he wondered, did he pack Ella's mittens in her backpack today?

"Here you go. Coffee, black. Just like you like it, like oil." His partner, Andrea, puckered her mouth and squished her nose to show her distaste.

"It keeps me going. Don't mock it." He looked at his watch. Only three more hours on this shift and he could pick up Ella from the after-school care center.

"Been a slow day, huh." Andrea scanned the street around her, as if she were hoping for someone to jaywalk or commit some sort of infraction, just to keep her occupied. She was relatively new to the station, having transferred in from Chicago. Even the busiest days in

Sweet River, Oregon, didn't compare to what she was used to. "Not many people committing crime around here at Christmastime."

Luke let out a slow chuckle. "Nope. Too much Christmas cheer. You should try it."

Andrea shook her head.

A short, round man approached the two, his hands heavy with bags overflowing with tissue. "Good afternoon, Officer Miller."

"Hello, Doctor Hersh. Preparing for the holidays?" Luke tipped his hat to the man.

"Of course." He lifted his bags in gesture. "We are planning our annual Christmas caroling in a couple weeks. Will we be able to persuade you to join us this year?"

"Very kind of you to ask, but I'm not sure we're ready for that." His voice was quiet.

"I understand. Well, if you change your mind, you know the offer stands." He gave a small bow to Andrea and disappeared around the corner.

"You don't go Christmas caroling?"

Luke shook his head and hid his face in the coffee cup. After a long sip, he said, "Not my style."

"Hard to believe from the man that has a dancing Santa pin on his uniform." She looked up at him, curiosity beaming from her face.

"I'll do the decorating. For Ella. I want it to be special for her. I just haven't found that thing that makes me feel the Christmas spirit."

He knew Andrea had been told about his past. About the perfect life that he lost. She had never spoken about it to him before, but he knew she knew. He could tell by the way she looked at him.

She looked away and drank her coffee. "Looks like it might snow soon."

❅

Luke ran through the door at five minutes before six. Ella was sitting at a table making a Santa out of cotton balls and red construction paper. As soon as she saw him, she jumped up and ran into his arms.

He scooped her up and squeezed her. "I'm sorry I couldn't get here sooner."

"It's okay, Daddy. I know you were only trying to make the world a safer place."

He waved to the woman in charge then took Ella's backpack from a hook on the wall.

"I made us a Santa to hang up at home." One of Ella's front teeth was missing, and it always made Luke smile when he saw that little gap there.

"That's perfect because I think tonight you need to write your letter to Santa."

Ella's jaw dropped. "Great. I know just what I'm going to ask for."

Luke helped Ella put her jacket on. Now that it was dark, it was getting colder. But it also meant he could take the long way around town and drive through the neighborhood with all the fancy Christmas lights.

Once Ella was safely buckled into the car, they went off on their adventure. He took his time winding through the neighborhoods. She gasped at the lit-up snowmen and the Santas on roofs. She giggled when they drove by the house with Santa's feet sticking out of the chimney. When they came to a house with wooden reindeer and lit-up snowflakes hanging from trees, Ella pressed her face against the window.

"Do you think it's going to snow soon? Wouldn't it be great if we had a snow day tomorrow?" Ella asked.

The car in front of him had come to a stop. "It'll snow soon enough."

"Look how the moonlight makes the snowflakes sparkle. They look like real giant snowflakes."

The car in front of him was still not moving. He tapped on the horn.

The driver waved and moved forward.

Luke and Ella drove in silence, making their way down the festive streets until they came to their own road.

"Are you going to write your letter to Santa tonight, too?" Ella asked.

"Well, sweetheart, Daddy's don't write letters to Santa. He already gets enough letters from all the children that write to him."

"I'm sure he would understand if just one daddy wrote him a letter."

He pulled over and parked on the side of the road then went to help Ella out of the car. "What is it that you think I should ask Santa for?"

Ella put her finger to her chin. "Well, if only one daddy is allowed to write a letter, then I think you'd better ask for something big."

"Something big? Like… a tractor?" He took her backpack and held her hand as they walked up the stairs to their second-story apartment.

"No." She shook her head and thought for a moment. Luke unlocked and opened the door. "Like a house of our own."

He froze. She had never mentioned that she wanted to live in a house. They used to live in a house. But that was *before*.

"You want to live in a house?"

"Yes. With a chimney for Santa to come down. And a big yard for us to run around."

"That sounds pretty spectacular." Maybe it *was* time for them to find a home. He had been saving up for a while, and combined with what he got when they sold the last house, they could find exactly what they were looking for.

"But Daddy?" She looked up at him, concern darting through her brown eyes. She looked so much like her mom.

"What is it?" Luke asked, bending down.

"I still want my room to be right next to yours." She gave a big smile and leaned in, pecking him on the cheek. Then she ran off to her room.

✿

"Fluffy the Dog?" Andrea repeated.

"Yes. I can't find them anywhere. And it's on the top of her list. Right after a house."

"A house?" Andrea took a bite of her granola bar.

Luke waved his hand in dismissal.

"I've looked online and called every store within miles. Sold out everywhere. My only shot is the toy store on Louisiana Boulevard. They said they are getting a shipment in today at three and they expect to sell out within minutes."

"Why don't you get her a real dog?"

Luke glared at Andrea. She lifted her hands in defense. "It was just an idea. You don't need to go all grinch on me."

Luke rolled his eyes.

"Go change. I'll give you a ride. We can use the siren and get there faster." She laughed as she knew Luke would never approve of using the siren for personal purposes. He was the most upstanding man she'd ever met. She couldn't help but feel for him and his desire to make his little girl happy.

When Luke came back out of the station, Andrea had the car ready to go. He slid into the passenger seat and rubbed his chin. "You think I should get a house?"

Andrea didn't answer right away. Luke eyed her. It was a simple enough question. Maybe he shouldn't have asked. But she was his partner. She was supposed to know him better than anyone else. Even if she was new and had only been there for six months.

He thought back to the last house they lived in. *Before.* It had been perfect. A sweet one-story with a white picket fence. Rose bushes lined the sidewalk border and a swing hung from the maple tree out front. The living room was small but quaint—ideal for a family of three. It had been everything they had ever wanted. Look how that turned out.

"I think it would be nice for Ella to have a place she felt was her own." Andrea said it nonchalantly. She didn't even look at Luke.

Ella. She probably didn't even remember their house. She had been so young when it all happened. Andrea was right. Ella deserved to have a home of her own.

"She said she wanted a house with a chimney for Santa." He rubbed his chin again.

"She would love picking out the paint for her bedroom."

He couldn't help but smile. Ella was always so enthusiastic about everything. "Yeah. I think you're right. I may start looking around."

"If you're quick about it, you might even get in before Christmas."

They sped down the highway, Luke checking his watch every few minutes. He knew it was only a stuffed dog, but he would do anything to make Ella happy. She brought him so much happiness; he just wanted her to have the best life possible. If that meant standing in a long line waiting for a stuffed dog, then so be it.

Andrea pulled the car into the parking lot. "There doesn't seem to be a line."

"Good. Then this should be really quick." Before he stepped out of the car, he turned back to Andrea. "Please don't use the speaker to announce my arrival this time."

Andrea began laughing. "Come on. It was only once. And it was funny."

Luke shook his head slowly and left the car. He entered the store and his heart dropped. There was a large group of people clustered behind a strip of yellow tape. It was worse than a line. It was a recipe for pure pandemonium. There was nothing that bothered him more than unnecessary chaos. He didn't want to have to race anyone for a stuffed dog, but it seemed the circumstances gave him no choice.

There was a blonde woman with scraggly hair in the front that kept eyeing the door. She'll probably try to steal something, he thought. It was a little cynical, but it came with the job, to be constantly looking for the thing that didn't belong. Then he remembered the talk the sergeant had with him the other day, when he assigned him to the shelter Christmas project. He needed to look at things differently. They were there to help the people they might normally be cautious of under different circumstances.

He looked at her again. Maybe she was watching the door because she was waiting for someone. Maybe she had somewhere to be. Maybe she was afraid that whomever she was buying the dog for was going to walk through the door. The woman caught him watching her and suddenly looked self-conscious. She smoothed her hair back and pulled her coat tighter around her waist. Normally, Luke would see this as suspicious behavior. Instead, he smiled at her. Probably just someone down on her luck.

She looked surprised. She glanced around her, to make sure he wasn't smiling at anyone else. She gave a small but tired smile back and seemed to relax, loosening her grip on her coat.

Luke searched the crowd around him for the quickest route to the front. Before he could come up with one, he heard a cheer and the crowd lunged forward.

Someone elbowed him in the ribs and as he was recovering, a short balding man sidestepped in front of him and raced to the front, grabbed a stuffed dog, and ran. Luke approached the pallet that was nearly empty but for one, last, Fluffy the Dog. "Yes," he cried, pulling his clenched fist to his side. He darted toward the pallet and reached out, his hand landing squarely on the stuffed dog. But when he went to retrieve it, he found that someone else was holding on to it for dear life as well.

3

Caroline

aroline pulled a paper with the names of four children from her purse. A smile spread across her face as she made her way down the toy-store aisle, searching for gifts on their lists. Her eyes widened as she entered the car aisle. *A set of Hot Wheels, a remote-control car, a race track.* She placed each one in her cart, diligently checking them off her list, before moving on to the next item. She walked through the store, eyeing the bright packages and the red and white decorations strung from the ceiling. Finally, she reached the doll aisle and strolled her way through. *A doll that cries, a play stroller, a doll house.* She placed them in her cart and checked items off her list again. As she worked her way through the store, her heart raced slightly faster each time she found an item she was looking for. The kids would be so excited opening their gifts on Christmas Day.

When she reached the bottom of her list, there was only one

missing toy: a stuffed dog that jumped and barked. She swallowed. This one was going to be tough. It was for the youngest girl in the family, and Caroline knew that she had been in the hospital for part of the year. She really wanted to make this Christmas spectacular for her, but it was the most sought-after toy this season. She wandered her way to the front of the store to find an employee. "Do you have any of the *Bark and Jump Fluffy the Dogs?*"

The employee laughed. "Yeah. They're about to open another crate."

"Great. I'll take one." She reached for her wallet to pay for her cart full of toys.

"Of course. Just tell them." He pointed to a group of people anxiously hovering behind a taut yellow line of tape.

Caroline exhaled; her confidence depleted. She pushed her cart toward the crowd and found a spot behind an older woman. The crowd was deep enough that she couldn't quite see what was happening on the other side.

After a few minutes, a cheer rose from the crowd and they all surged forward. When the older woman in front of her nearly fell, Caroline reached for her arm and helped her to her feet. She smirked at Caroline as she righted herself, then ripped her arm free and made her way for what was left of the pile of Fluffy the Dogs. She grabbed one, held it high in the air, and did a leprechaun-like jump before scurrying toward the registers.

Caroline barreled her cart forward, her sights set on the last of the Fluffy the Dogs. She was inches away, about to take hold of the dog, when a hand came out of nowhere. She reached faster, but they both grabbed it at the same time. Caroline gripped the dog with all her might, but the man tried to pull it away.

"I'm sorry but that's mine," Caroline asserted.

"I don't think so. See, my hand is on it, too." His voice was deep, with a certain confidence that made Caroline determined to hold the dog even tighter.

"I've been here in this crowd waiting and—" she continued.

"So have I."

"An older woman fell over so I helped her and then—"

"Oh, playing the martyr, are we?"

"No. I just mean, that it should be mine because—"

"Because what?"

Caroline tightened her grip on the dog. The man made another attempt at taking possession of it.

"I just need that dog. It's for a little girl that would really appreciate it."

"You think this is for me?"

"I don't judge." She shrugged.

He rolled his eyes. "You seem to have enough in your cart already."

"Also, not for me. Obviously."

"I don't judge, either." He smiled.

Was he flirting with her? He *was* handsome in a rugged, tough-guy sort of way.

"I'm shopping for… a friend."

His eyebrows lifted. "Looks like you have a lot of friends."

"I will have a very sad friend if I don't get that Fluffy the Dog."

"As will I."

They each let out a sigh. Caroline's shoulders slumped.

"Ah, come on. Don't do that," he said.

"Don't do what?"

"Don't act all defeated, as if losing this dog would mean the end of the world."

"Well, maybe it would to this little girl."

He watched her momentarily. It was as if he were reading her mind. She could feel her conviction starting to wane, and her grip on the stuffed dog started to loosen.

Then, he let go.

She tilted her head to the side and smiled sincerely. "Thank you."

He nodded once, then walked away.

She watched him. A slight pang of guilt tugged at her. The child he was buying the dog for really wanted it, too. What made her think that the little girl she was shopping for had more of a right to it? She had no way of knowing what this man and his child's story was. She turned to call after him, but he was gone.

❄

Once she got to her car and loaded everything into her trunk, she pulled out the other list. The one that Sarah had given her. The one with the addresses of the houses she was to look at and decorate for the Christmas Tour of Homes. Her heart felt heavy. She hadn't decorated for Christmas in years. She much preferred to spread Christmas cheer through the spirit of giving and helping others. She plugged the first address into her navigation system and begrudgingly set off on her way.

The first home was a large two-story brick house that had been painted white. It had a grand sweeping lawn with brick steps leading to the stately front door. There was definitely space for something on the lawn, but she refused to consider the inflatable decor that many homeowners enjoyed. That's fine for them, but it wasn't the look she was going for, for this event. She pulled her notebook out of her bag and unclipped the engraved pen, then turned to the page marked with a ribbon. She wrote:

Lawn?

There was a medium-sized area without grass that was covered in mulch. She would have to do something with that area. She added to her list:

Potted plants?

On either side of the steps leading to the front door, there was a small, rounded hedge. She tapped her pen to her lips for a moment. She'd have to come back to that one. Tall and skinny windows lined the front of the house. She knew immediately what she would do with those—a cluster of greenery with a single candle centered in each window would look amazing and channel that peaceful Christmas feeling she was hoping for. She stepped back and took a photo of the home, then zoomed in on the hedges, the circle of mulch, and a window.

She knocked on the door. Footsteps sounded from the inside. An older man opened the door and greeted her with a cheery smile. He was tall and chubby, with white hair. His beard shone, and his eyes had a sparkle to them. He wore a red baseball cap and a red T-shirt with jeans that were probably pulled up too high. In fact, he looked a lot like Santa. Caroline took a moment to gather herself. Were her coworkers playing a trick on her?

When the man's smile faltered, Caroline knew that this was, indeed, this man's home.

"You must be from the Tour of Homes." He extended his hand.

She took it in hers. It was warm and soft. "My name's Caroline."

He laughed and said, "I know."

Caroline paused. Cute. He was getting into character. She smiled and played along. "Of course."

The man shook his head. "Mary told me."

Her cheeks reddened.

"Come in. I'll show you around."

Caroline stepped into the home. Her heart nearly stopped when she realized there wasn't any furniture. Not a single chair.

"There's no furniture?" She tried to sound polite, but she could feel the panic coming through her voice.

"We just moved out last weekend. The good news is you have a clean slate for whatever you decide to do. Let me share with you some of what we've done in the past." He moved into the home and started talking.

Caroline followed him from room to room, listening to

the very detailed descriptions the man gave, but only writing some down. He had suggestions for every room, including the bathroom. When they came to the garage, he paused and took a deep breath.

"We used to keep a big red sleigh in here. The kids that came to visit loved it." He chuckled.

Caroline wrote in her notebook:

Big red sleigh

The man was looking toward the empty space fondly.

"It must be hard to not be able to decorate this Christmas. It sounds like you really enjoyed it." She hugged the notebook to her chest and watched as the man scratched under his hat then straightened it back up again.

He turned to Caroline. "Not really. It's not the decorating that makes Christmas special. It's the spirit of giving." At that, he turned and walked back to the living room. "Now if you'll forgive me, I've got an appointment to get to. You're welcome to stay as long as you like, just be sure to lock up before you go. There's a key under the rock out front. It was a pleasure meeting you."

With a newfound vigor, she watched him leave. She had no idea how she was going to pull it off, but she had to do this home justice. She had to decorate it to the brim, and she had to bring the joy of Christmas. But how?

She took a few more pictures of the home, mainly the fireplace and the stairs, as well as the island in the kitchen. She wrote her ideas in an email, attached the photos, and sent it off to Sarah and the team. Hopefully they'd be able to come up with something good. By the time she was leaving the house, it was starting to get dark.

❋

Caroline made her way through the neighborhood, taking note of how the houses were decorated. She had rarely paid much attention before, as she was always more interested in the homes themselves. She loved to notice the little differences from house to house. Like how the eaves sloped at sharper angles in one home and barely slanted at another. She noticed how the windows let you catch only a little glimpse of what was in the home, or exposed the owner's lives for everyone to see. She noticed how the sun or moon would reflect differently off front doors, determining how welcoming the home appeared.

These little details were why Caroline was good at her job. When she listened to her clients talk about their dream home, she listened for the mood of the home. Each house had a mood, just like people did. It was only a matter of figuring that out and then finding a home with a matching mood.

But these Christmas decorations had no mood. They were simply decorations. So she had to resist her urge to look at the houses and force herself to focus on the decorations. She saw three-foot-tall candy canes and reindeer pulling sleighs suspended in the air. She saw gingerbread men marching two by two, and the Grinch hiding in a tree. She saw a carousel of elves and bright neon snowflakes. None of it was what she was looking for.

By the time she pulled onto her street and in front of her house, she was sure she was in over her head. Why Mary thought Caroline was the person for this task baffled her. Regardless, she was good at her job, and she wanted to impress her boss. She would have to come up with something. Christmas was less than a month away.

4

Luke

Luke wasn't thrilled. He took Caroline in; the perfectly combed shiny brown hair, the determined blue eyes, the polished nails and high heels. Who goes toy shopping in high heels? Yet he was drawn to her. He wanted her to have the stuffed dog. Surely there was somewhere else he could get the dog for Ella.

He let go of Fluffy.

His heart sank and skipped a beat at the same time. What was he thinking? He had to walk away.

He walked out of the toy store and to the car empty handed. He was shaking his head when he reached the car. When he slid into the seat, Andrea eyed him suspiciously.

"What happened? Those vicious moms beat you to the stuffies?"

"I don't want to talk about it." It was the truth. He didn't want to talk about it. Because he couldn't stop thinking about it. About her.

He scratched at the stubble on his chin. He had no room to judge. He had let the dog go. He let his daughter's main Christmas gift go because he had been distracted by a woman.

"You sure you don't want to talk about it? You seem a little bothered."

"Yep. I'm sure. Just drive. I'll find another way to come up with the dog."

Just then, Caroline came sauntering out of the store, the toys piled high. Sitting at the very top of the pile was the prized dog.

Andrea was watching her. "Oh. I see."

"Can we go now?"

She started the car and they quietly rolled out of the parking lot.

As they drove away, Luke watched Caroline pile the toys into her trunk. She probably lived in a huge house with kids that had their every wish granted. Not that he wouldn't do the same for Ella, if he could. It's only stuff, he reminded himself. He provided Ella with love and a safe place to live, and that should be enough.

"Let's go to the homeless shelter," Luke said.

"What?" Andrea asked.

"The sergeant put me in charge of making sure that all the families get taken care of. I'd like to check on it. Add a few names to the list."

"He put you in charge of that?"

Luke looked at her. "You surprised?"

"Not at all. You do wear the Santa pin."

They pulled up to a squat, plain building with few windows. Andrea parked the car in the red zone out front, but when Luke just sat staring at her, she pulled into a parking spot about a block away. Luke popped the trunk open and pulled out a large cardboard box. A breeze blew the flap open, exposing flashes of red and green.

"What you got there?" Andrea tilted her head toward the box.

"Just some decorations for the shelter. Everyone deserves some Christmas cheer." He dug his hand around in the box briefly before taking out a small, shiny wreath pin. He held it out to her. "Even you."

They made their way toward the shelter. Andrea was visibly uncomfortable. She threw her shoulders back and was constantly taking inventory of the area through the corners of her eyes.

"You can relax. These people just need a little help." Luke's free hand was in his pocket as he walked slowly down the street. Every now and then he would nod at a man or woman passing them on the sidewalk.

When they approached the building, he jogged ahead of Andrea and skipped up the steps to hold the door open for a woman that wore three coats and had holes in her shoes. As she walked in through the doorway, she beamed at Luke as if she had won the lottery. Luke bowed his head to her.

Once she was inside, he called to Andrea, "Come on, Jones. We've got work to do."

She walked up the steps, straightening her wreath pin. Once inside, it took a moment for his eyes to adjust. It was dark, and the only lights were fluorescent ones that flickered every now and then. A baby cried down the hall, and the air smelled faintly of bleach and cinnamon. The clomping of their boots echoed through the building until they came to a door propped open by a stack of files. They entered the room; though the wall heater clicked and rattled, there was a chilly draft.

"Hello?" Luke called as he looked around for the woman whose desk sat in front of him. What was her name again? Lory?

A shuffling sound came from an open door on the far wall.

A head peeked around the door frame. She squinted her eyes momentarily, then looked Andrea over, taking in her police uniform. Andrea tugged on her collar.

Clarity registered in the woman's eyes and she popped out from behind the door. "You must be Luke, my police ambassador."

He held his hand out to shake hers. "Glad to meet you in person. This is my partner, Andrea."

"I'm Lauren," she said as she took his hand.

Lauren. That was her name.

A popping sound came from down the hall, and Andrea instantly turned her head, her hand reaching for her gun.

"Don't mind her. She's new to town." He slapped Andrea on the back, then said to her, "The children's ward is right down the hall. Sometimes people donate balloons and the kids get a little carried away."

Andrea relaxed, and she extended an arm to shake Lauren's hand.

"You're familiar with our shelter then?"

Luke shrugged. He was sent to the shelter on occasion to pick up a perpetrator but always came back to spend time with the kids. He didn't want them to see police as a threat. He wanted them to know officers were there to protect them, too.

"I've spent some time around."

"Well, we are very thankful you've found your way to the Family Relations Department. We try our hardest to serve everyone we can, but sometimes it's hard to find out about those families that still have homes but are really struggling."

"I've got some families that could use your help. It's amazing what you all do here, giving people the Christmas they deserve."

"We couldn't do it without your help." She leaned forward and tilted her head.

Luke pulled a folder from the box and handed it to Lauren.

She took it and placed it on her desk, then leaned farther forward to sneak a glance into the box. "What else do you have in there?"

Luke lifted the box and handed it to her. "Just some Christmas decorations I thought the shelter could use."

"You sure you don't want to keep those for your new house?" Andrea whispered to Luke. He nudged her with his elbow and smiled at Lauren, as though Andrea hadn't said anything.

"You have a new house?"

"No, No." Luke shook his hands in front of him.

"He's going to start looking for a new house, though. Hoping to be there by Christmas." Andrea placed a hand on Luke's shoulder. "He's trying to find the perfect place for his little girl."

"Isn't that exciting?" Lauren said, sharing Andrea's enthusiasm.

Luke blushed. "I haven't quite started to look yet. Though it would be nice to celebrate Christmas with my daughter in a new home."

"One with a chimney. For Santa," Andrea added.

Luke cleared his throat. He was never one to mix his business life with his personal life.

Lauren held up a finger. "I think I have just the person to help you with that." She unlocked a drawer in her desk and pulled out her purse. After rooting around in it for a moment, she presented a business card to Luke. "Give her a call. She'll help you find the perfect home."

They said their goodbyes and stepped out of the office. Andrea turned for the exit, but Luke went the other way.

"Where are you going?" she called after him.

"Children's ward."

He approached an older woman sitting at a desk. When she looked up, her face brightened. "Officer Miller! What a pleasure to see you." She jumped to her feet and reached across the desk to hug him. "I didn't know you were coming today. I hadn't heard of any—"

"Just here to say hello to the kids." Luke slipped his hands into his pockets.

"Well, I know of a few faces that will be happy to see you." She led the two of them to the door, unlocked it, and let them in.

Once inside, Andrea found it difficult to go on. The room was large and cold. Along one entire wall were sets of bunk beds. The rest of the room was filled with row upon row of cots. Each one had a set of sheets, a blanket, and a pillow. Several beds had worn stuffed animals sitting upon them.

Andrea had slowed, almost to a stop.

"You okay, partner?" Luke called to her. When she nodded, he motioned with his hand for her to follow him. "Come on. The kids are this way." He pushed open a heavy door that led to a large, concrete playground. A few children looked to see who had arrived. News spread quickly, and soon, there was a group of them surrounding Luke and Andrea.

"Mister Luke! You came back," said a young boy of about six years who was missing his two front teeth.

"Of course, I did. Look what I brought you." Luke pulled a bunch of candy canes from his jacket pockets and began handing them out. He gave a handful to Andrea to pass out as well. As each child received their candy cane, their eyes lit up and joy poured from their smiles. It was likely the only gift they would receive this year.

Once they all had their candy canes, Luke took a ball from a nearby bin. "Who wants to play?"

They spent the afternoon playing kickball with the children, until it was time to pick up Ella. When they left, they promised to come back soon.

As the heavy door shut behind them and they walked back to the car, Andrea was silent. Her shoulders were relaxed, and her step was light. It was humbling to spend the afternoon with kids that were thrilled to get a candy cane. Luke thought back to his afternoon at the toy store and the woman with her shopping cart full of toys. He didn't get that stuffed dog for Ella. That didn't mean her Christmas was ruined.

He had other plans for his Christmas with Ella, he thought, as he patted the pocket that held the business card Lauren had given him.

5

Caroline

aroline pushed open the office door and was greeted with soft Christmas music playing over the speakers. "Carol of the Bells" was one of her favorite Christmas songs and always put her in a cheery mood. She much preferred it over the modern songs that often left the Christmas out and brought in the romance. Who had time for romance at Christmas anyway?

She approached her office and nearly froze. Sarah had truly decorated her door, as promised. In fact, she had gone above and beyond what she had promised. There were layers of gold, green, and red tinsel draped across the ceiling from one end of the outside of her office to the other. Several large, gold stars hung down. She had even gone to the trouble of attaching a few strings of flashing multicolored lights in the shape of a Christmas tree across the one hallway window that she had. The bright-red bell hung over the center of her door. Caroline stood there, her jaw hanging open. Sarah approached.

"So… what do you think?" The cheer emanated from her face. Her big blue eyes filled with anticipation.

"It's lovely," Caroline managed to squeak out. "It's very… festive."

"I just figured the person in charge of the decorating committee should have the most decorative office."

Caroline tried to see this from Sarah's perspective. Sarah lived to decorate for the holidays and was sincerely thrilled about being selected for the decorations committee. She only wanted to spread cheer.

"It's great. I'm sure we'll all enjoy it. Thank you, Sarah."

Sarah did a little jig in place and rubbed her hands together. "Yay! I'm so glad you like it."

Caroline opened the door to her office, and the bell shook and started to play "Santa Claus Is Coming to Town." She took a deep breath, entered her office, and sat down, waiting for the song to stop.

Sarah popped her head in, cringing. "Okay, maybe the bell is a bit much. I'll just turn it off."

Caroline smiled and they both laughed. She turned her laptop on and went through the presentation she made the other day after her visit to the house, to make sure she hadn't forgotten anything. She put a few finishing touches on it, then headed to the conference room.

Someone had already put out a tray of cookies shaped like reindeer, Red Hots attached to noses and all. There was a warming bowl full of hot cider that filled the room with a heavenly scent. Next to that was a bowl of eggnog. She suspected Sarah had something to do with all of it. Caroline poured herself a small cup of eggnog and took a sip, enjoying the thick, sugary drink as it slid down her throat.

Slowly, the team members entered. Chris, from accounting, who was already wearing a Santa hat, came in first. He took a couple of cookies and some cider. Then came Alexandra, an assistant to one of the brokers. She was wearing a bright-green sweater with large bulbous ornaments hanging from it. She got herself a cup of eggnog then sat down, opened her notebook, and began jotting something down with a pen that had an elf hat on the end. Following Alexandra came Nick, Rebecca, and Victor, all new agents who were still learning the ropes and excited about the opportunity to meet potential clients. Nick poured three cups of apple cider for them, and brought a cookie for Rebecca. She smiled sweetly as he handed her the cookie, and Caroline wondered if there was something more there. Maggie, one of the senior brokers came in next, carrying her own cup of coffee, her face buried in her phone.

Finally, Sarah entered and sat in the chair next to Caroline. She had brought a notebook that she had decorated for the holidays. She held it up to show Caroline and said, "You can never be too prepared."

Caroline smiled, eager to get started and, thus, finished. Just as she was about to summon everyone's attention, Sarah stood up and called for everyone to have a seat.

"We have a very big task ahead of us, and I would like to say how happy I am to have Caroline as our spirited leader. I'm sure you all have wonderful ideas, and I can't wait to hear them all." She sat down and nodded to Caroline to continue.

Caroline cleared her throat. "Thank you for that, uh, introduction, Sarah, and we will get to everyone's ideas in a moment. First let's take a closer look at one of the homes we are tasked to decorate." She flipped on the projector and a photo of the home was projected onto the wall.

"Wow. Whose listing is that?" Victor whispered to Nick.

Maggie looked up from her phone. "Mine."

"We will need to decorate both the exterior and interior of the home, in a fashion that will make it appeal to both home buyers and people that are looking for tips on holiday home decor."

"Leaning more toward the home buyer," Maggie chipped in as she momentarily looked up from her phone again.

Caroline went through the pictures, allowing everyone to get a sense of the mood of the home, then opened the meeting up for comments and ideas.

"How about a sled run on the front lawn?" Alexandra suggested.

"Or a snowman contest," Victor enthused.

"What if we call it a 'White Christmas' and have icicle lights hanging from all the trees?"

Caroline held up a finger. "That's actually not a bad idea, Rebecca. Except that there aren't many trees in front of the house. Let's keep it in mind for another house."

"Maybe we could fill it with all sorts of life-size gingerbread houses that people can walk through." Nick rubbed his wiry beard as he made his suggestion.

Rebecca looked at him with wide eyes. "That sounds lovely." She leaned toward him.

There was definitely something going on there, Caroline thought.

Sarah was on the edge of her seat, furiously jotting all the ideas down.

Chris shook his head. "Not in the budget."

Sarah frowned and crossed out what she had written.

"I'm sending these photos to all of you. When we meet tomorrow, I want each of you to have at least one idea for each photo. For inspiration, I want you to look at Christmas cards and think about what a small-town Christmas would have been like in the past. We want to be subtle, but beautiful. Classy, but accessible. Fun, but sophisticated. More than anything, I want you to try and channel the spirit of Christmas into these homes."

As she spoke, they all wrote furiously in their notebooks, except for Maggie, who watched Caroline and nodded until she was done talking. Then Maggie typed into her phone.

"I am going to see the second house today. Who's coming with me?"

Everyone looked down at their hands, folded in their laps. Sarah threw her hand in the air, as if she were going to float out of her seat. Caroline looked past her, but everyone avoided eye contact. Maggie stood up and tapped her watch, indicating she had a client to meet with. Chris slid out of his chair and mumbled that he had a finance meeting in an hour.

Caroline looked to Sarah, still eager to be called on. "Guess it's just you and me."

Sarah squeezed her shoulders to her ears in glee. "I'll go get my bag."

Caroline filled a to-go cup with apple cider and headed for the door. As she got into her car, Sarah popped out of the office wearing a Santa hat with antlers.

Caroline wondered if she was serious. "I'll drive. But maybe leave the antlers. We want to make the sellers feel like they are in good hands."

Sarah appeared crestfallen as her eyes looked to the ground.

"You can wear them in the car. Just not into the house."

"Okay." This seemed to cheer her up. She jumped into the passenger seat, and as soon as Caroline turned the car on, Sarah started flipping through radio stations.

"What are you looking for?" Caroline asked.

"A Christmas station."

"Setting number five."

Sarah tapped the five, and a country version of a Christmas oldie streamed through the speakers. "Country? I never would have pegged you for country."

Caroline shrugged then gestured to Sarah's hat. "I never would have pegged you for a reindeer."

The drive to the house was silent, except for Sarah belting out each and every Christmas song as it played. When they pulled up to the curb in front of the house, Sarah dutifully removed her hat and hid it underneath her seat. They both stepped out of the car. The days were getting colder and frost was forming every night. Caroline wrapped her arms around her thick parka jacket and rubbed them. Sarah tightened her scarf around her neck and took out her notebook. Caroline eyed it, and Sarah flipped the cover over so no one could see the festivity it radiated.

The two women took the home in. It was a lovely gray Cape Cod with large picture windows and white trim. The entryway had a small arch leading to a single brown wooden door. The second story had a pointed gable on the right and a couple of windows on the left, likely an attic that had been converted to a bedroom and bathroom. It had a certain charm about it that made Caroline feel comfortable at once.

There was a small black gate leading to a brick walkway across the front yard. Several trees and low-lying bushes were artistically planted on either side of the walkway. Sarah stepped forward and pushed the gate open, then stopped. Caroline joined her to see what the problem was. She saw instantly.

The bright midmorning sun hit the leaves on all the trees at the perfect angle, so the frost that had begun to melt shone brilliantly. It was breathtaking.

"Are you thinking what I'm thinking?" Sarah whispered, as if speaking any louder would disturb the beauty.

"Winter Wonderland," Caroline whispered back. She took out her phone and snapped several pictures while Sarah wrote furiously in the notebook.

When they were done, they rang the doorbell. A young woman with a very pregnant belly answered the door. "Hello," she said with an Irish accent. "I've been waiting for you. Please come in." She gave them free rein of the home and asked them to make a list of anything they wanted her to remove.

The home was scarcely decorated, with no signs of children's toys or a nursery anywhere. The dark floors and accent woods throughout the house were perfect for continuing the Winter Wonderland theme inside.

As Caroline took photos, they brainstormed all the white decorations they could come up with, and Sarah wrote them down. They went swiftly through the house, and graciously left the mother-to-be to take a nap.

"I'm excited about this one." Sarah read over her notes quietly, her lips moving as she skimmed the pages.

This one? Caroline was surprised that Sarah was excited about *this one.* She thought Sarah was excited about any and every-thing Christmas.

"We just need to come up with something to bring in the Christmas mood. Something that shouts *Joy!* or *Noel!*"

Sarah first watched Caroline for a moment, as if she was trying to decipher what she had said. After a few seconds, she nodded, then wrote something down in her notebook.

When they returned to the office, Caroline sat in her chair, closing the door behind her and setting off the bell singing "Santa Claus Is Coming to Town." She took a deep breath and her phone rang.

Sarah shouted, "Sorry! I forgot to turn it off!" from outside. There was some clattering and a bumping against the door, then the music stopped, then started again.

Her phone rang a second time. Caroline didn't recognize the number. "Hello. This is Caroline." She used her most professional voice, hoping that whoever was on the other end of the phone couldn't hear the music playing in the background.

"Hi, Caroline. I was told you could help me find the perfect house." It was a male, and his voice was confident and calm.

"Of course. Why don't you tell me what it is you're looking for."

"I want a home for my daughter and myself. One with a chimney for Santa."

6

Luke

uke had done it. He had called the agent, and now he was getting ready to go and see a house. It all seemed very real suddenly. Was he ready to have a home again? Maybe he should cancel. Would truly moving on be too painful?

"Where are we going, Daddy? What's the big surprise?" Ella looked up at Luke, wonder spread across her face.

Luke kneeled on the floor so he was her height. "I was thinking we could go look at a house. See if we might want to buy it."

"A house? For you and me?" Her hands were clasped in front of her. Luke nodded. She jumped up and down, her long straight hair bouncing. "Where is it? Does it have a big yard? Is my bedroom near yours? What color is it?"

"Whoa, slow down there. We are only going to look today. Let's see what we can find, okay?"

"Thank you, Daddy!" She threw her arms around his neck and

squeezed. His heart warmed, and he knew then that the time was right. Ella deserved to have a home. She may not have a mother, but she could still have a home.

The drive to the house felt like an eternity, though it was only a few miles up the road. The real estate agent, Caroline, had said there were a few houses around that fit his description.

He followed her directions exactly, and they soon found themselves in front of a small but cute house with a black SUV parked out front. He helped Ella out of the car and they stood on the sidewalk, hand in hand.

"What do you think?"

Ella studied the house. "It's cute. It has a chimney." She looked back at him.

Luke nodded. The house was small. Much smaller than he would like. There were two windows on the front of the house and a screened-in porch peeking out from the side. The shrubs along the stone path leading to the front door were bare and colorless.

"Should we look inside?"

Ella bobbed her head up and down. She pulled on his hand as she ran up the pathway and came to the door. She looked at Luke, who jerked his head to the side, encouraging her to knock.

She knocked twice.

The door swung open to reveal a woman standing with one hand on the doorknob, the other held out, as if presenting the home. "Welcome to your—" She stopped midsentence.

Luke's heart dropped. It was her. The woman that he let take his daughter's stuffed dog. The woman he couldn't stop thinking about. "It's you."

"*You're* Luke. I'm your agent." She shrugged her shoulders as if to say, What a small world.

She was just as pretty as he remembered her. In fact, she was probably prettier. Today she had her hair pulled back into a ponytail. She was wearing a dark-blue pantsuit that made her look elegant, even in this house that he now realized was dreary inside.

"Daddy, is everything okay?" Ella looked up at him, her smile temporarily faded.

"Everything is fine," Caroline jumped in. "Your dad and I met the other day—"

"At the grocery store." Luke gave Caroline a warning look.

"Your dad let me have the last bunch of bananas. It was very nice of him." Caroline looked to Luke, her eyebrows raised.

Was she trying to apologize?

"She really needed those bananas." Although he was talking to Ella, he was looking at Caroline.

Ella looked from Luke to Caroline; her eyebrows furrowed. She shook her head.

"Can we see the house now?" Ella tugged at her dad's sleeve.

Caroline stepped aside, allowing them to enter. Ella stood close to her dad as he cautiously made his way in, looking around skeptically.

The living room was dark and small. There was just enough light coming in through the windows to see that the carpet on the floor was a light brownish-green and worn where people used to walk.

"It needs a little work. There is a fireplace, though." Caroline stood to the side, her hands calmly laced in front of her.

Luke stepped closer to the fireplace. The hearth consisted of dark bricks, and a cold draft flew in every time the wind blew. He could hear the chimney cap rattling.

Ella stepped closer to Luke and whispered, "I don't know if Santa can fit through that chimney."

He rubbed her back gently.

"How about the bedrooms?" he asked.

"Right through here. They are on either side of the bathroom, so you can both have plenty of privacy."

Ella wrinkled her nose and looked at Luke. "What do I need privacy for? I'm six."

Luke and Caroline both started laughing. He glanced into the tiny bathroom and slid his hands into his pockets. "I don't think this is really what we're looking for." Luke wasn't sure this agent understood what they wanted. Maybe he should find someone else.

As if she read his mind, she stepped forward. "I can see that now that I've met both of you. I'm guessing you want something a little brighter, a little homier. Maybe a bigger chimney?" She looked at Ella, who nodded her head. Then she continued. "Maybe a nicer view? The bedrooms a little closer together? Perhaps a family room where you could play games?"

Luke hadn't mentioned any of these things when they had talked on the phone. It made him nervous that she could read him so well. He rubbed below his lip.

"There's a coffee shop right up the block. Maybe we can meet there and have some hot chocolate while we discuss exactly what it is that you're looking for?" Caroline's head was tilted, exaggerating her high cheek bones and perfect posture.

Ella tugged on Luke's sleeve. He looked down at her and saw those pleading eyes he could never resist. He rubbed below his lip again. "Okay. We'll follow you."

The coffeehouse was a small, quaint log cabin turned cafe. Christmas ornaments hung from the ceiling, and each table was decorated with mini fir trees in pots adorned with gold stars. The walls were of light-colored wood and the windows were thick and pockmarked, as if they were made of melted sugar.

"I highly recommend the gingerbread hot chocolate," Caroline suggested to Ella.

Ella licked her lips and her eyes grew. "Does it come with whipped cream?" she asked.

"Only if your dad says it's okay." Caroline looked to Luke. It was almost as if she was trying to make it up to him.

"Sounds delicious." He rubbed Ella's head.

"Why don't you two go find us a seat while I put our order in. There are crayons and paper on that table over there." She pointed to a table in the corner.

They followed Caroline's finger, gathered some crayons and a picture of Santa, then made themselves comfortable in a big booth with plush green leather seats.

"Is she going to find us a house, Daddy?"

He sure hoped so. But he didn't know. He didn't even know if he could trust her. The only thing he did know was that he definitely wouldn't be able to stop thinking about her now.

Caroline joined them at the table with her coffee in hand. A man followed closely behind with a tray. He put a coffee with a candy cane on the side in front of Luke and a bright-red cup overflowing with pink whipped cream in front of Ella. There was a gingerbread girl sticking out of the whipped cream. Ella's eyes widened when she leaned forward and smelled the warm drink. When she leaned back, she had whipped cream on her nose. They all laughed.

"Why don't we make a list of your wishes for your dream house and see how close we can get to that?" Caroline opened her notebook and set it on the table beside her coffee. "I know you want a chimney big enough for Santa to fit through. Why don't you tell me more now that I have both of you here?"

Luke rubbed his chin, thinking about where to start. How do you explain to a stranger that you want a house that feels like home, without being able to describe what it is that makes it a home? While he was trying to gather his thoughts, Ella chimed in.

"I would love a yard. A really big yard so my daddy and I can run around and play hide-and-seek. A yard big enough to have birthday parties in." She glanced at her dad, beaming. "A big tree, to climb, or swing in, is a definite must."

Luke was shocked at the way his daughter was able to articulate exactly what she wanted. She had clearly put a lot of thought into this. His heart ached for her. Why hadn't she ever said anything?

"The living room has to be big. Big enough to fit a really tall tree in it. My daddy loves getting big Christmas trees. One year we got one that was nine feet tall. It almost touched the ceiling." She brought her hands to her mouth and giggled, then grew quiet. "That was our last Christmas with Mom."

How could she remember that? She was only three years old.

Caroline flashed him a look, then quickly looked away.

"The most important thing is that my bedroom is near my daddy's. He doesn't like to be alone at night."

Caroline smiled at Ella. He wondered what she was thinking.

"Those all sound great, Ella." He had to interrupt her before she said any more.

"I'm not done. I would love a two-story house. I've always wanted to be able to look out from a window and see the world."

"Well, Miss Ella, that's a pretty tall order. I'll see what I can do." Caroline jotted a few things in her notebook. Then she looked at Luke. "How about you, Luke? What is it that you want in your home?"

Although she asked completely professionally, there was something about the tone of her voice that made him think that there might be more to what she was asking.

He took a gulp of his coffee and leaned back in the booth. "I think Ella pretty much covered it."

Caroline folded her hands in front of her and watched Ella drink some of the hot chocolate, then lick the whipped cream off her upper lip.

"On second thought, there is one more thing." Luke leaned

forward, resting his elbows on the table. "I want some space. I want to be able to look out the window and see land. Not people."

Caroline nodded. "I think I've got a pretty good idea of what you're looking for. I'm going to take a look around and see what I can come up with."

Ella turned to Luke. "Daddy?"

He looked at her. "What is it?"

"Do you think we'll be in our new house by Christmas?"

He swallowed hard. He knew it was near impossible to buy a house that quickly, but he didn't want to let his little girl down. He would do anything for her. He looked to Caroline to see what she would say.

Although she kept an upbeat attitude, he was sure that he saw her shoulders droop a little. "Don't know, Ella. I will do my best."

This seemed to appease Ella, as she just shook her shoulders and went back to drinking her hot chocolate.

Caroline waved goodbye, but as she left, Luke had an uncontrollable urge to chase after her. She left an emptiness at the table that he hadn't realized she had filled, until she was gone.

7

Caroline

aroline took a deep breath. She pulled the seatbelt across her chest and buckled it, but she still felt like she could go flying at any moment.

Luke. How could it be him? Things like this happened for a reason. She knew it was no coincidence. But what was the reason? She sighed. Putting a face to the girl that was supposed to get the Fluffy the Dog pained her. Ella was a sweet, optimistic girl. And she wouldn't be getting her number one wish-list item for Christmas.

If Caroline had anything to do with it, she would be getting a house, though. So would Luke.

She looked down at her hands. They were shaking. Every time she thought of Luke, her heart gave a little flip. She laughed and shook her head. Then she started her car and set off for the third house she had to decorate.

Following the directions Maggie had given her, within ten

minutes she pulled onto a wide street with tall trees lining it. She checked the number again, then slowly made her way up the street until she came to the address. The home was breathtaking.

Once she parked the car, she was able to take in the large, circular driveway, laid with bricks that shone like gold. At the center of the driveway was a spectacular white French country home with well-lit windows all along the front. There was a pillar on either side of the entrance. The door was painted black; the top half of it all windows. Flanking the entry were two larger windows, framed by black storm shutters, each with its own flower box. Freshly planted bright-red poinsettias bloomed. There were small hedges along the front of the house, adding a pop of green.

The bottom floor had wings on both sides, distinguished by additional large, bright windows, allowing everyone to see the inviting golden light that shone from within. The middle of the house had two stories. The second story soared over the first, with warm golden-brown wood shingles and a chimney shaft at either end. There were three windows, each perched perfectly inside a dormer. Cream-colored curtains hung inside, pitched at a precise angle.

Topping each wing of the house was a flat roof, lined with decorative railing—the perfect place to have cocktails with friends or sit and watch the stars.

She imagined wreaths hanging on each window and red ribbons twisted around the pillars. She could almost see Santa peeking out one of the second-story windows. She took at least a dozen photos, then approached the door. She found a note telling her to let herself in using the lockbox.

The house was warm inside, a result of the fire burning in one of the fireplaces. She took photos of the living room then moved on to the kitchen. It smelled of yeast and saffron and… pumpernickel? She took photos of the large hearth around the open fireplace in the kitchen and of the long table with benches on either side of the dining-room table. She could almost smell the pine coming from the centerpiece that she imagined would look amazing there. She moved quickly and quietly through the house, ideas popping into her head faster than she could gather them.

Where was this inspiration coming from?

Caroline glanced at her watch. How long had she been here? It was starting to get dark and she had to get back to the office for the second decorating-committee meeting. She tossed her phone in her bag and made for the door.

❋

When she arrived at the office, the team was already in the conference room waiting. Chris was standing, eating a cookie and watching his phone intently. Maggie was in the corner on a call, and the Three Amigos, as Caroline had dubbed Nick, Rebecca, and Victor, were sitting at the table chatting. Sarah and Alexandra were nowhere to be found.

Caroline put her bag down and cleared her throat to get everyone's attention. Chris put his phone away and took a seat, Maggie ended her call and sat down, and the Three Amigos looked to Caroline for direction.

"Where are Sarah and Alexandra?" Caroline asked. Just then, the two of them came barreling in, Sarah towing a laptop.

"Sorry we're late. We had a few finishing touches we had to deal with." They looked at each other and smiled. They were up to something.

"Great. Let's get started. Who would like to share their ideas for our first house?"

Nick raised his hand. Caroline nodded at him.

He motioned to his small group. "We were working together and we came up with some ideas for the front of the house. We were thinking each window should have an arrangement of pine branches and pine cones along the bottom of the frame. In the center we could put a candle."

Caroline nodded. This was exactly what she was looking for.

When the committee had brainstormed their ideas and was ready to move on to the second home, Sarah stood up. "Alexandra and I have been working on a little something." She turned to Caroline. "I took many of our ideas and Alexandra used a program to demonstrate how the house will look once it's fully decorated."

As Sarah spoke, Alexandra fidgeted with the laptop's cables until she had everything plugged in. She pushed a button as Sarah turned out the lights, and suddenly, projected on the wall there in front of them, was a beautiful rendition of the home Caroline and Sarah had visited. But this rendition had lights strewn all about the front yard, bringing to fruition the Winter Wonderland that she and Sarah had thought up.

Everyone gasped.

For the first time, Caroline was excited about this project. More and more ideas flitted through her head. She couldn't wait to see what everyone would come up with.

Still, she wanted to incorporate the Christmas spirit. They needed to find that thing that made a heart feel like it belonged. The thing that made people recall Christmas with such fond memories. It wasn't the decorations or the music or the frantic search for the perfect gift that made Christmas special. It was that feeling. That warm and cozy sensation that left people feeling like the world was a wonderful place. That thing that left them with a sense of peace and hope.

Caroline was determined to find a way to infuse it into every house on the tour.

That night when she was home, sitting on her sofa with a blanket tossed on her lap, she couldn't stop thinking about Luke. No matter what she thought about, he kept creeping back into her mind. She took a sip of her tea, and it reminded her of Ella and the whipped cream. When a commercial came on with Santa getting stuck entering a home, she thought about how Luke was determined to get a house for Ella where Santa could slide down the chimney. When the dog next door began barking, she thought about how Luke had let her have Fluffy the Dog and how their hands had brushed for a brief moment. Just thinking about it sent a chill down her spine.

Finally, she turned the television off and opened up her laptop. She pulled out the list of things that Ella and Luke wanted and started her search. Several homes fit the bill, but there was one in particular that she thought he would like. It was set on an acre of land and was near a horse stable, something she was sure Ella would be thrilled about.

Caroline emailed Luke to see if he was available the next day to see it. When she hit send, she realized her hands were shaking again. She smiled to herself and was about to put her computer away when an email from Luke came through, almost as if he had been sitting, waiting to hear from her.

He was available.

Her heart did a little flip again, and she rolled her eyes at how immature she was being. She put her computer away and went to bed.

❄

The next morning, she was up early and ready to go. Was she excited about the decorating? Or was she excited about Luke? She refused to admit that she was doing anything more than her job. Even though when she walked to her closet to pick out what she was going to wear for the day, she couldn't help but wonder which outfit Luke would like best.

Instead of wearing her regular pantsuit, she opted for a pair of jeans and boots. She wore a nice warm white sweater and a beige scarf that matched the color of her boots. She had noticed that Luke and Ella were both dressed very casually, and she wanted to make him feel at home in the house she was showing him today. She had learned years ago that if her clients felt she couldn't relate to them then they wouldn't trust her. If they didn't trust her, then she wouldn't ever find a home that they were comfortable in.

So today Caroline went with what she thought would make Luke feel at home.

She arrived early at the house to wander through it and open curtains and straighten beds, maybe fluff a few pillows. She liked the house. It was warm and cozy, with just enough space that it didn't feel small. The bedrooms were on the second floor, with two right next to each other, a third down the hall. The kitchen was snug, but it should be fine for a father and his young daughter.

A few minutes before Luke was due to arrive, Caroline found herself in front of a mirror checking her hair. It was down today and flowed loosely to her mid back. It wasn't a look she often sported when working, but something told her it was the right look for today. Was she trying to impress Luke? She kept pushing that thought out of her head. Instead she told herself that leaving her hair down simply looked better with the sweater she was wearing.

After she reapplied her lipstick and smoothed some flyaway hairs, she went to peek her head out of the curtains to see if Luke had arrived yet. When she pulled the curtain back, Luke was right there, trying to look inside.

Shocked, they both stepped back, laughing.

Caroline opened the door. "I was only checking if you were here."

He chuckled. "No one answered the door, so I thought you hadn't arrived yet."

Their laughter quieted and left them standing, looking at each other. After a moment, Caroline stepped back. "Come in. See the house. Tell me what you think."

Luke removed his hat as he walked through the doorway.

Caroline felt something in her stomach, though she wasn't sure what. Whatever it was, she liked it.

"Here's the living room. It has a nice big fireplace. Santa would definitely fit through there." Caroline's marketing pitch rushed out of her as she walked through the house, pointing out every little thing she could think of. She wasn't sure why she was talking so much. She normally let the client lead the showing. But Luke did something to her.

He looked carefully around every room they saw, nodding as she talked. He held his hands clasped in front of him, occasionally twisting or squeezing them together. She couldn't tell if it was when he liked something, or didn't like something. Perhaps it was a nervous habit he had. But why would he be nervous?

When they had made their way through the house and were left standing on the back porch looking out at the yard, Caroline started to get nervous herself. He hadn't said a word. She had to know what he thought of it.

"What do you think?"

He was looking out toward the tree in the yard and appeared to be deep in thought. She had moved something in him, but she wasn't sure what.

Finally, he turned to her. "Do you want to go for a horseback ride?"

Caroline didn't know what to say. He hadn't commented on the house. He hadn't even given her any hints about whether or not he liked it. Now he was asking her to go horseback riding? She thought about all the work she had to do back at the office and the planning that still needed to be done for the Tour of Homes.

He was watching her weigh her options. He wasn't smiling, but he wasn't serious, either.

She felt that thing in her stomach again, then said, "Yes. I'd love to."

8

Luke

uke had no idea why he had asked Caroline to go horse-back riding. When he saw the stables on the way to the house this morning, he had this overwhelming urge to go. Maybe it was because he wanted to spend more time with her. His thoughts had strayed to her even more since they met at the house showing. He didn't want to spend the rest of the day thinking about when he would see her again.

He wanted to spend time with her *now*. That would do it. It would answer the question of who she really was and he could go on with his life. Go back to it being just him and Ella, and get rid of this persisting idea that he needed to get to know this mysterious woman.

Caroline had looked beautiful standing there on the back porch. The sun had been shining perfectly on her hair, which gently fell down her back. Part of him wished she had left it up;

he was having a hard time taking his eyes off her with it down. Now here they were, getting on a couple of horses and heading out onto the trail.

They rode in silence, their horses matching each other's cadence like old friends. The sun had vanished behind some clouds, and he could see the breaths of the horses as they sauntered down the trail.

Caroline sat in the saddle like someone that had been on horses her whole life. She had a confidence about her that drew Luke in, though he couldn't tell if it was pure determination or a wall to keep people out.

"It's the perfect morning for a horse ride." He tried to fill the silence as he watched her on her horse.

She looked at him. "I'd forgotten how relaxing it is to ride." Her eyes seemed to get bluer in the cold, and her cheeks turned a pleasant pink.

"You ride a lot?" He kept his voice casual, as if he was simply making conversation and not trying to solve the puzzle that she was to him.

Caroline nodded. "We always had horses growing up. It was one of the things I looked forward to more than anything; coming home from school and spending all afternoon at the stables. Then I grew up, and… I guess life got in the way."

"No wonder you look so comfortable."

Caroline grinned. "Do you and Ella ride often?"

"I haven't taken her in a while. Probably not since she was three or so."

Caroline looked at him. He could feel the question in her eyes, even if she didn't ask.

"Ella's mom loved horses. She passed away when Ella was three. Horseback riding brings a lot of those memories back to the surface."

"I'm sorry."

"We used to put Ella on the horse in front of us and pack a picnic. We'd be gone for the whole day." Luke couldn't help but smile as he thought about all the good times they had. "I was left with some amazing memories. I just wish Ella could remember them, too."

Caroline smiled at Luke. "She's a very special girl. You're doing a great job raising her." Her voice was soft and kind. Luke couldn't help but notice that it was very different from when he'd met her at the store and at the dark and dank house. He was talking to the *real* Caroline.

"Thanks. She makes me want to be a better person. This whole house thing, it's for her."

"You don't want a home?"

He noticed she had changed house to home. "We have a home. It's a house she's hoping for." He glanced at her out of the corner of his eye. She was not fazed by his comment. "Do you really think it's possible to be in by Christmas? It's a long shot, isn't it?"

She seemed to think for a moment before answering him. "I think it's possible, if we find the right house with the right circumstances."

"I would love to be able to have our lights and a Christmas tree up at a new house. We could finally pull all the decorations out of storage."

"Oh, you're one of those." There was a bite to her voice, but her eyes were playful.

"One of those what?"

"One of those that decorates every surface they come across. From the kitchen sink to the bathtub."

"What's wrong with a little tinsel dangling over the kitchen window? Or a Santa hat hanging from the towel rack?"

Caroline slowly shook her head. "Please don't give me any ideas."

Luke's eyebrows shot up. "You need help decorating?" He wasn't necessarily volunteering, but he certainly wouldn't say no if asked. "Because I'm the king of Christmas decorating. We go all out. We always have the brightest shining apartment in town."

She laughed, tossing back her head. "It's not my house that needs help. I don't decorate my home. I've been tasked with heading the decorating committee for our first Christmas Tour of Homes. I'm in way over my head."

Caroline's horse was a few yards ahead of Luke's when she turned around to look at him.

He wasn't laughing. "You don't decorate? And you're supposed to be helping me find my Christmas home?" He led his horse to catch up with Caroline's. "Do I need to find a new real estate agent? Maybe one that believes in Christmas?"

Caroline's head was lowered, but he could see her eyes through the hair that had fallen across her face. She was staring at him. "I believe in Christmas. I just don't do all the decorating. Christmas should be about more than decorating. It should be about kindness, and hope, and giving."

"And decorating."

She shook her head. "Nope."

"Do you have a Christmas tree?"

She shook her head again. "It's all too commercial."

He threw his hand to his forehead. "It's Christmas. How can you believe in Christmas and not have a tree?" He let out a sigh. "How about a wreath? Please tell me you at least have a wreath."

Caroline looked away.

"Man. Maybe I do need to find a new agent." They rode their horses in silence for a few moments. "How did you end up in charge of decorating a huge event if you're such a grinch?"

Caroline rolled her eyes. "Apparently my selling point on a home was where to put the Christmas tree. My boss heard about it, and well, here I am."

"So, you're decorating them all in black?" He chuckled.

"Very funny. I know what Christmas decorations look like. I just choose not to decorate my home with them."

"At least I don't need to find a new agent," he joked. "Were you deprived as a child? Or did your parents overdo it?"

"Neither. My parents loved Christmas. It was our favorite time of year. They did everything they could to make sure that every kid in our neighborhood had the best Christmas possible. They were very well loved by everyone for what they did at Christmas."

He watched her quietly.

"I've always loved Christmas, but after my parents passed, I really couldn't find it in my heart to decorate anymore."

"I'm so sorry. I had no idea." He felt like such an idiot. If anyone knew what that kind of pain was like, he did. He held so many beautiful but painful memories. He should have recognized it when he saw it.

She smiled, the lines in her cheeks bending softly. "It's okay. It's been about ten years. I guess I just fell out of the habit and never picked it up again. When I see people decorating, it feels like they're doing it for the show. I like to focus more on the spirit of Christmas."

"So why don't you bring that into your home tour?"

Her eyes lit up. "That's exactly what I'm trying to do. We have some ideas for the houses, but I'm having a hard time incorporating the spirit."

She looked down at her hands holding the reins.

"Maybe you just need a little inspiration." There he went again, offering to help. This time, though, he knew he wanted to. He was pretty sure he would do anything she asked him to.

"That's *exactly* what I need, a little inspiration."

She looked at Luke and his heart flipped. They rode side by side for a few moments, holding each other's gaze.

A breeze blew through the forest, and the trees protested with a chorus of creaks. Another breeze blew through, and it began to snow. Small flake after flake dropped from the sky, landing in their hair and eyelashes, melting with the warmth of their skin. Caroline held her hand out to her side to allow the snowflakes to dance onto her palms and through her fingertips.

Luke watched her with a longing in his heart.

"I think you've got your inspiration."

She tilted her head back and opened her mouth, catching a snowflake on her tongue. "If only I could channel this into the tour."

"Snow? I'm pretty sure there will be some."

"No." She shook her head, the flakes flying off. "The feeling you get when the first snowfall of the season floats down around you." She looked up at the sky, joy emanating from her face.

Luke wished he could bottle that look, that sensation.

"It is pretty great." He watched her, and couldn't help thinking that he wanted to be there to witness another first snowfall with her.

He shook the thought out of his head. What was wrong with him? He just met this woman a couple of days ago, and here he was already planning for the future. He needed to change the subject.

"So, who were all the toys for?"

She lowered her hands back to the saddle. She was fully at ease, looking as peaceful as he'd ever seen anyone look.

"What toys?"

"The cartful? The Fluffy the Dog? The one you had to have?"

"They're for my family." She put her arms back out to her sides as the snow started coming down a little harder.

Luke felt like he'd been punched in the stomach. Of course, she had a husband and kids.

"How do they feel about your unwillingness to decorate for the holidays?"

She looked confused. "They don't know. I deliver a tree to them along with their toys. Why should it matter to them that I don't decorate?"

He was confused. She delivered a tree to who?

Caroline must have seen the confusion on Luke's face. "You thought I meant *my* family."

Luke nodded. "Those toys weren't for your kids?" He tried to hide the happiness, but his voice only came out dry and flat.

She shook her head. "I adopt a family every year. It's one of the ways I spread the Christmas spirit. My way of celebrating Christmas."

It all came together at that moment. Lauren at the shelter recommending Caroline. The cart full of toys. "That's how you know Lauren."

Caroline whipped her head to Luke. "How do you know Lauren?"

"I'm the police delegate for the homeless Christmas program." They looked at each other. Yet another way their paths were bound to cross.

Luke's horse whinnied. "I guess we'd better get back to the stables." He could almost swear that a wave of disappointment crossed Caroline's face momentarily.

"We should."

They rode back in silence.

When they reached the stable, Luke tried his hardest to stall. He wanted to spend more time with Caroline. There was something about her that he couldn't get past. He stood silently in front of her.

"So." Caroline moved close to Luke.

"So." He wanted to ask her out to coffee or dinner or anything, but he didn't know if it was appropriate.

"I'm assuming the house we saw today wasn't the house for you." She smiled, looking into his eyes.

He swallowed hard. "I don't think so. It didn't feel right."

Caroline nodded her head slowly. "Is there anything different you'd like me to look for in the next house?"

"Maybe a house with a little more Christmas spirit."

Caroline's mouth spread into a wide smile. "I'll work on that." She hesitated for a moment. "I guess I'll let you know what I find when I get back to the office." She stepped away from Luke slowly.

He nodded, not sure of what to say to keep her from leaving. She opened the door to her car and slid in. Luke ran after her. When he reached the car, she rolled down the window.

"If you need any help with the decorating, let me know."

"Thanks. I will."

He watched her drive away, her tires leaving a trail behind her. The snow accumulated on his shoulders, but he didn't notice. He was too busy thinking about when he might see Caroline again.

9

Caroline

"I've got it!" Chris exclaimed as he walked into the meeting twenty minutes late.

Everyone turned and looked at him. He stood in the doorway, waving a clipboard above his head. His round belly tugged at his green sweater, barely skimming over his belt that dutifully held up his khakis. His round glasses accented his thick eyebrows and his balding head.

"Please, come join us," Caroline said from a chair at the front of the room. She motioned to a skinny brunette woman sitting next to her. "This is Jessica from Anderson's Furniture Store. She's here to make sure we get what we need for the tour."

Chris bowed his head briefly to Jessica then made his way to the front of the room. He turned to Caroline. "I've found some Christmas spirit for us."

She lifted her eyebrows. The anticipation of something with

Christmas spirit made her giddy. Time was ticking away, and she still hadn't come up with how to incorporate the spirit into any of the homes.

He pulled up a chair next to Caroline and placed the clipboard face down on the table. He held his hands splayed out in the air in front of him, as if he were looking in a window. "I've got a red sleigh." He clapped his hands together for dramatic effect.

Caroline sat up straighter. "A sleigh?"

Everyone in the room leaned in. "The first house you visited, you said he used to have a sleigh in his garage. Well, I found us a sleigh." Little drops of sweat clung to his upper lip.

Caroline felt her cheeks tighten. She gazed up to the ceiling as she thought about what to do with the sleigh.

"We could park it on the lawn under a tent," Alexandra suggested.

"Kids could meet with Santa inside," Victor added.

Sarah bounced in her seat. "We could decorate the tent to look like Santa's barn." She rubbed her hands together then wrote furiously in her notebook.

Caroline nodded. "I like it."

Jessica sat, watching.

"We could hand out candy canes to the kids," Victor continued.

"And a Santa's decorating-tips card for the parents." Maggie held up her hands as if she were holding a banner.

"This sounds great." Jessica shut her notebook. "Just send us a list of any furniture you need to borrow and we'll get it going. I'm really excited about this." She stood up and shook Caroline's hand as they walked to the door.

Once Jessica was gone, Caroline clasped her hands in front of her chest. "Great teamwork everyone. Victor, Sarah, and Alexandra, I want you to come up with everything you need to make that tent look like Santa's barn. Maggie, you work on the decorating tips, and Chris, you find us a Santa."

Chris raised his right hand just enough to get Caroline's attention. "I was thinking that maybe I could be Santa?" He held up the clipboard for her to see. Fastened to it was a photo of him dressed as Santa.

The room went silent. Chris had always kept to himself more or less. No one took him for the type that would want to be socializing, especially with children. Caroline felt the Christmas spirit growing in the room. "I think that's a great idea."

Chris nodded and left the room with an extra bit of pep in his step.

Satisfied that everyone was working, she packed up her bag and headed out to meet Lauren for lunch.

Caroline was seated at a table up against a large window overlooking the street. Snow dotted the branches of the trees and was piled along the edges of the sidewalk. There was a soft shush each time a car drove by. Caroline sipped her mocha latte and twisted the candy cane in her hands as she brainstormed how to bring the Christmas spirit into the homes. She was excited that one house was taken care of, but she still had three more to deal with, one of which she hadn't even seen yet.

As Caroline was glancing at her watch, Lauren plopped into the chair across from her, unwinding her scarf. Her dark curly hair was pulled into a ponytail today, and she looked extra festive, with tiny red and silver stockings dangling from her ears.

Caroline pursed her lips together and shook her head. "Lovely earrings."

"I wore them for you. Keep thinking if you see enough of it, you'll eventually start joining me."

Caroline shook her head. "Not happening."

The waitress came by and took their order.

"Why didn't you tell me you referred a tall, dark, handsome stranger to me?"

Lauren narrowed her eyes at Caroline. "A tall, dark, handsome stranger? Tell me more."

"Luke. Your police delegate." Caroline's voice was flat.

"Oh, the guy with the daughter. You're right. He is handsome. Consider it my Christmas gift to you." Lauren giggled. "Have you found him the perfect house?"

Caroline shook her head. "No. He's not that easy. I've shown him two houses so far, and he didn't like either. One was too small and dark. I'm not sure what was wrong with the other. He didn't really say. We went horseback riding instead."

"You went horseback riding? You haven't done that in ages."

"I know, and it was great. I had forgotten how relaxing it is. Especially in the snow."

"Sounds romantic," Lauren teased.

Caroline blushed, then looked down at her drink, cupping it in her hands.

"Wait. You like him, don't you?"

"I just met him. How can I like him?"

Lauren wagged her finger at Caroline. "I know you, and that's the 'I met someone' face."

Caroline tried her hardest not to smile. "You said it yourself. He's handsome."

Lauren nodded.

"And he's so good with Ella. She's the driving force behind his house hunt."

"You sound like that's stressing you out."

"I feel like I have to get them their dream house. How can I not?" Caroline sighed and took another sip of her latte. She picked the candy cane back up and twisted it through her fingers again. Lauren eyed her suspiciously.

"I feel like there's more to this. What aren't you telling me?"

"He's the self-proclaimed King of Christmas Decorating."

Lauren shrugged. "You could use a little more red and green in your life. Maybe it will rub off on you." She smirked. "What else aren't you telling me?"

"I took his daughter's dog."

Lauren squeezed her eyes shut and wagged her finger at Caroline again. "You did what?"

"Remember the guy at the store I told you about? The one that wanted the Fluffy the Dog and let me have it?"

Lauren opened her eyes wide. "That was Luke?"

Caroline nodded her head slowly. "Now I feel awful because I have a face to put with the little girl that won't be getting her wish-list toy this year."

Lauren's shoulders dropped. She rested her chin on her hand. After a moment she sat up and held both her index fingers up in front of her. "First, you shouldn't feel guilty because that dog is going to another little girl that will love it just as much. Second, he *let* you have it. You can't feel bad when he gave it to you."

Caroline sighed.

"Except you like him and so you do feel bad."

Caroline nodded. "I just need to find them the perfect house and it will be fine."

Lauren lifted her eyebrows in agreement.

"Speaking of the perfect house, I have one more house I need to see for the home tour. Want to come with me? I could use some of your decorative Christmas eye."

"Of course."

The waitress arrived and placed two steaming bowls in front of them. They were filled to the brim with a creamy sauce that sent the heavenly aroma of chicken, thyme, and cooked vegetables floating up. Specks of green parsley dotted the tops of their bowls, while dumplings poked out from under the chunks of chicken.

"The perfect meal for a snowy day." Lauren shoveled a spoonful into her mouth.

"If I could only figure out how to channel the warm-and-fuzzies this meal gives us into the home tour."

✻

A stream of smoke billowed out of the chimney that sat slightly left of center near the front facade of a quaint little house.

"Is this it?" Lauren asked.

"I think so." Caroline paused as she pulled her gloves out of her bag and looked the house over. "It's cute."

"It looks like a gingerbread house."

They sat in the car with the heater on. The front door stood at the center of the house, directly underneath a pointed arch. The door itself was made of dark wood, and it had a circular window sitting in the top half. On either side of the door hung a sconce. To the right, the roof peaked, a small window hovered over a large but dark set of three paned windows. The gray roof above sloped steeply. To the left of the door were two windows hidden behind a round, reddish hedge. Peeking out of the roof was a square dormer with a large window, bright curtains hanging inside.

"It's like a cross between a cathedral and Snow White's cottage." Lauren giggled.

Caroline jabbed her with her elbow.

Snow sat atop the ridge of the roof and covered the hedges, leaving some to look like oversized snowballs. "I think this one might take a lot of creativity."

They stepped out of the car and Caroline handed Lauren her notebook. "Here, help me out. Write down whatever we talk about."

Lauren took a red-and-white striped pen with fuzzy little balls dangling from the end out of her purse.

"Really?"

"You need all the help you can get with this one."

Caroline cocked her head. She fumbled with her camera and, giving up, took one of her gloves off. She took photo after photo of the outside of the house, trying to find an inspiring angle. After a few minutes, she looked to Lauren. "Let's just go inside."

A man in a black suit opened the door and showed them around the house. The living room was nice, but subtle. Nothing too special. The furniture was old and antique looking, with beautiful rugs that appeared as though they'd never been walked on.

Next they entered the dining room. Caroline's heart stopped. It was the most stunning room she had ever seen. The entrance was a pointed arch carved from exquisite wood with dark streaks throughout. The same arch on the dining room side of the wall was a massive cream-colored ornamental casing. It had pilasters leading to the top of the arch. Above the arch were intricate patterns of lace and flowers weaving their way to the ceiling, where a delicate series of horizontal rails were laid out. The ceiling was coffered. It was painted a deep celadon, with dark wood detailing that made the room feel even taller than it was. Along the floor lay a red Persian rug, with bright pops of green and gold, and deep undertones of magenta and sienna. A long, shiny table ran the length of the room. Place settings had been put out, with chairs spaced a perfect three inches apart. The china was an immaculate white with a single line of green winding its way along the edge of each piece. In the center of each, an elegant rendering of holly.

The room was ethereal. Caroline felt herself getting choked up.

They moved on to the kitchen through an inconspicuous door that blended in with the wall. Caroline was sure nothing could measure up to the room she had just seen. The kitchen, however, was magnificent in its own right. Lauren's jaw dropped as she entered.

Over the stove top was a noble hood made of a polished brass with straight edges. There were flowers molded into the center.

The stove itself was a sight. There were eight burners and two large ovens below with numerous red knobs. Light-green-and-cream granite counters ran along two sides of the room, with light-green cabinets above and below. In the center of the room was a large island with a single sink at the end. Caroline felt weak in the knees simply thinking about the wonderful concoctions that must come out of that kitchen.

"This is unquestionably a cook's dream kitchen." Caroline motioned for Lauren to write as she took pictures from every angle. The man in the suit, whom Caroline now presumed to be the butler, smirked as they made their way through the kitchen. He then took them through the rest of the house. No other rooms were quite as phenomenal as the dining room or kitchen, but they were all tastefully decorated.

"I have no idea how I'm going to decorate this one. How do I do those two rooms justice?" Caroline fidgeted with her camera as they stood outside the house trying to reconcile the outside appearance of the home and the inside majesty of it all.

"I think I know who can help you with this."

Caroline sighed. "Who?"

"The King of Christmas Decorating."

10

Luke

Luke had found the perfect house. At least, that's what it looked like on the internet. He squinted as he leaned in to see the pictures better. It was a beautiful two-story home, set on five acres, and had numerous trees on the property. What more could he ask for? Although the interior pictures looked nice, he should probably try to see it in person. He turned the computer monitor toward Andrea so she could see.

"Want to do a drive-by?"

She pressed her lips into a fine line and lifted her eyebrows.

"Don't look so concerned. I only want to check out a house before I ask Caroline to take me to see it. We have plenty of time before our shift starts."

"Can I drive?"

Luke hesitated. He drummed the table with his fingers, then nodded. "Fine."

Andrea clapped her hands together and said, "Let's go."

She raced down the street and slipped onto the highway. "Where is this place?"

"It's the first town over the county line. Looks like it's called Brambling Falls."

As they sped down the highway, Luke didn't say much. He should have been thinking about the house, but instead, he was thinking about what Caroline would think about the house. He was eager to share it with her. He wanted her opinion. He tried to shake this urge off, but the more he tried to think about anything else, the more he found himself thinking about Caroline and what she would say about the trees and the wraparound porch. He tried to picture Ella swinging underneath one of the big oaks on the property, but it turned into him and Caroline sitting on the porch, drinking wine while Ella swung under a tree.

"You're awful quiet today," Andrea observed.

Luke scratched at his neck. "Just got a lot on my mind."

Andrea cleared her throat. She knew her partner well. She had to know there was something going on. "How was your day off?"

"Just looked at a house."

"And?"

"And it wasn't the right one." He shifted in his seat.

"What was wrong with it?"

"Is this an investigation?"

She smirked. He knew he was caught now.

"Just tell me already. Or I can try to figure it out on my own."

Luke rolled his eyes. That was the last thing he wanted. His partner snooping around this… he wasn't exactly sure what it was. He sighed. Maybe she could offer a female perspective on the whole thing.

"This house—" he began.

Andrea cleared her throat.

"Fine. Caroline, the real estate agent. She's getting to me."

"Getting to you how? Like you think she's up to no good?"

He shook his head. "No. I just…" he paused. "I can't stop thinking about her."

Andrea grunted.

"We went horseback riding yesterday. I hadn't gone in years because I thought it would be too painful. But it wasn't. I had a good time."

Andrea watched him. He realized this was the first time he had talked about his feelings for his wife with Andrea. It made him uncomfortable.

"I found this house and want her to see it. I just want to make sure it's halfway decent before I even suggest it to her." He ran his hand through his hair. "Man, when did I turn into such a schmuck?"

Andrea laughed. "You're not a schmuck. It's okay to want to impress a woman. Do you think the feeling is mutual?"

He threw his hands up. "I have no idea. This is our exit."

Andrea pulled off the highway and onto a quiet two-lane road. "Are you sure this is where we were supposed to get off?"

"That's what the directions say. One mile straight ahead." He pointed forward.

Both sides of the road were lined with tall pine trees. There was the occasional dirt road turning off that led through the forest and on to who knew where. After a few minutes, the trees opened up to a small town. It took Luke's breath away.

There were small buildings on either side of the road, with wooden plank sidewalks. Streamers of red and green tinsel were draped from the corners of each building to its center, where there was a wreath. Every building had Christmas lights and green garlands running along its roof. The streetlights had large red and gold bells hanging from them. Bright lights were strung back and forth from one side of the street to the other. Even the trash cans were covered in cheery red-and-green bags to make them look more festive. There were flyers in every window advertising a wreath-decorating contest and a Christmas tree on every corner.

"What is this? And how have we never been here before?" Andrea slowed the car almost to a stop.

"It's the best little Christmas town I've ever seen. Pull over." Luke was antsy to get out of the car. As soon as Andrea stopped, he swung the door open and jumped out.

"Merry Christmas," a woman walking a dog said. Taken aback, Luke mumbled a combination of "thank you" and "you, too."

They walked down the street until they came to a small square with a large Christmas tree in the middle. Luke stood there, staring up at the tree. This was it. This was the place he had always wanted for Ella. He could feel his eyes starting to water.

Andrea walked up beside him and put her hand on his shoulder. "You okay?"

He wiped his eyes with the back of his hand and cleared his throat. "Yeah. It's just cold. Let's go see the house."

They walked back to the car. Both of them were in awe of the festive town around them.

"Probably not a lot of crime around here, eh?" Andrea opened her door and plopped in.

Luke chuckled.

They continued down the sleepy road until they came to a small paved lane that led off to the right. The trees were closer together and birds were flitting about. They passed several driveways with mailboxes staked into the ground. Finally, they came to the driveway they were looking for. Andrea pulled over.

"Do they know you're coming?"

Luke shook his head.

"So, what's your plan?"

"I don't really have one."

"We do have our uniforms on. And the car. I'm sure we could pay them a little visit."

Luke whipped his head to Andrea. The emotion gone from his face. "Then when I come to see the house and they recognize me?"

"Okay. Maybe not the best plan."

He looked at the road ahead of them. It curved to the right and wound up a mountain. "Actually, let's follow the road ahead of us. See where it goes."

She drove the car up the mountain until they came to a turnout with a guardrail along the side. She dutifully pulled over.

He opened the door and slowly walked to the guardrail, where he looked out over the valley. The view was breathtaking. Swaths of green peeked out from under the light blanket of snow. There was a break in the trees where a river ran swiftly along the curves of the land. In the distance, where they had come from, was an opening with a house in the middle. It was a nice home from what he could see. However, he had no way of knowing if that was the home he was looking for.

Though the air was crisp and cool, it sent a warmth through his body that he couldn't explain. Luke took in a deep breath, letting the air, heady with pine, fill his lungs.

Andrea popped her head out of the car. "We've got a call coming in, Luke. We'd better head back."

He took one last look at the view while scratching his chin, then jumped into the car. "Let's go. But don't put the lights on until we get to the highway."

When Luke got off work that day, he decided to swing by Caroline's office. Not only could he tell her about the house, but he would get to see her, too. As he walked into the building, it occurred to him that perhaps he should have called first. She may not even be there. He stepped up to the front desk. A young woman in an ugly Christmas sweater looked up and greeted him.

"I'm here to see Caroline."

"Is she expecting you?" She tapped one of the ornaments hanging from the mini Christmas tree on the desk.

"Uh, no. Is that a problem?" He started thinking maybe it wasn't such a good idea to show up unannounced.

"Not at all. Let's see if she's available. Come with me." She led him down a hallway, stopping briefly to poke her head into a conference room, then continued down the hall.

When they reached an office that was smothered from wall to wall with tinsel, she stopped and knocked.

"I'm sorry, I think you misunderstood me. I'm here to see Caroline."

The door opened and Caroline stepped out. Luke grinned. The woman with the sweater walked away.

Luke pointed at the wall. "I thought?"

"Don't." Caroline waved her hand in the air. "Please, come in."

As he walked under the bell, he accidentally bumped it and "Santa Claus Is Coming to Town" blared.

"Sorry!" the receptionist called from down the hall.

Luke was in full laughter by the time Caroline had motioned for him to sit. "Overexcited assistant?"

"She means well." Caroline pulled out a chair for herself and sat. "This is a nice surprise. What brings you by?"

"I found a house." Although he tried to keep the excitement from his voice, he couldn't help but let it show. "I mean, I think I found a house."

"Isn't that my job?" Caroline clasped her hands in front of her.

He pulled a folded piece of paper from his jacket pocket. "I found it online."

He unfolded the paper slowly then passed it to Caroline. She took it from him, her eyes darting about the page until they came to the picture. Then she became very still. She cleared her throat.

"This is the house?" Her voice was quiet.

"Yes. I drove through the neighborhood today, and I think it might be it."

She continued to stare at the paper.

"Do you think you can get us in to see it tomorrow?"

She hesitated. "Tomorrow? I don't know. I have a lot of, I need to…"

There was a knock on her door and a young woman wearing a Santa hat peeked in. "Sorry to interrupt, but it's time for the meeting. Want me to tell everyone to wait for you?"

Caroline held up a finger. "Tell them I'll be right there." She looked back to Luke. "I'm sorry. I have to get going."

"I understand. Can you look into the house?"

"I'll see what I can do." She got up and left the office, taking the piece of paper with her.

Luke stood. What had happened? She was so eager to help him find a home, and they had a wonderful time yesterday. Then all of a sudden it was like she couldn't get away from him fast enough. He smoothed his hand across his chin and glanced at his watch. It was time to pick up Ella. He had been hoping he'd have exciting news for her today, but he'd better not mention it yet.

That night, after he had put Ella to bed, he received an email from Caroline.

I found a great house. Can you meet me tomorrow at noon?

He sat up on the sofa and responded, *Of course.*

11

Caroline

aroline plopped onto the sofa, kicking off her heels. She laid her head back and stared at the ceiling. It was all starting to get to her—the stress of decorating all the homes and now this. She sighed and pulled the folded piece of paper from the pocket in her work bag. She unfolded it and sat it on her lap.

A flood of emotions rushed through her and tears began to form. How did he find her childhood home? There's no way he could have known she had any connection to it. It had changed ownership at least twice since she sold it when her parents passed ten years ago. But he had found it, and now he wanted to see it.

If she showed it to him, she knew he would want to buy it. It was exactly the kind of home he was searching for. Ella would love the yard with so much space to play and imagine. Luke would love sitting on the wraparound porch, watching Ella explore.

She knew the interior layout by heart. She could walk through it with her eyes closed. In fact, she basically had on several occasions when she was a teenager, sneaking in after curfew.

There was an uncomfortable, hard feeling in her heart. If this was the perfect home for Luke and Ella, then why didn't she want him to have it? She had already booked a house to show him for tomorrow at noon. He had caught her so off guard when he showed up, she hadn't told him. Plus, he sounded like he had his heart set on the home on the paper, and she didn't think he would have been open to seeing a different one. Forget the fact that she, too, had been excited to see him. She wasn't thinking straight when he showed up at her door looking more handsome than usual, wearing his uniform.

She took a deep breath. She needed to buy some time before she decided what to do. So she did the only thing she could think of. She sent Luke an email asking him to meet her to see the other home. Then she took her favorite oversized mug out of the cabinet and made herself an enormous hot chocolate, topping it with a healthy helping of whipped cream and a handful of sprinkles.

❋

Caroline tossed and turned most of that night, leaving her with a headache the next morning. There was another decorating-committee meeting, and she was already running late for it, again.

By the time she made it into the office, the team was all huddled in the conference room going over their findings. Sarah had set up an inspiration board that she brought to each meeting. It was covered in old Christmas cards, samples of decorative fabrics, and photos of various holiday ideas. As the team chatted, Caroline reviewed their progress. A wave of relief came over her. The first house was shaping up. Now they had to shift their focus onto the second home.

They brainstormed ideas for executing the Winter Wonderland theme in the second home, assigning groups to manage the details of each room. Caroline shared the photos of the last two homes to get everyone thinking, so when they met again, they would have plenty of ideas.

When she glanced at the clock on the wall, she couldn't believe it was almost time to meet Luke. She grabbed her bag and left the team working together, with the exception of Maggie, who also had a house to show.

❅

Caroline drove through downtown Sweet River, past the church with the lights in the shape of a star hanging from the top of the bell tower. That's how you decorate with spirit, she thought. She kept driving down the main road until she reached the part of town where the lots were larger. The spacious yards left the homes more spread out. There was room to breathe here. She turned up the drive next to the large fir tree that the family had decorated for Christmas. Luke would love it.

Rather than opening up the house for Luke, she decided to wait in the car for him. She could already tell that he wouldn't be persuaded. There was no use in sprucing up pillows or lighting Christmassy candles. He would see right through all of it. She turned the radio to the Christmas station and dug through her purse to find her gloves.

A knock on the window of her car made Caroline jump. She looked out to find Luke standing there, laughing, wearing a Santa hat.

"Very funny," she said as she got out of the car. She lifted her chin to him. "What's with the hat?"

Luke rubbed his chin. "You'll see. Should we go in the house?"

As they walked up the drive, she got to work convincing Luke this was the house for him. "What do you think so far? Two acres, a fruit tree orchard, plenty of space."

He nodded. She led them up the stairs to a small patio and

unlocked the door. Caroline was thrilled when she saw that the entire house had been decked out for Christmas since the last time she had been there. It certainly wouldn't help Luke's case.

They wandered from room to room, Caroline letting Luke take the lead. He'd occasionally mumble something about liking a countertop or wanting to change a light fixture but was, for the most part, relatively quiet.

When they were done and found themselves back in the living room, Luke took a slow look around and shrugged. "I like it."

Not the excitement Caroline was hoping for, but it would do. "Did you want to put an offer on it?"

He rubbed his chin. "Do you think we could be in it by Christmas?"

Caroline paused. She knew the answer, but she didn't want to tell him. When people are selling and have decorated for Christmas, they don't usually want to leave before the holidays.

He must've known what she was thinking by the look on her face, because before she could answer, he changed the subject. "What did you find out about the other house?"

She fidgeted with her keys. "Not much."

He watched her intently. She wasn't sure if it excited her or made her want to run. He looked around the room again. "Let me think about the house."

She made for the door and he followed. After she locked up, Luke stood blocking the steps. "Do you want to grab some lunch? There's a place I've been wanting to try."

"Okay. I need to swing by my house first and pick up a few things for a meeting I have later."

Luke followed her to her house, and when she came back out, he was waiting for her outside his Jeep. As she approached him, he swung his keys around his fingers. "Mind if I drive? There's something I want you to see, and I would like it to be a surprise."

Caroline thought this felt suspiciously like a date. She liked the idea of it. "Lead the way."

He went around the car and opened the passenger door, waiting for her to situate herself before he shut it again. When he got in and started the car, pop music blasted from the speakers. Caroline laughed.

He turned it down. "Ella really likes the popular stuff."

"Anything but modern Christmas music." She smiled warmly, and if she wasn't mistaken, he relaxed a little.

"This place is about twenty minutes away. That okay?"

"Of course. I always like to try new places."

They talked about the weather and Ella's wish list, which made Caroline a little nervous. She was happy to hear that there were several other things besides Fluffy the Dog that Luke was able to find.

The farther out of town they went, the more Caroline recognized the landscape. Although she hadn't been there in several years, she knew the area they were headed toward. The farther they went, the drier her mouth felt. "Where is it we are going again?"

"It's right up the road. We're almost there. I hope you're hungry."

She swallowed hard. Her appetite had vanished even though it was lunchtime. She watched the trees pass, bringing her memories of all those times as a child she had been riding in the back seat of her parent's car. It had felt like the trees went on forever. They were like a fortress to keep her safe from the rest of the world.

When the trees opened up on the small town, Luke found the first empty parking spot and pulled into it. His face lit up as he took in all the Christmas decorations.

Even Caroline couldn't help but feel the excitement of Christmas when she looked around.

She stepped out of the car and inhaled deeply.

"The air feels different out here, doesn't it? It's like you're breathing Christmas." Pure happiness emanated from him.

She had to admit, it did feel more like Christmas here than anywhere else. But it wasn't only Christmas she felt. It was the Christmas spirit that was woven throughout every part of the town. It was just like it had been when she was growing up.

"Come on, I want to show you something." He took Caroline's hand and walked with her down the street until they came to the square with the large Christmas tree in it.

It was just as she remembered. Purple, yellow, and red lights adorned the branches. The traditional ornaments made by the town children were hung from the tree by beautiful sparkling ribbons crafted by the town seniors.

It radiated Christmas spirit.

"I thought it might help you find some inspiration for your home tour."

Caroline nodded, unable to find the words. She had been trying to keep him from a home that was no longer hers, that she knew would bring him happiness. Yet he had thought to bring her here to help her find inspiration. Butterflies flitted through her stomach. She saw the look on his face as he watched the tree sparkling in the sunlight. She knew what she had to do. She only had to find the courage to do it.

"Stand in front of the tree, I'll take your picture." Luke pointed to a spot on the ground and took out his phone.

"I... I don't know."

"All you have to do is stand there. You'll thank me later when you're wracking your brain for inspiration." He stepped back and held up his phone, ready to take a picture.

She acquiesced and turned around. When she saw the smile on Luke's face, she couldn't help but put her arms out and pose with a goofy smile. He laughed.

She turned back and looked at the tree. Her parents had brought her to the tree-lighting ceremony every year. It was a town and family tradition. Afterward they would sing Christmas carols as they walked down to the church, where they would decorate cookies. As a child, she thought life didn't get any better.

"I'm starved." He took Caroline's hand and led her down the street until they came to Cathy's Diner. "They're supposed to have the best apple pie in the state."

Caroline hesitated. She knew that if she walked into that diner everything would change. She would have to tell Luke all about the house and where she grew up. There would be so much explaining to do about Christmas.

"Don't you want to eat?" Luke's eyes pleaded with hers.

There was something about him that made her want to make him happy, no matter what the cost. She gulped and walked in with him, hand in hand. When they approached the counter, he asked for two menus. Moments later, an older woman with long gray hair pulled into a braid came out of the kitchen. She wore a light-pink shirt with black pants and a black-and-pink striped apron. Caroline waited for her to make eye contact.

A young waitress seated them in a booth near the window, where they had a clear view of the decorations up and down the street. The older woman came by to pour coffee into their cups, but when she looked up to ask if they wanted decaf, she nearly poured the coffee into Luke's lap. He jumped out of the way.

"Caroline? Is that you?" Her voice was warm and round. "Well, I'll be!" She put the pot of coffee down and lunged forward. Caroline leaped out of her seat and stretched out her arms. Cathy had always given the most loving hugs. It brought her right back to her childhood. They rocked back and forth in each other's arms.

Cathy pulled away and held Caroline's face in her hands. "Let me look at you. You're so grown-up." She lowered her hands to Caroline's shoulders. "What are you doing here?"

Caroline motioned to Luke. "My friend Luke brought me."

Cathy spun around and slapped her thigh. "I am so sorry. I

didn't even see you there. I was just so shocked to see our sweet Caroline back in town. Are you visiting for a few days?"

Caroline tilted her head to the side. "We're only here for a few hours. I'm in charge of decorating several large houses for a Christmas Tour of Homes, and he thought I would find some inspiration here."

"Well, of course. They certainly picked the right woman for the job." She slapped her thigh again. "I'm going to let your friend look at the menu for a minute, but should I get your usual ready?"

"I can't wait."

Cathy winked at them and went back to the kitchen.

12

Luke

Luke watched Caroline. He couldn't believe how she sat there all innocent looking, as if nothing had happened. He checked for signs that she was going to tell him what was going on, but she seemed oblivious, gazing out the window with a satisfied grin.

"Clearly you've been here before."

Caroline slowly lifted and lowered her head.

"Many, many times."

She nodded again.

"Are you going to tell me more, or do I need to start guessing?"

She smiled bigger this time. "It's a pretty long story."

He opened his hands then clasped them together, his elbows resting on the edge of the table. "Turns out I've got time."

She leaned back in her seat. "I grew up in Brambling Falls."

He nodded and his eyebrows lifted, encouraging her to go on.

"This town was everything to me. It was all I knew. When my parents passed away, it was so sudden. I didn't know how to live here without them. I decided it was time to leave, and I moved to Portland. It was great for a couple of years, but then I began missing small-town life. Moving back here was too… filled with memories."

Luke whispered, "Memories are great to have, but they can be painful, too."

She nodded. "I moved to a town in the county next door, and I've been there ever since."

"You never came back? Not even to visit?"

"I thought about it, but it was just too much."

"But the decorations. How do you grow up around this and not want to decorate every year?"

Her smile saddened. "The decorations are great. I love them, I really do. My parents would both help put them up. It was the most exciting time of year. But they always emphasized to me that the decorations didn't mean a thing if there wasn't a bit of Christmas spirit in them."

"So, you keep the spirit," he said, bringing his hands to his chin.

"And I left the decorating behind. It reminded me too much of them."

"This Tour of Homes must be hard on you, then."

She shrugged. "I don't know. It's been so long. I still miss them. I just don't know if I can find it in me to enjoy the decorating as much as they did."

He watched as the sadness filled her. There was a tapping in his heart that told him to change the subject.

"Tell me about Brambling Falls. What was it like growing up here?"

She shook her head; her shoulders lowered as her body seemed to relax. "It was great. Everyone here is so friendly. They all know each other. Even though I was an only child, I always felt like I had a bunch of brothers and sisters. My mom loved to take in any child whose parents had to work. There was always someone over. I was never lonely."

"Do you keep in touch with any of them?"

"I left it all behind when I moved. There are a few people I talk to every now and then that keep me up to date with everyone. Lots of small towns are full of gossip that drives people away. Brambling Falls, it's different. People really care about each other."

Luke lowered his head. "Really? A town where everyone cares?" One eyebrow was cocked. It seemed too good to be true.

"Okay, fine." She leaned in and lowered her voice. His heart sped up as she came closer. "There is Mr. Halloway. He's the town scrooge. But even he hands candy canes out to the kids every year at the tree lighting. You should see his house at Halloween. It is amazing. He goes all out. Flying ghosts, mysterious fog, spooky noises."

Her eyes sparkled as she spoke, and he found himself even more drawn to her than before. "He sounds like a real scrooge." Luke chuckled. He leaned back in his seat, watching her, encouraging her to tell him more.

"Christmas is amazing." She nodded her head. "What you see out here, it's only a small fraction of what really goes on."

His eyebrows lifted. He tried to picture her as a child. He was sure she must have been strong willed. Maybe even a little mischievous, but in a curious way. Definitely fun-loving. "There's more than all this?"

She held a hand up to Luke, as if telling him to hold on. "There are cookie-swapping parties. Gingerbread-house-building workshops. The movie theater down the street shows a different Christmas movie every week, complete with a hot cocoa bar." She pointed over her shoulder. "Carolers wander the streets after church on Sundays. City Hall displays all the trees decorated by the elementary school—each grade gets to decorate its own tree. Those wreaths from the wreath-decorating contest? They are hung along Main Street on lampposts. It's hard not to love Christmas growing up here."

Luke watched her for signs of sadness but saw none. She was in her element talking about this town. It undoubtedly lit her up. Deep down another thought bubbled. Ella would love it here. He imagined her gawking at the tree in the square, listening to carolers in her Sunday best, and learning how to make a gingerbread house, a task Luke was certainly not up to teaching. Then he pictured Caroline there, with them.

He shook his head. Where did that come from?

"It sounds wonderful."

"It is. The best part of it all isn't what you see. It's what you feel, here." She put her hand over her heart. "It's all done with so much love and kindness for one another." She was beaming. Her cheeks were glowing.

"It sounds like you really loved it here."

She nodded slowly, lost in thought.

Cathy came by and took Luke's order. He wanted a burger, but she said it was too boring and that she'd bring him a shepherd's pie instead. When Cathy left, he turned his attention back to Caroline.

"I'm sorry if today—"

"No. Today has been incredible. It's been way too long since I've seen Cathy, and I think I may have found some inspiration."

"Really?"

"Yes." She held up her hand with her fingers about an inch apart. "Just a tiny bit."

They laughed and chatted until Cathy brought out their food. She put the shepherd's pie in front of Luke and a pastrami sandwich with an extra helping of coleslaw in front of Caroline.

"I never would have pegged you for a pastrami kind of lady."

"What did you think I would order? A salad?"

Luke started laughing, crumpling his napkin in his hand before wiping his mouth. He nodded. "Yeah, most definitely."

"Well, there is a lot you don't know about me yet."

Yet. He liked the sound of that.

They finished their meal, Caroline telling Luke about the last of the four houses she had to decorate and how she had no idea where to start. Luke told her stories about the families he refers to the shelter, and how it would be his first time helping with the shelter's Christmas project. When he was about to pay the check, Caroline's demeanor changed. She became very quiet and wouldn't make eye contact with him. It reminded him of how she acted when he told her about the house he wanted to see. As a police officer, he was used to reading people's body language. Caroline was different, though. He didn't know if it was his emotions that were getting in the way, but he was unable to read her.

She brushed her hair out of her face and looked him directly in the eyes. His skin flushed and he swallowed.

"Are you okay?" He watched as she forced a smile, then nodded.

Luke sat and watched a moment longer, until he was convinced that she truly was fine. When they had hugged Cathy goodbye and promised to come back soon, they made for the car. As they approached it, Caroline slowed.

"There's something I would like to show you." She stopped and waited for him to follow her.

"Okay. Lead the way." As he walked beside her, he realized that he would go anywhere she asked.

What had gotten into him?

They passed the car and crossed the street. She led him down a path between a barbershop and a store that sold wood sculptures. The walkway was narrow, and under any other circumstances, he would have been suspicious. Once they came out on the other side of the buildings, his mouth fell open.

They were in a shaded garden dappled with a sprinkling of light snow. A gravel path wove through the space, which was spread with patches of poinsettias, holly, and some varieties of green shrubs. There was a gazebo at the end of the path with a small Christmas tree decked in gold ribbons. What stole Luke's breath, though, and left him still were the rows of luminaries that dotted the pathway. They glowed brightly in the shade of the trees, like beacons guiding lost souls to Christmas.

"It's as beautiful as I remember."

He held her hand tight.

"It's Christmas spirit."

He was quiet. He didn't want to ruin the moment. When a bird flew and landed in a tree nearby, he turned to Caroline and whispered, "I think you need to include luminaries on your home tour."

Her eyes grew wide as she looked at him. "I think you're right." The excitement in her voice made Luke excited, too. They were silent, standing inches apart, looking at each other. He could feel his heart pounding in his chest. Did she feel the same?

"We'd better get back," she whispered.

Luke nodded, then took her hand and led her back to the car. When they reached it, she put her hand on his arm.

"Thank you for bringing me here. It was nice to be back for a little bit."

"Of course," he said as he opened the car door and swallowed all the emotions that were threatening to form.

❈

When he dropped Caroline off at her home, he watched her drive off to her meeting, then sat in his car on the street for a few minutes. He thought about how the world had brought them together not once, but twice. There was something about her that made him so unpredictable. Why was he unable to get ahold of his feelings when he thought about her?

Before he knew what he was doing, he had his phone out and was searching for information on the Christmas Tour. He found it quickly—they were doing a good job advertising. He could see why Caroline felt so pressured about creating a first-rate holiday experience. Although, he suspected that she was the type that took it upon herself to make everything she was involved in a first-rate experience. He took a notepad from his glove compartment and wrote down the addresses. Glancing at his watch, he calculated that he had just enough time before picking up Ella. He shook his head and started the car.

13

Caroline

aroline closed the door behind her and sat at her desk. Butterflies danced in her stomach as she went over the trip to Brambling Falls. She had always thought it would be painful to go back. Today, however, she had actually enjoyed the trip. She had felt safe, secure. All the memories of Christmas and her youth lingered in her mind.

Luke had made sure that she experienced all the happiness that the town had to offer. He had been right. It was exactly the kind of inspiration she needed to pull this Tour of Homes together. There was a small pang in her heart as she remembered the Christmas her parents had taken Cathy in. They had heard she was sleeping in her diner after her house had sustained fire damage. Caroline's mom loved to cook, but she let Cathy bring home every meal from the diner that season because it was the only way Cathy felt she could repay them.

Luke had been so gracious with Cathy, casually allowing her to cook him whatever she felt he needed instead of what he wanted. He would fit in perfectly in Brambling Falls. He had been so thoughtful to take her there.

Then she remembered the house he wanted to buy. Had it all been a ploy to get her to fall in love with the town as well?

No. He didn't even mention the house. He had simply wanted to help her experience Christmas. He wanted to inspire her. Isn't that what he had said?

There was a knock on the door. Sarah peeked her head in. "Everyone is gathered in the conference room."

"Great." She began gathering her papers when Sarah stepped all the way into the office, hugging her clipboard close to her chest.

Sarah's head was cocked, her eyes narrowed, as she watched Caroline.

Caroline stopped what she was doing and looked around to see if she was missing something.

"What? Is my hair a mess?"

"No. It's just you're smiling a lot."

"Is that bad? Do I not normally smile?"

"You do. It's just a little different today. Like you know a secret or something."

Heat rushed to Caroline's cheeks.

"No secrets here." She angled her body away from Sarah and gathered a few more papers, most of which she didn't need for the meeting.

When she reached the conference room, Caroline plopped all her papers onto the table in front of her and looked out to the decorating-committee members that had been able to make it at the last minute. Chris glanced at his watch.

"Thank you all for meeting on such short notice, especially since we already met this morning. While I was out today, I was hit with some inspiration, and I wanted to make sure that we got started on it right away."

Rebecca sat at the edge of her seat, anxious to hear what Caroline had to say. Victor relaxed in his chair; his hands were folded across his lap. Where was Nick? Alexandra opened her computer, ready to bring whatever idea they had to life. Sarah, as usual, scribbled away in her notebook.

"Luminaries." She watched for their reaction.

Alexandra's eyes lit up and she frantically typed into her computer. Sarah nodded. Everyone else watched Caroline, waiting for more.

"We are going to line the circular driveway leading to house number three with luminaries."

The rest of the team slowly nodded their heads.

"But we need something more. We need something that will bring this beautiful house to life. I know Maggie isn't here, but she will attest to how amazing this one really is. If you haven't had a chance, drive by the home and think about where else the luminaries could go. Okay. Who wants to be in charge of supplies for luminaries?"

Sarah's hand shot up.

"Great. Victor, Alexandra, and Rebecca, I want you to come up with a clean, sophisticated look for the interior. I'm thinking something along the lines of fresh green boughs with pops of red ribbon. Maybe some holly and mistletoe. Some simple, classic red stockings. And the tree decorations should be uniform. Lots of red, green, and silver glass balls with red ribbons tied about."

They looked at each other, then huddled around Alexandra's computer.

Satisfied that everything was more or less on track for the tour, she headed back to her office and back to the clients patiently waiting for her to find their dream home.

That evening, Caroline made herself a cup of hot chocolate, turned on some traditional Christmas music, and made herself comfortable on the floor in the living room. Stacked all around her were piles of toys and rolls of wrapping paper. It was a tradition for her to get a head start on the gifts she bought for the families she adopted at Christmas.

She picked a toy from the pile, selected the perfect wrapping paper for that child, then wrapped it diligently, so no corners were torn and every edge was folded over. She placed the tape perfectly over the seams, then found the matching ribbon to wrap around the gift. Finally, she topped it with a colorful and coordinated bow. Once that was done, she put a Post-it with the child's name onto it, and attached it to the gift.

The making of the tags was an event of its own and was done once all the gifts were wrapped.

She made her way through the pile, enjoying every moment of it. It reminded her of when she was a child and how her mom would pick gifts out for all the kids in the neighborhood that she knew were having a hard year. Her mom had taught her how to wrap and how important the perfect bow was for each present. It was the one Christmas tradition she had carried with her. Though it made her miss her parents, it was what the Christmas spirit was made of—giving to those in need.

It was almost ten o'clock when she came to the final present, the one she had left to wrap with extra care and attention. She stopped and looked at it. Guilt surged through her. Fluffy the Dog sat there on her floor, staring back at her.

She thought about this family, which barely had a home. This family that was struggling to put food on the table and may not have a home in the near future. She wanted to do all she could to help them. Then she thought about Luke and Ella, and how Luke had let her have the dog, not knowing it was for a family in need. She thought about how he wanted a home for Ella so badly, and how she was the one denying him that. The one way she could repay him for letting her have the dog, and she wouldn't even talk to him about the house.

She let out a sigh.

She took the dog in her hands and placed it in front of her, then looked at the rolls of paper and picked out a sparkling red with images of Santa Claus checking his list. Next to him was a large bag full of toys with teddy bears poking out. She wrapped the dog as best she could, folding the paper around the awkward edges and taping them down carefully. When she was done, she found a soft cream ribbon and carefully wrapped it around the present. On the top, she put a bow made of many loops of glittery, red ribbon.

"Perfect," she said as she placed a Post-it on.

She sat looking at the wrapped dog for a few moments. She played back the trip to Brambling Falls with Luke over and over in her head. He had been truly excited about the town. He loved it as much as she had growing up there, and he'd only been there twice. She thought of all the memories she had made with her family. As painful as they were, she had them. Who was she to keep him from giving Ella a happy life filled with the kind of memories she herself had been blessed with?

She slid onto the sofa and turned on her laptop. She found the home's listing and sat there for a moment staring at the photo in front of her. It looked the same. The large, white front door in the center of a spacious wraparound porch that held memories of so many of Caroline's firsts. The winter jasmine her mom had planted when Caroline had been a toddler was still reaching its branches up the tall white pillars that framed the porch. Directly above the front door was the Juliet balcony off what used to be her bedroom. The gray siding was weathered, but still made the house look warm and cozy inside. The old branches from the oak tree in the yard reached out around the side of the house. Her eyes scanned the picture for signs of her parents that she knew weren't there. There was so much history. The house and her parents were practically one and the same.

It *had* been her home, and it still held her memories. Memories she wasn't sure she wanted to face, especially at this time of the year.

It wasn't fair for her to keep the house from Luke.

What would her parents want her to do? She had wondered that so many times before—when she sold the home, before she left Portland, and today when she was at the diner.

She bit her lower lip, letting it slowly slide out from between her teeth. Then she took a deep breath and emailed the agent handling her childhood home to set up a showing for Luke.

✻

The next morning, she woke up to the silence of snow. She rolled out of bed, threw on a thick robe, and pulled the curtain back, exposing her small yard. The metal bench on the brick patio where she often drank her morning coffee in the summer had an inch of snow sitting atop it.

She loved this about Oregon; the fresh piles of snow she woke up to in the winter months that urged her to sleep in. Not today. She had too much to do.

She made herself a cup of coffee and sat at her kitchen table, which overlooked her front yard. The road had already been plowed, and the faint whish of a car passing seeped in through the silence every few minutes. Once she was fully awake, she took out her phone and checked her email.

There, at the top of her inbox, was an email from the agent handling her childhood home. The owners were out of town for a few days. They could see the house today. She laughed when she read that the agent suggested coming by earlier to familiarize herself with the home.

Before she had a chance to stop herself, she was dialing Luke's number.

"Hey, Christmas Elf. I'm glad you called. Ella and I have something for you."

She paused, taken aback by his familiar way of greeting her.

"Hello?" he said, more serious this time.

"Yeah, hi. I'm here. It was a bad connection." She shook her head, thankful that he couldn't see the embarrassment rising to her cheeks. "I have a surprise for you, too."

"You first." His voice was strong and comfortable at the same time.

"All right. Are you ready? Are you sitting down?"

"Whoa. It's a big surprise then?"

Caroline cleared her throat.

"Okay, okay. I'm sitting. Go ahead."

"I can get us into the Brambling Falls house today, if you still want to see it."

The phone went silent. Then very quietly, he said, "Really? Today?" He spoke quickly, the anticipation getting the best of him.

She nodded, then realized he couldn't see her and laughed at herself. She needed to get it together if she was going to see Luke today.

"Yes. Really."

"Thank you. That's amazing. Ella and I will be ready to go in fifteen minutes."

"Hold on. How about I meet you at the house at noon?"

"Perfect. We'll see you then."

"Wait—what about my surprise?" Caroline was shocked at how forward she was being.

"Your surprise will have to wait until we see you." His voice was light. Was he flirting?

"See you at noon then."

Caroline hung up the phone and sat back in her chair. She finished her coffee as she watched the birds fly from branch to branch. She was filled with excitement and nerves. She couldn't decide if she was more excited about seeing Luke or more nervous about being in her old home.

Her breath quickened as all the possibilities rushed in. What if she can't hold it together? What if she can't keep the memories from flooding back? She inhaled deeply and closed her eyes.

She thought about Luke's deep voice and how it felt when he held her hand yesterday.

It will be fine, she told herself before getting up and getting ready for the day ahead of her.

14

Luke

Luke paced back and forth across the kitchen three times before Ella poked her head in.

"Daddy? Are you okay?" Her big eyes were filled with concern.

He bent down to her on one knee. "I'm fine. I have exciting news."

Her eyebrows lifted with his voice. "What is it?"

"We have a house to look at today." He watched her, waiting for a reaction.

Her head tilted. "One for us to live in?"

He shrugged. "Maybe. We have to see it before we decide."

She paused for a moment as if deep in thought. "Is Caroline going to show it to us?"

He nodded.

The smile grew on Ella's face. "Do we get to show her the surprise we came up with yesterday?"

"Absolutely. Let's see the house first. Then we can tell her about the surprise." Luke stood back up and walked to the window, looking out to the front of the apartment. He rubbed his chin. Ella tugged on his shirt and he turned to face her again.

"Can we have a picnic lunch today?"

"Of course." He leaned back on the counter, his arms folded in front of him. Ella continued to watch him. She clearly wanted something more. He raised his eyebrows at her.

"Can Caroline come with us?" Her voice was tiny and nervous.

He lifted her up and sat her on the counter beside him.

"You like Caroline, don't you?"

She nodded.

"You've only met her once, though."

She shrugged. "I mostly like her because you do, Daddy." She leaned over and hugged him tight. His heart melted, then sped up as he thought about what Ella said. He *did* like Caroline. Even his daughter could see it.

He put Ella back on the floor. "Get dressed so we can get going."

"Okay, Daddy." She crinkled her nose at him before running off and yelling down the hall, "Don't forget, I like ham-and-cheese sandwiches."

✳

Noon couldn't get there fast enough. He had taken Ella to the mall to see Santa Claus and do a little more shopping. But as soon as the clock hit eleven thirty they jumped in the car and were on the way.

Luke had been thinking about this moment since the first time he and Andrea had visited. He was full of nervousness by the time they pulled into Brambling Falls. Ella went quiet, her usual chattering absent, when she saw all of the Christmas that was around her. Luke pulled over and parked.

"Wow." Ella's mouth hung open.

"It's pretty amazing, isn't it?" Luke couldn't stop watching her. Her eyes blinked several times before she just stared out the window.

"Is this where Santa lives?" she whispered. Luke smiled back at her and shrugged.

"Let's go look at the tree."

She slowly unbuckled her seat belt and slipped out of the car. As she walked down the street, her jaw was slack. The decorations glimmered in the sunlight, making the walk even more magical.

When they got to the square, Ella froze. They both stood, staring in a daze.

"That is the most amazing tree I've ever seen." She stepped forward until she was so close that her nose could touch the lowest branches. "It smells like Christmas."

"It's pretty amazing, isn't it?"

Ella nodded her head slowly, her eyes closed as she inhaled deeply, trying to take in every part of the tree that she could.

They walked back to the car in silence. When they came upon a booth decorated with hanging gingerbread men and cut-out yellow stars, a child waved and asked if they wanted to buy some cookies and hot cocoa. Ella looked up at her dad with pleading eyes.

Luke laughed and bought two cookies for their picnic and two hot cocoas to drink on the way to the house. As he was paying, Ella poked his side.

"Daddy, you forgot one for Caroline."

He hadn't forgotten. He could never forget Caroline. He had just hoped to share his with her. "You're right. We need one for Caroline, too."

He bought another cookie, and they headed back to the car.

As they were driving up the road, Luke was filled with a mixture of feelings. What if Ella didn't like the house? What if *he* didn't like the house?

Then he thought of Caroline. He was excited to see her. She occupied his mind almost constantly, and the only way to alleviate it was to see her. There was also the whole issue of the surprise he and Ella had for her. He couldn't wait to see what she thought about it.

The road wound between the trees, with a river appearing between the trunks every now and then. Ella opened her window and stuck her head out.

"It smells like Christmas out here, too."

Luke inhaled. She was right. It really did smell like Christmas everywhere in this town.

They soon came to their turn. Luke took a moment to calm his nerves, then headed through the open gate and up the gravel driveway until it opened to a beautiful green lawn. In the middle of the lawn was the house. It sat comfortably among a few small trees, with a large oak tree hovering protectively behind.

"Daddy? Why did you stop driving?"

Luke hadn't even noticed he had stopped the car. All he saw was Caroline, standing on the front porch waving. His heart skipped a beat. It felt like he was coming home.

He cleared his throat and slowly pulled the car forward until he was at the house. Ella jumped out and ran up to Caroline, throwing her arms around her.

"You found us a house!" she yelled.

"It's your daddy that found this house," Caroline responded. There was a sadness in her eyes.

Luke made a mental note to check on her later when Ella was distracted.

As Ella let go and ran to the edge of the porch, leaning over to see around back, Luke stepped up the three stairs, taking his time. "I can't thank you enough for getting us in to see this house."

She shook her head. "Don't thank me. You found it."

Ella came running back. "It smells like Christmas here, too."

Caroline gave her a big, beaming smile as she squatted down to Ella's height. "It sure does. This house is surrounded by Christmas tree farms. On every side of the property, you'll find nothing but Christmas trees. You know what that means?"

Ella haphazardly shook her head.

"It smells like Christmas all year round."

Ella's eyes grew bigger. She looked at Luke. He laughed.

"Does that mean Santa comes all year round?"

"I don't know, Ella. I think you'd have to talk to Santa about that. Even he needs a break sometimes."

She giggled and bounded down the porch and around the corner. Caroline held her hand out, guiding Luke to follow. Ella's footsteps patted around the house, with Caroline and Luke close behind. When they reached the back patio that spread out into the yard, Ella stopped. She slowly took the large oak tree in.

She cocked her head. Caroline walked up and stopped beside her. "This tree has been here for a long, long time. There used to be a tree house in it with a ladder that led right up the trunk to that branch." She then pointed to another branch farther down the tree. "And that branch, right there, is perfect for a swing."

Ella looked up at Caroline, wonder in her eyes. She ran back to Luke and grabbed his hand. "Can we have this house, Daddy? Please?"

"Why don't we take a look inside first?"

Caroline led them to the back entrance. She pulled the screen door and it creaked open. She let Luke enter first, followed by Ella. They found themselves in a warm farmhouse kitchen. He was almost sure that he could smell gingerbread baking, but maybe it was from the cookies he still had in his jacket pocket.

The kitchen was large enough to feed a decent-sized family, with a table in the corner and booth-style seating along a window. The oven could fit a twenty-pound turkey easily, and the stove above it had six burners. He looked to Caroline, but she was staring blankly at the kitchen table. If only he knew what she was thinking.

He ran his hand through his hair. "This is great."

Caroline snapped out of her daze and smiled meekly. "Let's go see the living room."

She pushed open a swinging door that led to a warm room with a massive, deep fireplace. There was a wooden mantel that Luke longed to hang stockings on.

"Whoa. Santa could definitely fit through there." Ella wrapped her hands around her belly, then giggled.

The wooden floor let out small squeaks as they walked around. Luke looked out each window, taking a moment to absorb the views. He couldn't see any houses at all—just open land and trees.

Caroline led them through to a formal dining room with a large chandelier hanging in the middle and then to another room with dark-brown paneled walls. "This room has been used as a library in the past, but as you can see the current owners are using it as a family room."

There was something different about Caroline's voice that Luke couldn't quite put his finger on.

She led them upstairs to the bedrooms. There were three of them, two of which were right next to each other.

"Ella, there's something I want to show you." Caroline walked into the bedroom that was painted pink. Ella followed close behind. She led her to a set of French doors at the opposite side of the bedroom. Caroline opened them and rested her arms on the balcony railing overlooking the front yard of the house. Ella leaned out as well. Luke was close behind.

Caroline bent down so she was closer to Ella's height. She

looked out into the forest of trees and held a finger up. "Look out there. Do you see that tree that's taller than all the others?"

Ella nodded.

"That is the oldest tree in Brambling Falls. It's over one hundred years old."

Ella gasped.

"Every year on Christmas Eve, a bright-yellow star appears at the top. It's said that it helps Santa find his way to this town."

Ella's eyes glistened. She turned to Luke. "Daddy, did you hear that?"

He nodded.

Ella turned her focus back to the tree.

Luke watched Caroline and how she was a natural with Ella. He noticed how she had thought of all the things a little girl would love about this house. When Caroline turned around, Luke was still watching her. He blushed, but she just smiled, holding his gaze until Ella turned around and ran between them.

"Let's see the rest," she called as she left the room.

Luke wandered through the house, listening to all that Caroline had to say. When they had seen everything, she led them to the back porch again. Ella ran out to explore the yard, leaving Luke a moment to talk with Caroline.

He could sense there was something going on with her, but he wasn't sure how to ask. They stood on the porch in silence, watching Ella wander the yard, leaving footprints in the shallow snow. He wished he could wrap his arms around Caroline and tell her that whatever was plaguing her would be fine, but he could hardly find the words to ask her how she was doing.

"Are you okay?" He wasn't as smooth as he had hoped to be.

She must have been deep in thought, because when he spoke, it snapped her to attention. "Yes. I'm fine. I've got a lot on my mind." She hesitated a moment. "So, what do you think of the house?"

"I love it." He did. He was drawn to it even more now that he had been inside. It was more than the perfect house. It felt like home. It felt like everyone that had lived there had loved it. "Do you think we could be in by Christmas?"

She turned and looked at him. "I think it's a definite possibility. I can call them as soon as we're done."

Ella came running back, snow caked on her boots. "Can we have our picnic now?"

"Of course." They both turned to look at Caroline.

Ella ran forward and took Caroline's hand in hers. "You'll come with us, right? Daddy packed enough sandwiches for all of us. He even got you a cookie at the hot-cocoa stand."

Caroline's smile emanated warmth. "I'd love to join you. In fact, I know just the spot."

15

Caroline

Caroline hung up the phone, her heart racing with the possibility of a new home for Luke and Ella, but sinking at the memories nudging at the back of her mind. All they could do now was wait for the sellers to call her back.

She pulled out of the driveway, making sure that Luke was following close behind. She turned down the road toward town, but after about five hundred yards, she veered onto a dirt road where tires had cut a path through the snow. She followed it as it wound through groves of trees and between large stumps of old fallen ones. Finally, the road opened up to a small gravel parking lot. She pulled over and parked. Luke did the same.

Ella stepped out of the car while Luke went around to the trunk and pulled out a soft-sided cooler, followed by a large thermos.

Luke and Ella took the scenery in around them. They were in the middle of a grove of trees, nothing more. They looked skeptical.

"Don't worry. You're going to like this." Caroline led them to a small path between two rocks. She walked slowly, letting them breathe in all the Christmas air and take in their surroundings. Birds flitted from one tree to another, chirping as they did. Branches rustled as a slight breeze blew at the top of the tree canopy. The land began to slant downward, and the trees spread out. In the distance, water trickled.

As she walked the path, Caroline remembered all the times she had been there before. When she was a child, her dad had brought her here. He loved to tell her about all the birds that made these trees their home. They often brought paper and pencils and would sit together for hours, sketching all the different things they saw. Then, when she was a teenager, she and her friends would come and dip their feet in the cool river water during the hot summer months.

When they reached the bank, Caroline turned to face them. "Welcome to Town River." She spread her arms out.

"It's amazing." Ella walked up to the edge. Luke stepped forward to keep her from falling in.

"Don't worry. It's only about six inches deep here."

Ella stood with her hands in her jacket pockets.

"This is amazing. Thank you for bringing us," Luke whispered to Caroline.

She walked him over to the one picnic table in the area, protected from the snow by the large tree next to it. Luke tossed a blanket over the table and opened up the cooler. Caroline helped him take out the food. He had brought quite the spread. There were ham-and-cheese sandwiches made with croissants, and a fruit salad full of apples, orange slices, bananas, and kiwi, all topped with chopped almonds. He had carrots and bell peppers and a tub of hummus. There was a pile of pita bread. Next he put out the three gingerbread cookies he had bought at the stand. It must have been Derek and Sylvia's kids at the stand. She remembered all the days she had bought hot cocoa from Derek and Sylvia themselves.

Once they had everything spread out, Luke called for Ella to join them. They talked about Ella's school and Luke's work as they ate, and houses Caroline had seen and sold over the years.

"Why is it called Town River if it's not in the town?" Ella asked.

Caroline nodded. She loved how smart Ella was and all the questions she asked about the town. "That is a great question. When they first built the town, it was along this river, but a way down the hill." She pointed to the left. "See, the first people that came to Brambling Falls were looking for gold. It only made sense to build on the river. Back then, the town was so new they hadn't named it yet. They had to name the river, though, so people would know which river they were digging in. Since it had a town on it, they called it Town River."

"Is there gold in the river now?" Ella was intrigued.

Caroline shook her head. "No. No one ever found any, but people kept coming because it was such a beautiful area. After rainstorms kept flooding the town, they decided to relocate it to where it is today."

Ella seemed to think about this for a while. Caroline saw how Luke watched his daughter, amused by all her little characteristics.

She liked being here with them. She felt she belonged here, like she was a part of them, almost. She shook the idea out of her head. She wasn't sure how Luke felt about her, and if he bought the house, well, then she knew she'd have to say goodbye.

When they were done eating, Luke whispered something into Ella's ear. She jumped up and ran to the cooler, pulling a notebook out of the side pocket. She handed it to Caroline.

"What's this?" Caroline asked as she looked down at it.

"Look inside," Ella insisted.

She flipped the cover open, and there on the first page was a drawing of one of the houses on the tour. It was decorated with red ribbons and green wreaths and had been transformed into something sophisticated and fancy. Her jaw dropped. She looked up at them.

"This is amazing." She turned the page again, and there was another drawing of the same house, with different decorations.

"Keep going, there's more," Ella encouraged. Luke looked at Ella, rubbed her back, then looked to Caroline.

She flipped through the pages of the notebook. It was filled with drawings of all the houses on the tour, each with two or three different decorating possibilities.

"My daddy worked on it all night." Ella nodded, pride beaming from her face.

Luke cleared his throat quickly. "Ella helped until it was bedtime."

"It was my idea to have the carolers at a house. I love Christmas music and carolers."

Caroline, her head leaning to the side, looked at Ella. "Carolers. I think that's exactly what I need to bring Christmas joy to the house with the luminaries."

Luke came and sat next to her. "That's where I put them." He flipped through the notebook until he came to the page with the carolers. There, next to the long lines of shining brown paper bags, was a set of carolers—women in long dresses and men in top hats and coats. She couldn't believe he had taken the time to draw these for her. They were beautiful and inspiring. They were exactly what she needed to get the home tour going.

She looked up to find Luke sitting very close to her, his eyes settling on her every move. Her heart raced and a warmth radiated through her. "Thank you. This is—" She couldn't find the words to express her gratitude.

He was so close to her, his warm breath mingled with hers. "You're welcome." His voice was soft and deep. He stood up. "We'd better be going. You'll keep us updated on the house, right?"

Caroline jumped up and started to pack things away. "Of course. When I get back to the office, I'll draw up the papers. Can you swing by at around four today to sign them?"

Luke nodded. Ella was nearby, balancing on a log and humming "Rudolph the Red-Nosed Reindeer." When it was time to go, she skipped ahead of them until they reached the cars. When they had packed up the Jeep, Ella ran over and gave Caroline a big hug. She released her and skipped her way back to the door and jumped in.

Luke walked Caroline to her car. She watched him: how his hair ruffled in the breeze, how the cold turned his cheeks red. When they reached her door, they hugged. Her heart pounded, and she hoped he couldn't feel it through their thick jackets.

"Thank you," he whispered in her ear, sending chills throughout her body.

She smiled and nodded her head once.

Back at the office, Christmas music was playing exceptionally loud. As soon as Caroline stepped in, Sarah came running over. "We need to talk." Her voice was rushed and low. What had happened? Was there a looming disaster with the Tour of Homes? Her shoulders tensed and she took a deep breath, trying to prepare herself for what was to come.

Sarah led them into Caroline's office and shut the door behind them. "Santa Claus Is Coming to Town" blared through the door. Sarah rolled her eyes. "Sorry. I still need to fix that."

They both sat down. Sarah had her notebook pressed against her chest.

"What is going on?"

"It's Nick and Rebecca. They got into a huge fight, and now Nick hasn't been coming to the office."

Caroline shrugged. Her heart rate slowed. "Okay. What does that have to do with us?"

"They are both on the decorating committee."

Caroline shrugged again.

"Nick went to pick the first load of decorations up the other day. They are in his car. That is at his house." She stared at Caroline blankly.

Caroline sat back in her chair, her hands folded in front of her. "Okay. We can solve this." She thought for a moment. She had to take care of the house offer for Luke. She had to figure out how to decorate all these houses, get the supplies, and furnish an entire home. There was no way she was going to be able to do all of it on her own while dealing with other people's love lives.

Sarah sat staring at her, the notebook balanced on her lap, pen at the ready.

Caroline leaned forward in her chair. "First, call a meeting in fifteen minutes. I have some ideas I want to share with everyone. Then, I want you to figure out the whole Nick thing."

Sarah's eyebrows went up. "Me? I'm just an assistant."

"You are not just an assistant. You keep us running smoothly. Everyone loves you, Sarah. If there is anyone that can solve this Nick issue, it's you." Caroline smiled encouragingly.

Sarah bounced her head once. "You're right. I can do this." She jumped out of her seat and left the office. Once she was out the door, she grabbed a stepladder, reached for the bell and took it down, then threw it in the trash can, where it continued to blare "Santa Claus Is Coming to Town."

Caroline winced. She hadn't meant for the bell to be a total casualty, but if that's what it took for Sarah to gain confidence, then so be it.

She gathered the papers for Luke's house and set them aside for when he would come in. She grabbed her laptop and the notebook Luke had given her and set off for the meeting.

When she called for everyone's attention, Alexandra raised her hand. "Where is Sarah? We can't start without her."

"She will join us in a bit. She is taking care of something for me."

She shared the notebook, and they were able to finalize a design for three of the four houses. Everyone liked the idea of the carolers, and it left her with only two more homes to bring the Christmas spirit to.

"The number one issue we need to deal with is getting furniture into the home with the large lawn. We have the sleigh for photos with Santa, but no furniture. Rebecca and Alexandra, I want you to coordinate with Jessica from Anderson's to finalize the plans and then get it staged ASAP. Chris, can you find us some old-fashioned carolers?"

Chris nodded and wrote something in his notebook. "My friend Sylvia is in a caroling group. I will check with her."

Then it hit Caroline. Sylvia and Derek's hot-cocoa stand. "I think we should have hot chocolate and cider at one of the homes."

Rebecca cleared her throat. "What about the home with the amazing kitchen? Could we do warm drinks and cookie decorating out on the patio by the fire?"

Caroline thought it over. Her mom would bake Christmas cookies every year, and they sat together for hours decorating them. They would make red and green and gold frosting and top them with all the sprinkles they could find. She let out a small sigh as excitement fluttered in her belly.

"That's a great idea. Can you work on getting a donor for the cookies?"

Rebecca nodded.

They went through detail after detail, referring to the notebook often. Alexandra tweaked the designs in her computer as they came up with more ideas, until each home fit its assigned theme and looked sophisticated and graceful.

It was starting to come together. She felt relieved that they at least had more of a plan now, but the decorating would be a task in itself. She glanced up at the clock. They had been so involved with the planning that she hadn't realized it was time to meet with Luke.

She excused herself from the meeting and made her way to her office. She found Luke sitting there, in her chair, smiling.

He was holding a picture frame in his hands. "Is this you with your parents?"

She smiled. "It was taken the year I graduated from high school." The photo had the house, Luke's house, in the background. She carefully took the frame from him before he noticed. "Are you ready to sign some papers?"

He nodded. She pulled another chair close beside him. The weight of his stare while she prepared the paperwork made her both nervous and excited. Before she handed the papers over for him to sign, she said, "There are other houses in Brambling Falls that I could show you."

He shook his head. "We want this one."

A pain ran through her heart. She could tell him. He would understand. He had felt loss like she had. Guilt surged through her. If he did understand, he would be giving up his dream of a perfect place for Ella to grow, for what? Because Caroline didn't want to face the pain that came with the memories of that house? She couldn't do that to him.

"Of course. Just sign here."

When they were done, they both stood. She had never noticed how she had to lift her chin slightly to meet his eyes. When they reached the doorway, he stopped. "Thank you. I can't tell you how much it means to me to see Ella happy and at home somewhere. She really likes you."

"I like her a lot, too."

They stood smiling, holding each other's gazes, unaware of what was around them.

Sarah walked by and gave Caroline the thumbs up. "Situation solved." Then she pointed above them, where the annoying bell had previously hung. "I replaced the bell with some better decor." She walked around the corner, leaving them alone.

They both looked up. There, hanging above them, was mistletoe. When their eyes met again, Caroline bit her lip and rested her hand on her collarbone. "I'll let you know when I hear from the sellers."

Luke paused, as if he had something to say. Then he nodded and left.

<h1 style="text-align:center">16</h1>

<h1 style="text-align:center">Luke</h1>

Andrea handed Luke a coffee as she slid into the passenger seat of the police car. "So, you like her. What's wrong with that?"

Luke smoothed the stubble on his chin. "I didn't say I like her."

Andrea rolled her eyes, then settled them on Luke, not breaking her gaze.

He put the car into drive and pulled out onto the street. Andrea leaned back in her seat. "It's okay to be scared. Things won't always end the way they did last time. You and Caroline and Ella could live long, happy lives together."

Luke did his best to keep his emotions under wraps. It bothered him that Andrea could so easily see through him. Then again, it was what made her such a good cop. Being able to read people was pertinent to doing a good job in their line of work.

"Ella obviously likes her. She's finding you the home of your dreams. According to what you say, she's beautiful and smart. I don't really see the problem."

Luke shifted in his seat. "There's something bothering her. She's been acting different lately. I'm not sure what it is."

"Did you ask her?"

He rubbed his chin again. "Sort of, yes. I asked if she's okay."

Andrea looked directly at Luke again, her eyebrows lifted this time. "She's a woman. Not a perpetrator. You probably need to approach it a little differently."

"How does Dave ask if you're okay?"

"He just asks. That's different, though. We've been married twelve years. I understand all the little details of what he's trying to say when he only says three words. This whole thing with Caroline is new. You need to be a little more specific."

Luke let out a big sigh.

"How long were you married when she passed?"

He hesitated. He had loved his wife with every part of himself. It nearly broke him when she died. But he had found a way to make a life for himself and Ella. Maybe he didn't believe in fate or destiny or soul mates as much as he used to. Maybe his heart wasn't in the Christmas decorating as much as he led others to believe. It was hard going through life knowing it could all be taken away and that there was nothing that could be done to stop it. Even so, he had found a way to go on, changed as he was.

"Seven years. We had been together for ten. We were college sweethearts."

"So, it's been a while since you dated, then."

"Who said anything about dating?"

"Okay, Lover boy. Maybe you should ask her out on a date. Get to know her."

He thought this over. Was he ready to date? How would Ella feel about it? She really liked Caroline. So did he. Maybe it was time to open his heart to the possibilities again.

"How am I supposed to ask her on a date if I can't even ask her what's bothering her?"

Andrea rubbed her hands together. "Well, try by telling her you noticed something has been on her mind lately. Then ask her if she'd like to talk about it."

Luke nodded. "I can do that."

"Then you ask her out on a date. Like a real one. Not one where you both happen to be out so you casually end up horseback riding."

Luke chuckled.

"I know you, Luke. It's okay to put your heart out there. You'll find that when you're open to love, it finds you."

They rode in silence. When they came to a stoplight and sat there for a few minutes, Andrea continued. "So… the department Christmas party is coming up pretty soon. Are you bringing anyone?" She laughed heartily.

"You're the worst, Andrea. Subtlety has never been your strength, has it?"

"I find it's so much easier to just speak your mind. Life is too short to hold it all in."

❁

Ella was sitting on the steps of the school quietly twisting her backpack drawstring through her fingers. Luke's heart rate sped up when he saw her. Something was wrong.

"Are you okay?"

"Yes. I just want to go home." She stood up and threw her backpack over her shoulder.

"You're upset. Are you hurt?"

She shook her head, her pleading eyes looking up at him. "Can we please go home, Daddy?" Her voice wavered.

"Yes, sweetheart. Of course." He put his arm around her shoulder and led her back to the car.

She was silent most of the ride home. When they made it half-way, he couldn't take the silence any longer. "How was school?"

"It was fine."

"Did you learn anything new?"

Through the rearview mirror he saw her shrug.

They were silent the rest of the drive home.

Ella slowly dragged her backpack out of the car and pulled it along behind her until Luke came and took it from her. When they reached the top of the stairs, Ella looked out over the front of their apartment and across the street to the homes that stood there. Luke tried to figure out what she was looking at, until he spotted a Christmas tree, fully decorated and lit up, peeking out through one of the homes' windows.

He bumped the door open with his hip and turned to Ella. "Hey, what do you say we go get a Christmas tree?" He knew there was a small chance they would be moving before Christmas, but what if they didn't? It was time for them to start decorating, regardless.

She turned to him; her eyes lit up like the Christmas lights. She nodded vigorously.

"Go grab your jacket." He dropped her backpack on the sofa and waited for her in the living room. When she appeared, she was wearing a pair of reindeer antlers with blinking lights. Luke chuckled.

"Let's go." She ran out the door before Luke could say anything.

As they rode in the car, the radio blaring pop music, Ella spoke up. "Why don't we ever listen to Christmas music?"

Luke swallowed hard. He struggled to find the words to answer her. He didn't make a practice of listening to Christmas music. It reminded him too much of the Christmases they had spent as a family. The decorating was something he could do. He knew Ella loved it, and that was enough to make him get it done. Ella's mom had been the one that did it all before, and she had loved every minute of it. The warmth and love that she had put into the celebration of Christmas was incomparable to anything he could ever do. So he didn't even try. He just made the best of decorating for Ella.

But now she wanted to listen to Christmas music. She was certainly her mother's daughter.

"I mean, isn't that what you're supposed to do when you get a Christmas tree? It's not only about the decorating. It's about the spirit of Christmas, too."

"I think maybe you've been listening to Caroline too much."

Ella giggled. "I think she's right. There's not much point in all the decorations if there's no heart behind it."

Luke tuned the radio to a Christmas station.

As they pulled into the tree-lot parking, Ella began bouncing in her seat. "Are we cutting down our own tree, Daddy?"

"I was thinking we would pick what's already cut like we normally do." He turned to look at her.

Her lower lip protruded and she scrunched her forehead.

There was no point. Luke's heart was melting.

"I suppose we could cut one down." He thought back to the last time they had done this. Ella's mom was with them. She had them wander the forest, Ella packed into a carrier on Luke's back, until she found the most perfect tree for their home. She called it *the Tree of All Trees*.

Luke and Ella entered the tree farm, hand in hand, and set off in search of the perfect tree. "It can't be too tall. Or too fat. In fact, it has to be pretty small to fit into our apartment." She looked to Luke with a knowing smile.

He nodded. She checked every tree they came across. First, she would stand a few feet back, her head tilted slightly. Then, she would place her face between the branches so she could smell them properly. Next, she would run a few branches between her fingers. Finally, she would step back and say, "It's almost perfect, but there is something missing."

Deep in the forest, they came across a group of five or six people, all of them wearing Santa hats with bells hanging from the tops. Luke and Ella smiled politely and stepped aside to let the group, who was clearly on a mission, pass them. As the last person in the group approached, Luke's heart started to race.

She looked just like Caroline. She had the same wavy brown hair that fell down her back, and her blue eyes sparkled in the same way. That's when he realized it *was* Caroline. Why was she wearing a Santa hat, of all things?

"Luke?" she said, stopping scant inches from him, forced close by the narrowness of the path. "What are you doing here?"

"Caroline!" Ella came running up to them.

Caroline kneeled and hugged Ella. If Luke wasn't mistaken, Ella held on a little longer than she normally did.

"Nice hat." Luke tucked his hands into his pockets.

Caroline stood up and was about to take it off when Ella said, "Leave it on. I like it. If you're looking for the Tree of All Trees, you need all the Christmas spirit you can gather, or you'll never find it."

A chill ran through Luke as Ella's words registered. Could she remember that's what her mom used to call it? Somehow the memory didn't hurt as much when it was coming from Ella.

"Well, I'd better keep it on then, because I need to find *four* perfect trees."

Of course, she was looking for trees for the Tour of Homes.

"I'm sure you'll find them. You're all wearing hats." Ella giggled.

"That's exactly what Sarah said when she told us to put them on." Caroline laughed, too.

"Daddy, I just had a great idea. Can Caroline come over tonight and decorate the tree with us?"

Luke rocked back and forth on his heels, then scratched his

chin. He looked from Ella to Caroline, then back again. "I don't know. I'm pretty sure she's busy tonight." He knew how she felt about decorating, and she was already faced with decorating four homes. He wasn't sure she would have the heart to turn Ella down, either.

Caroline shrugged. "I think I can come by for a little bit."

A weightlessness spread across his chest. She sounded like she actually wanted to come and decorate. Or was she only being nice? "Are you sure? We would understand if you—"

"It's the least I can do, after those amazing designs you made for our team." She reached out and placed her hand on his upper arm.

Jolts of electricity shot through him.

"Caroline, we found one," someone in the group called from down the path.

"I'd better be going." She patted Ella on the head and waved to Luke then disappeared through the trees.

"Let's go find our tree." Ella sped up ahead of him.

The tree farm spread out over a few acres, and Luke was sure they had seen every single tree growing there before Ella found the perfect one. It was short, and its branches were uneven, but Ella thought it would make the decorations look that much better.

They cut the tree down and Luke carried it to the car. Ella skipped along singing a variety of Christmas carols that Luke didn't even know she knew the words to.

Maybe Caroline could help him figure out what had been bothering Ella when he picked her up from school. He carefully tied the tree to the top of their car and climbed in. Ella stuck her head over the seat and whispered into his ear, "Thank you, Daddy. This is going to be the best Christmas ever." Then she kissed him on the cheek and climbed back into her seat and buckled up.

17

Caroline

A light snow was falling when Caroline parked in front of Luke's apartment. She eyed the Santa hat on the seat next to her. She had been embarrassed when Sarah had insisted that everyone wear the hat. When she saw how excited Ella had been about it, though, she thought maybe she should wear it again. She slipped it on her head and made her way up the stairs to the front door.

When she raised her hand to knock, the door opened. Luke stood there, wearing a matching Santa hat, and a wide grin. He nodded slowly. "I had a feeling you would be wearing that hat."

"Ella seemed to like it." She shrugged.

Luke stepped aside and motioned for her to come in. "Have you eaten dinner yet? I've got chili on the stove top."

"Sounds delicious."

She followed him into the kitchen and he took her jacket.

Caroline had never been to their home before. She wanted to look around and see what made him tick, what was important to him, but she knew it wouldn't be polite. Instead she pulled out a chair and sat at the counter.

"Where's Ella?"

"She's finishing up her homework. She'll join us in a minute." He poured a cup of tea for himself then held out an empty cup for Caroline. When she took it, he filled hers to the brim. He put the pot back on the stove and rested his elbows on the counter across from her. "I was hoping you could maybe help me out with something."

She wanted to reach out and touch his elbow, and tell him she would gladly help, but restrained herself. "What is it?"

"When I picked up Ella from school today, she was upset about something. She wouldn't tell me what. I was hoping that since you're a girl and she's a girl, you could maybe talk to her and figure out what's going on?"

She was flattered that he trusted her enough to check in with Ella. "Of course. I'd be happy to."

He reached his hand forward and let it land on hers. "Thank you."

They stayed there in the kitchen, hands overlapped, for a few moments. Warmth radiated through her body. Their faces were inches apart; she could almost feel his breath.

"You're here." Ella came running into the kitchen and hugged Caroline again. "You're wearing the Santa hat, just like my daddy."

Caroline felt the blood rush to her cheeks. She nodded. "I hear your dad made chili tonight. Is he a good cook?"

Ella nodded. "He's the best."

She climbed onto the seat next to Caroline as Luke placed bowls of tomato, onion, and cheese on the counter. Then he filled a bowl with chili and placed it in front of Ella, and prepared two more heaping bowls for himself and Caroline.

Ella talked about the hunt for the Tree of All Trees and how she finally found the right one, then asked Caroline how her search went. Caroline told them about how Nick and Victor couldn't agree on whether they wanted a short and fat tree or a tall and skinny one for one of the houses and that they ended up flipping a coin that eventually got stuck in a tree.

Ella giggled her way through dinner. The only sign that she was upset about anything came when Luke was gathering the bowls and putting them in the sink. He asked her if she had finished her homework. She nodded, and quieted from her usual chatter. Luke looked at Caroline out of the corner of his eye.

The pain and concern in Luke's face were obvious. Caroline reached out her hand and placed it on Ella's back.

"Why don't you show me where these decorations that your dad has been telling me about are."

A wide smile reappeared as Ella jumped down and took Caroline's hand, leading her to the several large boxes that were stacked in the hallway.

The boxes were so large that someone could barely squeeze past them. What had she gotten herself into? She should have known this was going to test her no-decorating policy, after all the stories he had told her about his decorations. Not to mention the amazing designs he had come up with for the home tour. Only a true expert could have thought up those designs.

She felt a little light-headed and her legs were wobbly.

"Dad, you'd better come in here."

Luke came rushing over. "What is—"

He took one look at Caroline and grabbed her hand. "You'd better come sit down. You are very pale."

He led her to the sofa and helped her sit. Ella showed up on her other side with a cup of water. Caroline smiled and took a sip.

"I'm sorry. I don't know what's come over me. Maybe we should get started decorating."

Ella disappeared around the corner, and there was the sound of boxes being shuffled around.

"You don't have to do this. I know it's not really your thing." Luke sat next to her, holding tightly on to her hand.

Caroline didn't know what had come over her. She wanted to be there. She wanted to be a part of their decorating. It had been years since she had decorated on her own. That was different. She thought about the houses and the Tour of Homes that loomed over her. She would have to decorate all of those homes. This had seemed like the perfect way to ease into it.

Ella came around the corner, her little body leaning on a box that inched across the floor each time she gave a heave. When she made it halfway to the sofa, she enthusiastically took off the lid and pulled out one plain green decorative ball.

"I think you can handle this." Ella handed the ball to Caroline.

She took it in her hands, turning it over as if it had some sort of significance. It was the most generic Christmas tree ornament she had ever seen.

"The ugly box," Luke and Ella said in unison before bursting into laughter.

Caroline couldn't help but giggle herself.

"When Ella was little, she wanted to play with all the decorations on the tree," Luke began.

"I kept dropping them and breaking them." Ella shrugged.

"So, I went out and bought a box of ugly ornaments that she could play with and not worry if they broke." Luke looked at Ella, pride beaming.

"He didn't realize that he bought unbreakable ones. So, all these years later, we still have them."

"Now it's kind of our tradition to put up the ugly, unbreakable ornaments first." Luke walked over to the box and pulled out a red-and-white Santa. His hat wasn't painted on quite right, and it made his head look funny. "We call this one Three-Eyed Santa."

Ella burst into giggles again. She took the deformed Santa from her dad and placed him on the tree.

"It's your turn now. Go ahead, put up the ugly green ball."

Caroline got to her feet, ornament in hand. Ella reached out to her other hand and took it, leading her to the tree. Caroline reached up and placed the bulb on a branch that didn't have much greenery.

"See, Daddy. I told you that branch would look beautiful with an ornament on it."

"You're right, Ella. It really does."

When Caroline turned back to look at Luke, he wasn't focused on the branch at all. Instead, he was looking at Caroline. A warmth she couldn't explain came over her.

Luke pulled another ugly ornament out of the box and Ella started laughing. Caroline couldn't imagine anywhere else she would rather be.

They spent the rest of the evening drinking warm cider and decorating. Caroline even suggested that they put Christmas music on as they decorated.

When it began getting late, Luke looked at his watch and suggested that Ella get ready for bed. She skipped out of the room, to return five minutes later in footed pajamas, a book in hand.

"Can Caroline read to me before you kiss me good night?"

Luke looked to Caroline. She stood at the tree, hanging a small golden star. She wiped her hands on her pants and walked toward Ella. "I'd be happy to."

"I'll be waiting right here." Luke filled his cup with cider and made himself comfortable on the sofa. "You and I can finish decorating tomorrow."

An ardor filled Caroline, one that she hadn't felt in a long time.

Ella took her hand and led her past the boxes and into her bedroom. The walls were plain white, but the windows were surrounded by soft pink curtains. Her bed was covered in a fluffy lilac bedspread whose ruffles cascaded down the sides. There were framed pictures of Ella and Luke on the walls. One picture was of a much younger Ella and a beautiful woman. They were both laughing. For a moment, Caroline felt like she was intruding.

"That's my mom. My daddy took that picture." Ella climbed into her bed and pulled the covers up to her chin.

Caroline sat at the foot of the bed. "You must miss her."

She shook her head. "I don't really remember her very much." She was quiet for a moment and appeared to be off in deep thought. "But I do miss having a mom."

Caroline nodded in agreement. "I miss having a mom, too."

"Why don't you have a mom?"

"She died a long time ago. And I still miss her."

Ella was quiet again. "There's a Christmas mother-daughter tea coming up at school." She played with the covers at her chin. "I wish I could go."

Caroline's heart sank. She knew the pain this child must be feeling, but there was nothing she could do to make it better. This also likely explained why she had been upset after school.

"Do you think you could talk to your dad about it?"

Ella shook her head. "My Daddy was really sad when she died. He tries hard to be both a mom and a dad. I don't want to make him sad again."

Caroline reached out and patted her knee. "I can understand that." She truly could. There was something about Luke. Something that made her want to make him happy.

After a moment of lying there silently, Ella said, "I think I'm ready for that book now."

Caroline read her one of her own childhood favorites, Corduroy. When she was done, with her eyes half closed, Ella whispered that she was ready for her dad.

❄

Caroline sat on the sofa, sipping her cider as she waited for Luke to come back out. When he did, he was smiling. "She seemed a little happier. Did she tell you what was bothering her?"

She didn't answer immediately. She didn't want to betray Ella's trust, but she also wanted to be able to help her. She put her cup on the side table next to the sofa and folded her hands in front of her. Luke watched her patiently. She had to tell him.

She cleared her throat quietly. "There's a mother-daughter Christmas tea coming up at her school."

Luke drew a breath and released it through a clenched jaw. He dropped his head against the back of the sofa.

"I could go with her. I mean, I just met her, but if she needs someone there with her, I could go." The words spilled out of her mouth before she knew what she was saying.

Luke's eyebrows popped up. "You would do that?"

She shrugged. She knew how it felt to want to have your mom around. She was an adult and had a hard-enough time with it. But a child… Ella was a great kid, and she deserved to have someone there with her for the Christmas tea.

She looked at Luke, hope spreading across his features; his forehead relaxed and his shoulders no longer looked tense. She nodded encouragingly. "Of course."

"Thank you." His hand fell to the sofa cushion, covering hers. A warmth traveled through her body and landed in her cheeks. The light from the tree glimmered on the two of them, settled close on the sofa. "I'm really glad you came to decorate with us tonight." His voice was soft and husky.

Decorate. Caroline remembered all the work she had to do tonight to prepare for the decorating meeting tomorrow. She lowered her head. Luke pulled away from her slightly.

"I had a great time, but I should really get going."

"Of course." He jumped to his feet and held out a hand to help her up.

When they reached the door, before opening it, he rubbed the back of his neck. Caroline smiled and stepped over the threshold. She was surprised at how quickly he escorted her out. Was he anxious for her to leave? She put her gloves on, trying to buy a few more minutes, though she wasn't sure what to say. Finally, she turned to Luke and smiled, then waved, and made for the stairs.

"Caroline?"

Her heart raced. She turned back to him.

"Would you like to go to dinner sometime?" He held her gaze, awaiting her answer.

Her heart drummed in her chest. First, she slowly nodded, then she said, "I would love to." She bounded down the stairs, containing the laughter that so badly wanted to escape.

18

Luke

When he pulled into the station, Luke's head was still buzzing from the night before. He found Andrea in the hallway, leaning against the wall waiting for him.

"What's up?"

"We've got some families to check on." She pushed off the wall and handed him a stack of folders as they walked to their car.

He shrugged. "Okay."

She stopped when they got to the car and turned to Luke. "You seem a little distracted today."

He couldn't help but let a smirk show.

"Ah. You asked her out and she said yes."

"Get in the car." He laughed as he said it and slid into the passenger seat.

"Did you ask her what was bothering her?"

Luke paused. He hadn't. He had been so sidetracked by Ella's problem that he had completely forgotten that something had been bothering Caroline.

Andrea took his silence as confirmation that he hadn't. "Well, I guess you'll have plenty of time to ask her when you're out on your date then."

He would. Although he didn't remember her being very upset at any point last night. He rubbed his chin. "She's taking Ella to a mother-daughter tea at school."

"That's great." Andrea's voice was very matter of fact.

"Do you think that's dangerous? Is it too soon? I mean, we barely know her."

"I trust your judgment, and you seem pretty fond of her."

"What if it doesn't work out?"

"You mean between the two of you?" Andrea cocked her head as if confused. "That doesn't mean she won't still make a great role model for Ella."

"You're right. She has a good job, a level head on her shoulders. She cares about people. She takes good care of herself."

Andrea was suspiciously quiet. Luke stopped himself from going on, but it was too late. She had already caught on. Her eyebrows were raised and her lips were shut tight.

"Yep. Go on."

Luke shook his head. "I can't believe I walked right into that one. She's great. I admit it. That's why I asked her on a date."

Andrea reached over and patted him on the shoulder. "I'm proud of you, partner."

Luke rolled his eyes, but he knew Andrea was right. This was a big step for him.

❁

As Andrea turned left onto a narrow street, she told Luke to find the exact address they were looking for.

"It's this one," he said as he pointed to a small, white one-story clapboard house. The wood was deteriorating, and there was graffiti along one wall. The front yard was dirt, with a concrete path leading to a set of concrete stairs that opened to an empty patio where the front door stood.

Andrea parked and they made their way to the door. Neighbors peered from behind curtains but quickly disappeared when Luke or Andrea looked their way. Luke visited neighborhoods like this on a regular basis, but it still shook him. To see that some people had to live like this broke his heart.

"Don't look so solemn, Miller." Andrea knocked on the steel screen door. "We're here to spread Christmas cheer, remember?"

There was a clicking sound coming from the other side of the door before it slowly creaked open a few inches. A woman's face peered out. "Can I help you?" Her voice wavered.

Police were not normally welcome in this neighborhood.

"We'd like to talk to you about Christmas," Luke started. "May we come in?"

She watched them warily, as if she was weighing the truth behind what they said. Then slowly, she opened the door and unlocked the metal screen. She had a toddler on her hip.

"Come in," she said as she held the screen door open for them. "Please, have a seat." She motioned toward a small living room with a single sofa that had tears along the back. There was no coffee table, no side chairs. Just a fireplace with a small fire burning in it. Yellowed sheets hung over the windows as makeshift curtains.

They followed her to the room and sat. She stood across from them. Luke got to his feet, and motioned for her to sit instead. She did.

"We came by to see how we could help make Christmas a little easier for you this year." Luke tried to take the policeman out of his voice and talk as he would with Ella or Caroline.

The woman looked at him in disbelief. "You want to help me?"

Luke nodded.

Andrea continued. "We know this can be a tough time of year for people, and we want to help make it a joyous time for your family."

The woman swallowed. "What do I need to do?"

Luke smiled. Andrea asked her what items she would like for her home and what her kids would want for Christmas.

"Food would be nice. My mom used to bake for us every Christmas, and I haven't had the money to do that for my family. My children could use beds. They are sleeping on a mattress on the floor right now. I would love for them to have a bed."

A small child came running out of an adjoining hallway. "Mommy, I'm hungry." Her voice was small and sweet. It reminded Luke of Ella when she was younger.

Andrea wrote something in her notebook.

The woman excused herself for a moment and left for the kitchen. A cupboard opened in the next room, and she returned with a piece of bread, handing it to the child. She looked up at her mom. "Can I have some cheese with it?"

The woman sat back down and whispered to the girl, "Not until Friday. Then we'll have more food, okay?"

The little girl nodded and ran off to where she had come from. Luke was having a hard time keeping himself composed. He rubbed the back of his neck.

Andrea stood up. "All right, thank you, ma'am."

The woman stood to watch them leave. Luke wasn't sure she believed why they were there. They waved goodbye, and the toddler on her hip waved momentarily, then put her hand back in her mouth.

When they reached the car, Luke took the driver's seat. He turned the car on and made a U-turn, determination across his forehead.

"Where we going?" Andrea asked.

"To the store. Let's get that family the Christmas they need."

"Luke, we're supposed to pass their information on to the shelter, and they will find someone to adopt them for the holidays."

"Can't we adopt them? You and me?"

Andrea tapped her fingers on her notebook, then flipped it open and read whatever she had written. After a moment she looked back at Luke. "Let's do it."

❄

Andrea pushed the shopping cart through the store, following Luke as he grabbed things off shelves and put them in the cart. He piled the cart with toys, candy, and books he thought the kids would like. Then he moved on to the clothing section and put in jackets and dresses. Finally, Andrea stopped him.

"I think we're missing the point here."

Luke froze and looked at Andrea. "What do you mean? They need all this stuff."

Andrea nodded. "Yeah, they do. But it's just stuff. Isn't Christmas about more than stuff?"

Luke's shoulders drooped. She was starting to sound like Caroline.

"What do you have in mind?" Luke was almost afraid to ask.

"Do you remember what she said about her mom?"

"You mean the baking thing?" Luke shrugged.

"Yes. Let's get them some food and some baking things, and let the shelter take care of the rest. We can't adopt every family that needs help out there."

Luke looked back at the toys he had piled in the cart.

"Okay, we can give them a few of the toys, too." She shook her head, letting out a joyful sigh.

Luke carefully put the majority of the items back where they belonged as they walked to the baking section. They found two bread pans, a cake pan, a couple of baking sheets, some measuring cups, and a mixing bowl. Then they went to the grocery section and loaded up with flour, eggs, milk, cheese, granola bars, fruit, and anything else they thought the kids would enjoy.

They packed everything into the car and set off for the home.

This time when they knocked, and the woman looked out the window and saw them, arms full of bags, she quickly opened the door. They wriggled their way through the entry and stood there, waiting. The woman's hands flew to her mouth. Luke's heartbeat slowed, and there was an ache in his throat. He didn't know what to say.

"This is for us?" She burst into tears and led them into her kitchen. The countertops were clean, but bare.

Luke handed her the bag with the bakeware in it. She slowly pulled a pan from it then placed her hand on her heart. As she went through the bag, Luke and Andrea put her groceries away for her. When they were done, the woman just stood, the mixing bowl clasped in her hands. "I don't know what to say. Thank you."

Luke swallowed hard. Tears were threatening to pour from his eyes. He wanted so much for Ella, and all this mother wanted for her children was food and a comfortable place to sleep.

Luke nodded while Andrea hugged the woman. They turned to leave the kitchen and found four small children standing in the doorway, watching them.

Luke wiped at his eyes with the back of his hand. He reached for the wrapped gifts that were on the kitchen counter and handed them out to the children, one at a time. Then Luke and Andrea squeezed past as the children ran and hugged their mom.

"Merry Christmas," they both said as they waved and walked out the door, leaving the mother crying in the embrace of her children.

The lump in Luke's throat was solid, and he was sure it would be there a while. This was the spirit Caroline was always talking about. This was the part of Christmas that brought joy and could change people's lives. He was beginning to remember what he had missed the past few years.

Now it was time for him to help Caroline.

"I've got some more Christmas cheer I'd like to spread. Can we swing by the Christmas tree lot?"

❊

Luke balanced the tree on his back as he walked up the path to Caroline's house. He wasn't surprised to find the yard neat and tidy, with colorful flowers reaching for the sun through the light layer of snow. He took the two steps up to the patio in one large leap and looked for a good place to leave the tree. To the right of the door, there was a bench with a bright-red cushion on it under a picture window, with an eave protecting it from the snow. To the left, there was an open space barely big enough for a person or two to stand. He propped the tree there, securing it in its stand, and tied the message he had written and placed in an envelope to the tree.

He stepped back. There was a flutter in his stomach as he gripped his hands together in front of him. She seemed to have a good time decorating last night. She was ready for a tree of her own. He was sure of it.

Finally, he took one of the ugly ornaments they had started with last night and hung it securely on the tree above the envelope.

"Hey, Romeo, can we get to work now? We've got some patrolling to do," Andrea whisper-yelled from the window she had opened.

Her words rolled off him like melted snow. He grinned as he looked at the tree, then tucked his hands into his pockets and jogged to the car, ready to take on the rest of the day.

19

Caroline

The first thing Caroline did when she got to the conference room was make herself a cup of hot cocoa, complete with whipped cream and sprinkles. Next she went to the front of the room and turned on some Christmas music. Then she waited for everyone to join her.

They trickled in one by one, each as pleasantly surprised as the next. They followed suit, making themselves hot chocolate and taking a seat, waiting for the meeting to start. When the clock struck ten, everyone was seated and waiting. They were more quiet than normal and watched her curiously, as if they were afraid that whatever spell had overtaken her would soon disappear.

She tried not to laugh.

"That feeling you got when you entered the room? That's how I want people to feel when they walk through the homes we are decorating. I want them to sense that unexpected Christmas joy as soon as they set foot on the path leading to a home. The question is, how are we going to get them to feel that?"

"The luminaries are a nice touch." Sarah held her pen in the air as she spoke.

"I think Santa and his sleigh will do it, too," Chris said softly.

Caroline looked to the ceiling of the room, as if drawing inspiration from the heavens. "What if we have Christmas tree decorating at one of the homes?"

Sarah jumped in her seat and clapped her hands quickly together. Alexandra nodded. Rebecca looked thoughtful for a moment, then spoke up.

"We could have kids string popcorn."

"Yes. That's what I'm looking for." Caroline nodded.

Sarah scribbled on her notepad.

"What else can we come up with?" Caroline led them as they brainstormed more ideas and made lists of supplies. To her surprise, she found herself enjoying coming up with ideas and how to add them to the homes. She thought about how much Luke would have enjoyed the meeting and wondered what kind of ideas he would have contributed. Every time she looked down at the notebook he had given her, her heart raced. It was in large part thanks to Luke that this home tour was coming together.

The sun was starting to set when Caroline got in her car to go home. As she made her way down the road, her phone rang. She switched on the speakerphone button, and Lauren's voice came through.

"Hey. How's it going? I saw you called earlier."

"I just wanted to check in." She paused a moment. "And let you know I had a great time with Luke."

"Really?" Her voice was cautiously optimistic.

"Really. I'm taking Ella to a Christmas tea at her school."

"I'm so happy for you. It sounds like you really like him."

Caroline didn't answer, but a warmth filled her as she replayed the night in her head. A phone rang in the distance. "Are you still at work?"

"Yes. I've been swamped with planning the shelter's Christmas Eve dinner. It's going to be amazing this year, but I won't bore you with decorating details, and I should probably answer that call."

"Sounds good. Get some rest." She clicked off the line.

She turned on the radio and switched it to the Christmas station, a small smile involuntarily taking over. She took her time driving, appreciating all the bright lights that decorated the homes as she wound through the neighborhoods. She pulled over to the curb and parked in front of her home, which was dark, with no lights outlining the roof or twirling down the porch posts.

She got out of the car, her thoughts returning to the Tour of Homes and how to best go about decorating four large homes in the span of a few days. She stepped up the two stairs and slid her key into the lock of her front door. There was a strong scent of Christmas tree, just like she had known growing up in Brambling Falls. Now on alert, she noticed the modestly sized tree on her patio. Attached to it was an envelope, and an ugly ornament. Her lips parted, and she reached out to touch a branch.

She pushed open the door and put down her purse, then ran back out to the porch, giddy as a kid on Christmas morning. She did her best to pick up the tree and carry it into her home without tripping over the threshold. Once she was in, she looked around. Where would the tree go? She had never before had a tree in this house and hadn't ever thought about where to put one.

It would fit next to the fireplace, but then it blocked part of the television. Not that she ever watched it. She looked back toward the door. It would fit perfectly in front of the window, where all the neighbors could see. She giggled when she thought about what they would say when they saw she had put up a tree.

It didn't matter. Part of the Christmas spirit was sharing our joy with others.

She moved a few things away from the window then dragged the tree across the floor, leaving a trail of needles behind her. She stepped back and tilted her head to one side first, then the other. She moved the tree a few inches to the left then stepped back and looked again. She dusted off her hands and placed them on her hips.

She reached out and held the ugly ornament, still attached to the tree, then let it dangle. She opened the envelope and read what Luke had written.

To help inspire your Christmas decorating. Thank you for last night.

—Luke

Her heart flipped as she read it.

There were a few boxes of decorations that she had taken with her when her parents passed away; they were hidden in the attic somewhere. She changed into a pair of yoga pants and a sweatshirt and pulled down the stairs that led to the attic. Once she reached the top step, she yanked on the string attached to the light bulb, switching it on. She made her way through the cobwebs and dust until she found a pair of boxes labeled Christmas. She carefully took them downstairs one at a time and placed them in front of the tree.

The smell of home wafted out as she lifted off a lid. She was instantly engulfed in memories of eggnog, candy canes, and gingerbread houses. Her heart felt heavy, but something in the box shimmered and caught her eye. As she peeled back the tissue it crumpled in her hands. There it lay in the box. A tree ornament of a ballerina in a shiny pink tutu, with a dove sitting on her shoulder. Her mom had given it to her after she saw The Nutcracker for the first time. Her chest heaved. She got to her feet, trying to catch her breath, and hung the ornament at eye level. She tapped it with her finger, and the dancer spun in a circle as if she were on stage. Caroline smiled.

She pulled back another piece of tissue and uncovered several ornaments. There was a wooden nutcracker, a frog wearing a Santa hat that she had bought her dad at a school fair, and a glass wreath with a picture of her as a child in the center. She placed each one on the tree, finding exactly the right spot, then taking a moment to admire them. Peeling back another layer of tissue, she discovered a row of glass snowmen—one for every year she lived at home. They varied in size and shape and color, but they were all snowmen that signified the same thing: every year you could start afresh. Mom always said, "Every year is a new chance to reinvent yourself, like a snowman from freshly fallen snow."

She ran her finger across the snowmen. They were cold to the touch. The first one wore a pink snow hat that read Baby's First Christmas. The next one had a pacifier. Her heart squeezed in her chest. Her parents would never have wanted her to stop celebrating Christmas. They would have wanted her to build herself up, like a snowman at the start of winter. They would have wanted her to go on celebrating as they had.

It was so painful to not have them there, celebrating with her.

The sharing of joy and taking care of other's needs came easy to her. But celebrating it herself? She wasn't sure she was ready.

Memories of Christmas breakfast in the breakfast nook, just the three of them, played in her mind. They would get out of bed, place the baby in the manger, then sing a Christmas carol for Him. Next, her mom would make pancakes filled with red and green sprinkles, topped with whipped cream and a drizzle of fresh-made orange-cranberry sauce. When breakfast was done, they would find themselves in front of the Christmas tree. They would take turns handing each present to the person it was for, then watching them open it. In the afternoon, the neighbors would get together and sled, sing carols, and drink eggnog. That's where Caroline had learned that the true joy of Christmas was in making others happy.

They were memories that were so dear to her, she wasn't sure she wanted to remember them. Knowing her parents were gone meant she couldn't make more of the same memories.

Now Luke was going to buy the house and those memories would be front and center in her mind any time she saw him. She wiped her eyes with the tips of her fingers, then carefully folded the tissue over the snowmen and closed the lid. As she passed through the living room on her way to the bedroom, she stopped near the stack of presents by the fireplace. Suddenly she felt an overwhelming desire to make her parents proud.

One by one, she moved the presents from the fireplace hearth to under the tree, arranging them as she added more. She couldn't stop; each one she moved made her more determined that those kids would have the best Christmas ever. As she stacked and restacked, more memories came to her: her dad opening the baseball glove she got him, her mom opening a scarf Caroline had knit her. Caroline opening a beautiful doll with long, wavy brown hair that she had seen in a shop window but had never had the courage to ask for because she knew it was expensive.

The weight of all the memories was more than she could bear. Still, she hadn't thought about them in so long. For the first time in a long while, it felt like she had a past. It felt like there was a tiny piece of her parents with her there, under the tree.

She grabbed a stack of paper and feverishly cut out stockings, reindeer, and trees, then affixed sequins and glitter to them. She wrote each child's name in fancy script until every present under the tree had a unique tag.

She took a deep breath and stepped back, looking at the tree. It seemed to radiate even brighter than before. She swallowed, one hand over her heart. Then she whispered, "I miss you, Mom and Dad."

❄

Snow had fallen steadily all night long, and Caroline awoke to the sound of the snowplows clearing the roads. She lay in bed for a few minutes, watching the sunlight reflecting off the snow-clad trees and into her bedroom, as it danced on the wall. She reached her arms above her and stretched, running the day's plans through her mind. Another decorating-committee meeting. She let out a sigh. They were getting there. In a few weeks it would all be done and over with.

New clients were coming by the office today to talk with her about the kind of home they would like to find. She made a mental note to check all the current listings and see if Maggie had any new homes to sell that hadn't been listed yet.

When she thought about the end of the day, a smile swept across her lips. Luke was taking her out. Her heart leaped with the potential of what was there, then sank when she thought about the home he had his heart set on.

She rolled out of bed, grabbed her robe from the chair, and wrapped it tightly around her. She was headed for the kitchen to make herself a cup of coffee when she passed the tree. It stood glowing from the sun behind it, glorious. The presents in merry reds, cheerful greens, and royal golds warmed up the room. She looked out the window at the crisp, white ground.

It felt different in her home today. It felt like there was the promise of something. She might make it through this Christmas after all.

First, though, she needed to put lights and more ornaments on the tree.

20

Luke

After dropping Ella off at school, Luke found himself driving past Caroline's house. Adrenaline rushed through his body when he noticed the Christmas lights glimmering off the tree and through the window. He slowed his car, carefully watching to make sure she didn't spot him. He thought back to a few nights before, and the glow he had seen on her face when she helped them decorate their tree. Maybe there was hope for her yet.

He turned the corner and headed for work, lost in thoughts of Caroline. Ella seemed to truly like her, which meant a lot to Luke. When his wife passed, he thought he could never love anyone again. Seeing Ella, though, and how she viewed the world so positively and full of possibilities, he had begun to see things differently. If a little girl can lose her mom and still move through this world with love and hope, then he should be able to as well.

His wife had loved Christmas and put her heart and soul into all of the festivities. Luke hadn't found the way to emulate that feeling. The way she made everyone feel around the holidays was inimitable. Every cookie she baked was full of love, every card she wrote carried heartfelt wishes. Every ornament she hung on the tree shone as if it had been made solely to greet the Holy One on His birthday.

After his wife had passed, he had studied the homes around them. He had watched how all the other dads diligently put up lights and cut down Christmas trees. He had watched as they went on late-night shopping trips fulfilling their children's biggest wishes and set out cookies for Santa. Ella may not have had a mother that first year, but she certainly had an amazing Christmas.

Every year after that, he made sure that, even though they had moved to a new town and into a small apartment, Ella had an incredible Christmas. Their home was always filled with Christmas cheer and festive decor. Yet there was always something missing. It was the spirit that Caroline spoke about. He could give Ella all the decorations in the world, but he couldn't find it in his heart to feel Christmas the way his wife had before she died. The way Caroline did now.

As he pulled up to the station, Andrea was already waiting for him. He stepped out of the car and placed his hands on his hips.

"What is it?"

"Just trying to get us out of here on time. Wouldn't want to make you late for your date tonight." Andrea winked.

Luke rolled his eyes. "You talked to Pam."

Andrea shrugged. "It's a small town. Word gets around."

"It's not that small."

They walked together to the patrol car. Luke slid into the driver's seat with Andrea following into the passenger side.

"Have you heard about the house yet?"

Luke shook his head. "Caroline said they were out of town and wouldn't be able to respond for a few days."

"How do you feel about it?"

"I feel like I put a bid on a house and I'm getting a little impatient waiting for an answer."

"Yeah. I get that, but do you think you'll get it? What does your gut tell you?"

He stopped at a red light and gazed heavily Andrea. "Are you going to give me another lecture about this whole intuition thing?"

"It's not just women's intuition. Men have it, too. You simply have to be tuned in."

"I'm tuned in to work right now."

"Maybe you should ask Caroline what her gut tells her. She probably has a good idea about what's going to happen."

Luke paused for a moment. That wasn't a bad idea. He should ask her what she thought. Even if he didn't believe in women's intuition, she had a lot of experience selling houses and would surely have an idea as to how this one was going to go.

Though she'd been very quiet about the house since they visited, she had been a wealth of information when they were there.

"What is it?" Andrea asked.

Luke shook his head. "Nothing."

"Have you already asked her about the house?"

"No. She's very… quiet about it."

A call came through on the radio, saving Luke from any further interrogation.

❉

The day went quickly, and Luke found his nerves more jittery than he had anticipated when he stood on Caroline's front patio, staring at her door. He cleared his throat to help muster some courage. This was the first date he had been on since becoming a widow, and he was having a hard time remembering what it was like to be single and dating. He took a deep breath and knocked.

There were footsteps, and the floor creaked before the door opened. Caroline stood there in jeans and a fitted purple sweater that made the blue in her eyes deeper than he'd ever noticed. Her smile radiated happiness. At once, Luke was at ease. All his nerves were gone and he knew this was where he was meant to be.

"So, you liked the tree?" He smirked.

Caroline nodded. "I loved it. Thank you. Would you like to come in and see it?"

Luke stepped into her home and hints of cinnamon, fresh laundry, and pine tantalized his senses. She led him to the Christmas tree, where they both stopped, staring.

"You even started decorating it."

Caroline nodded. There was something about the way she was standing, one arm stretched across her stomach gripping the elbow of the other, loosely at her side, that made her appear sad and lost in thought.

"Ella picked this one out for you." He reached forward, pointing at the ugly ornament dangling at the center of the tree.

"That was very sweet." He could see her take a deep breath. "I still have a couple more boxes to put up."

He wanted to save her from this sadness, however distant it was. "Shall we go?"

Caroline grabbed her coat off the sofa and followed him out the door. When they reached the car, he opened the door and waited for her to make herself comfortable before closing it.

"Do you know how to ice-skate?" he asked as he opened his door and slid in beside her.

Her face lit up. Her eyes sparkled. "I haven't been skating in a very long time."

"Well, tonight we change that."

"There was a pond near my home where we would go ice-skating every year. It was a really big deal. One of us was assigned every day to go down and check if it was frozen over enough to skate. When we got the word, there was a big celebration."

"Really?" He wanted to ask her where this pond in Brambling Falls was, so he could take Ella one day. But he also wanted to hear about her and her childhood. He wanted to figure her out, get to know all the little things about her. He could ask about the lake another day. After the house was his.

"It was amazing. There was always hot cocoa and freshly popped popcorn. We would build a fire and roast marshmallows." Her voice was soft and soothing. He hadn't heard her this relaxed before.

"I wish I would have been there."

Caroline looked at Luke, smiling, and his heart leaped.

"It sounds like an amazing place to grow up. Your childhood was a winter wonderland."

Caroline giggled. "Well, I don't know about that. We did have some pretty amazing winters, though."

When they arrived at the skating rink, Caroline slipped her hands into her pockets and her smile disappeared. "Oh. I think I forgot my gloves at home."

Luke leaned in close. He was so close that he could smell her—a faint scent of cinnamon and pine. His heart raced. She was leaning in closer as well. He paused, and Caroline leaned back. He let out a sigh as quietly as he possibly could and extended his arm to the glove box.

"I've got you covered." He opened the glove box and pulled out a pair of Ella's mittens, leaving them on Caroline's lap. She laughed.

"Ella's mittens? Are you sure she won't mind?"

He shook his head. "Not at all. She'd be honored. I'm sure. As long as you don't mind not being able to use your fingers."

"Well, I guess I'll just have to rely on you to keep me up if I fall." She fluttered her eyelashes at Luke then hopped out of the car. "Come on. I can't wait to get out there." She was bouncing from foot to foot, waiting for him.

Luke was nervous again. What had he gotten himself into? She was going to skate circles around him. Not that he didn't like an independent woman, but he was really hoping to impress her tonight, and he wasn't so sure that this was going to do it anymore.

He caught up to her and slipped his hand in hers. They rented their skates and found a nearby bench. Luke couldn't help but notice how the reflection from the ice danced on her cheek as she tied her skates. Caroline looked up, catching him staring at her.

"What is it?"

"Nothing. I just like to see you happy."

"There's ice. I've got skates on my feet. I'm with you. What's not to be happy about?"

His heart warmed. He tied his final lace and was up on his feet, reaching out a hand for Caroline. She took it and followed him to the rink.

"I hope I remember how to do this." She tentatively stepped onto the ice with one foot, then the other. Luke stepped close beside her, ready to catch her if she were to fall.

She teetered for a moment, adjusted her position, then glided smoothly. Luke slid along beside her.

"You're a natural," she said, watching him.

"I've clocked a lot of hours on the ice keeping Ella on her feet."

Caroline spun around so that she was skating backward, facing Luke. The wind blew her hair across her face. "I'm really glad you brought me here. I've forgotten how good it feels to slide across the ice." She pushed off with a foot and turned away from him, gliding across the rink. When she reached the other side, she forced her toe into the ice and stopped. She put up a hand and wiggled her muffled fingers toward Luke, beckoning for him to join her.

His heart sped up as he watched her, a sly grin on her face. He pushed off, and went flying toward her. She stood her ground, unafraid of the momentum he was gaining. He gathered himself as he skidded toward her, preparing to jab his toe into the ice, as he had seen an instructor teach Ella once. He swallowed hard, and as he approached, he held his breath. He did exactly as he had seen, and stopped abruptly, his nose two inches from Caroline's.

Her breath warmed his lips as she looked at him. He looked her in the eyes and felt himself moving closer. His lips were about to meet hers when a group of teenagers sped by, bumping into him. To avoid bumping heads with Caroline, he lifted his, breaking their moment.

She cleared her throat, and as their eyes met, they both laughed. His heart pounded in his chest at the missed moment. He inhaled deeply, then took hold of her hand and pulled her back onto the ice.

21

Caroline

The wind swept across Caroline's face as they skated around the rink. Each time she would steal a glance at Luke, he would smile, as if he knew she was watching him, waiting for that perfect moment to return. She slowed her pace, and he matched her cadence as they made their way around and around the rink. There was a Christmas tree at one end; next to it was a small covered booth where hot chocolate was sold. The front of the booth was laced with a string of white lights that illuminated the snow and ice.

"Thirsty?" she asked.

He nodded and led her off the rink. When they switched out of their skates, he took both her hands in his and faced her. "I want you to try this."

Luke's eyebrows lifted and there was a jolt of *something* that shot through her as she wondered what he was thinking. She looked away, afraid that he could read her mind. They walked hand in hand to the hot-chocolate booth where they each ordered a drink. There were red and green buckets full of crushed candy canes, chocolate chips, and cinnamon. There was chocolate syrup for drizzling and sprinkles in every color of the rainbow. Nearby, a large bowl held a pile of marshmallows.

Caroline watched as Luke stacked a few marshmallows on the lid of his cup. When she went to drop one in the hot cocoa he stopped her, and said, "Just wait." Then he winked and led her down a narrow path through a small patch of trees.

When they reached a stone pit with a large fire roaring in it, Luke brushed off one of the logs surrounding it and motioned for Caroline to sit. He took her drink and set it down with his then draped a blanket that was folded on a nearby log over Caroline's shoulders.

"I'll be right back."

Caroline sat, listening to the fire crackle in front of her. She couldn't control the thoughts rushing through her mind. Here she was on a date with this amazing man. She thought back to when they first met at the toy store, fighting over that last stuffed dog. Never in her wildest dreams would she have guessed that she would end up on a date with him, let alone help him find his dream house.

His dream house.

Her heart sank. All this was going to end soon. She was almost sure that the sellers were going to accept Luke's offer. When they found out Caroline grew up in the home, they had insisted on speaking directly with her, instantly taking a liking to her. Though they hadn't given her their final answer yet, she knew from experience that sellers didn't normally get excited about working with an agent and then turn down an offer.

She squeezed her eyes shut. The irony wasn't lost on her: the one thing that kept her from wanting to be in the house was the exact same thing that was going to help Luke get the house. The brush behind her snapped and she quickly turned.

Luke stood there with two long sticks in his hands. He handed one to Caroline and sat next to her, wrapping the blanket around himself as he did.

"I know you've roasted marshmallows before." He slid one onto the end of her stick, then another onto his own. He reached out with the stick over the fire.

"Is this what you wanted me to try?"

Luke half smiled. "Just wait and see."

She watched how he carefully turned the stick in his hands, cooking each side of the marshmallow until it had a golden shimmer to it. Caroline liked her marshmallows a little crispier. Just as her marshmallow was about to start burning, he reached over and gently pulled her stick out of the fire.

"I like mine crispy." She went to put the stick back in the fire, not taking her eyes off him, wanting to see how he would react to her defiance.

"The next one you can burn as much as you like. This one needs to be just a little toasty." He took her toasted marshmallow and slowly slid it off the stick, his fingers jumping on and off so as to not get burned. Then, he removed the lid of her hot chocolate, and dropped the toasted marshmallow in.

"Oh." Caroline sucked in her breath and tried to fish it out.

"Trust me," Luke said as he replaced the lid and then dropped his marshmallow into his own drink. "In a minute, it will be pure heaven." His eyes lingered on her as he said *heaven,* sending her heart into a frenzy.

He held her gaze as he placed a new marshmallow on her stick and guided it back toward the fire. "This one you can cook as long as you like."

Caroline watched him. His eyes were a deep green with flecks of gold floating about. The wrinkles that flanked his eyes reminded her of his past and how much he had lost. A loud pop from the fire broke Luke's gaze and he rested his arm around Caroline.

"Can I have my hot chocolate now?" She giggled like a little schoolgirl asking for permission.

"Have at it."

She held the cup to her lips and took a sip. The chocolate had a slight toasted sweetness to it, nothing like the flavor of the mushy marshmallows that normally end up in the cup. She nodded her head.

"The best part is yet to come." He smiled, looking away.

She couldn't help but agree.

Luke cleared his throat. "So, what do you think about the house offer."

She froze. It all came back to her and the warm, fuzzy feeling dissipated. "They are still out of town."

"Right." He was silent a moment, then continued. "How do you feel about it?"

She steadied herself. What was he asking? He couldn't possibly know that she grew up in the home. "How do I feel about it?" She wanted to say, *I feel like you should find another house so we can give this a try.* Instead she shrugged. She didn't want to get his hopes up about the house even though she had a good feeling about it, for him. "I think you have a good shot at getting it. We won't know either way until we hear back from them."

He slowly nodded.

Maybe she could talk him out of it. Maybe she could find him another house that he loved just as much. It could even be in Brambling Falls. Just not *this* house. "What is it about the house that makes you want it so bad?"

He exhaled deeply, then looked at the ground. "I want the house for Ella. She deserves to have a place she calls home. The house I grew up in was always lively and noisy. It was only me and my two sisters, but we had so much fun. We were always coming up with some sort of adventure, and my parents embraced it. They let us take over the house. I want that for her. I want that for me. I want to have a noisy house full of kids someday."

She swallowed. He wanted more kids. She couldn't help but let a small smile escape. "Couldn't you have that in any house? There are other homes in the same area I could show you."

He shook his head. "There is something magical about this one. I could feel that it's always been full of love."

A chill went down her spine. It had been filled with love. And wonderful memories. Memories that were so amazing that they were hard to think about because they couldn't be relived.

"Plus, think of all the ways you could decorate that house for Christmas. I know decorating for Christmas isn't really your thing, but can't you see it lit up with lights?"

A mix of emotions swirled around inside her. "I can see it." It didn't matter how much she wanted to be with him. It didn't matter how much she wanted to be part of his life with a noisy house full of kids. This house was meant to be his. It definitely wasn't her place to stand in the way of that.

"Waking up in that house this Christmas morning, that would be the most amazing gift I could give Ella."

Her heart sank farther into her stomach. She tried to change the subject. "You have two sisters?"

He nodded. "My older sister lives on the East Coast. She moved there after college. She's married and has three boys. They would love to play in that yard."

Caroline looked down.

"My baby sister lives in Portland. She's the one that usually comes down for the mom stuff at school, but she just had a baby. We were planning to go up and see them, but if we get this house, then maybe they could come down here." The smile on his face spread even wider.

It seemed everything was linked back to the house. All of his happiness relied on getting this one house. Her house. Would he change his mind about it if he knew that she would disappear from his life if he got the house? She shoved the thought out of her mind. She couldn't tell him. It wasn't about her. It was about him and his family and their future.

"I think your marshmallow is probably crispy enough."

She looked at the dark ball hanging off the end of her stick and laughed. Luke pulled the stick toward them and blew on the marshmallow a few times in an attempt to cool it down. Once it was cool enough to touch, he slid it off the stick and held it up to her mouth. She leaned in and bit half of it off, the gooey center between her lips. When she was done chewing, she said, "You can have the other half. I want you to experience what a real toasted marshmallow tastes like."

He put the other half in his mouth and laughed. "It tastes a bit like charcoal."

They bounced together, both trying to control their laughter. Once they were able to calm themselves down, she found they were sitting much closer together.

The wind picked up and Caroline's hair caught across her face. Luke reached over and brushed it away. Her heart raced as he leaned in closer. His lips met hers and sent a shiver through her body. When he pulled away, his cheeks were rosy. The fire had died down considerably and it was getting colder.

"What do you say we go get a bite to eat?"

"That sounds fabulous." She stood up as he folded the blanket and put it back on the log.

"Don't forget the hot chocolate. I told you the best is yet to come."

Her heart leaped at his words and she obeyed.

As they walked back to the car, Luke was quiet and Caroline sipped on her drink.

"Have you gotten to the bottom yet?"

She tilted the cup back until the last sugary drops slipped into her mouth, then nodded.

"Okay, here's what you do." He flipped open the lid of his own cup and tilted it until the marshmallow, still intact, slid to the edge. "Now you have to put it in your mouth in one big bite." He popped it into his own then wiggled his eyebrows.

She narrowed her eyes at him. Then followed his lead. Once the marshmallow slid between her lips, she stopped, her cheeks puffed out like a chipmunk's. Luke looked at her and chuckled.

"Bite into it slowly," he tried to say, his mouth still full.

Caroline bit in and the marshmallow immediately exploded, sending out a gush of warm, thick chocolate. Luke was right, it tasted like heaven. He watched her, amused by her expressions. The heat rose in her cheeks. She continued to chew until it had all dissolved.

"That was amazing. It was as if it turned into a chocolate truffle."

"One of Ella's creations." He reached down and took Caroline's hand in his. "Maybe it can be one of your new traditions. Hot chocolate marshmallow truffles while decorating a Christmas tree?"

"Let's not get too carried away." The warmth of his hand around hers spread through her body, creating a buzz she wasn't used to feeling.

"Okay. Baby steps." His thumb caressed her hand and filled her with hope, allowing her to forget about the house and the sure demise of their future. "Let's go get a bite to eat."

22

Luke

Luke pulled his car over to the curb in front of a green door with a small *open* sign in the slightly larger window. Above the door was a plank of wood with the words Luigi's Pizza carved into it.

"Here we are." He got out of the car and walked around to open Caroline's door. She stepped out and scrunched her eyebrows as she looked at the restaurant in front of them.

"Pizza?"

Luke's confidence waivered for the second time that night. She had a way of making him doubt himself, making him feel like he had to stay on his toes. He rubbed the back of his neck in an attempt to build confidence. Why did she get to him like this? He wasn't normally thrown so easily. In fact, he was known for being the one that always kept his cool. He was the one that everyone counted on to be logical and levelheaded.

"Did I let you down with the hot chocolate?"

Caroline tilted her head to the side and placed a hand on her cheek. "You think you can wow me twice in one night? That's pretty ambitious."

"I can try." He took her hand and pulled her toward the restaurant. When he opened the door for her and she walked in, he couldn't help but watch her. It had been so long since he had felt this way about someone; he nearly forgot he was capable of feeling it.

There was a menu posted by the door and when Caroline saw the long list of gourmet pizzas, her jaw dropped.

"How long has this place been here?" Her eyes were wide as she looked around.

Luke shrugged. "I'm not sure. It's been a police favorite for as long as I've been here."

As if on cue, two men in uniform walked up to them and patted Luke on the back.

"Hey, Miller. Good to see you. Who's your friend?"

Luke straightened his back, suddenly aware that he had no idea what to introduce Caroline as. She wasn't his girlfriend, but the word "friend" didn't seem quite right, either.

"Hey, guys. This is my real estate agent, Caroline."

Luke froze. His agent? Sure, she was. But she was also more than that. He looked to her, to see if she caught what he said.

She was squinting at him, but as he made eye contact, she looked away. She held out her hand and shook theirs.

"Andrea mentioned you were looking for a house. How's that going?"

Luke was going to let Caroline take over the conversation, but she was quiet. Was it because he had referred to her as his agent?

The two men looked back and forth between Luke and Caroline, waiting for one of them to say something, anything.

"The house hunt is going well. We are just getting started aren't we, Caroline?"

A softness spread through her eyes at that moment. "Yes. We are just getting started." He wasn't sure she was completely referring to house hunting. It felt as if someone were grabbing hold of his heart and squeezing.

"We thought we'd take a night off from looking at houses and grab a bite to eat."

The two men exchanged knowing glances and took this as their cue to leave.

"It was great meeting you, Caroline. Luigi's is great, but make him take you somewhere nicer next time. Somewhere you can sit down, maybe with tablecloths?" The taller of the two men punched Luke playfully in the arm, then they left. Caroline laughed.

Luke put his hands out to guide Caroline toward the ordering counter. As she eyed the extensive menu, he gave her suggestions on which ones were good (the Vegetable Pile pizza and the Margherita) and what was best skipped (the Sardine and Sausage).

In the end, they ordered a small Margherita pizza with a side of potato wedges. When Luke asked for it to go, Caroline looked disappointed.

"Aren't we going to stay here and eat?" She held her hand out, motioning to the many wooden family-style tables lined with benches and patio chairs.

He shook his head. "I've got something I'd like to show you while we eat."

Luke loved surprises. His favorite thing was to bring Ella little surprises every now and then. It had begun after his wife had passed. He wanted there to be something for Ella to look forward to, so when he would pick her up from school or day care, he'd have a surprise for her. It was always something little, like a sheet of stickers, or a pack of crayons he picked up from a restaurant.

The look of sheer joy on her face when he would give them to her was irreplaceable. He couldn't get enough of it.

Now, he found himself wanting to surprise Caroline every opportunity he could get. He would give nearly anything to see that same look of sheer glee from Ella's face on Caroline's.

"You really do know how to plan—" she stopped herself, as if she wasn't sure what to say next.

"Plan?"

"An evening out with your real estate agent." Her face was serious but the glint in her eyes let him know she was teasing him.

He rubbed his chin. "I'm sorry. I fumbled. I didn't know what to call you."

"That's okay. It was fun watching you stumble." She slipped her hand into his.

They walked to the car hand in hand, Luke placing the food in the back seat before they drove off.

Caroline looked out the window. "Where are we going?"

"It's a secret."

"Should I close my eyes?" she joked.

He smiled. "Last time I tried to take you somewhere new, it turned out you grew up there. I had to get a little more creative this time." He reached across the center console and placed his hand on top of hers.

"I'm intrigued."

The smell of the pizza wafting out of the back seat was nearly unbearable. Luke hadn't eaten lunch because he was too busy trying to wrap up everything at work and get Ella settled before he left. His stomach growled, and he hoped Caroline didn't hear it.

They drove a long way down a main street before turning onto a small winding road that led down into a valley. He wove along various streets, the houses going from quaint one-story cottages to larger two-story homes, until they became near mansions with yards that practically spanned half a block. Finally, they came to a stately set of gates, framed by thick hedges that went on as far as the eye could see. There was a guardhouse in the middle of the road, with an old man in a beige uniform. When he saw them, he motioned that he'd be over in a minute.

"Is this Verdant Gardens?" she whispered, as if it were too much to say out loud.

"Have you ever been?"

She shook her head. "It's the most secluded gated community in the state. These houses are owned for generations. You have to be invited to get in."

The guard peered into the car and Luke rolled the window down. "Oh, hello, Officer Miller. We've been expecting you. You can go on in. Enjoy your evening. Be sure not to miss Peppermint Lane. I think you'll find it quite charming." He winked at Luke.

Luke thanked the guard and waited for the gates to slowly roll open, then pulled the car forward. As the gates closed behind them, it was as if they had been transported to a different world. The street was lined with ponderosa pines and Douglas firs. There were bright patches of red flowers popping up through the light layer of snow on the ground. The houses were set a good way back on the vast lawns and gave off a warm glow from their precisely hung Christmas lights.

Luke watched Caroline. He liked the way she tried to hide her amazement by tightening her forehead, but the sparkle in her eyes gave her away.

They continued down the lane until they came to a small visitors' parking lot with four spaces and a picnic table nearby. It was centrally located in the community and was the perfect place to carry out what he had planned.

"Have you been here before?" she asked.

He nodded. "For work." Very few outsiders had been inside. The wealthy families that resided here had done so for over a hundred years. With that kind of wealth often came family secrets that were fiercely protected. Crime was rare in the neighborhood, but the occasional police call still had to be made, and the Neighborhood Board was very particular about which police officers they allowed in. Luke had become one of the trusted few. Because of his long-established rapport with several of the elderly women who lived there, he had been granted a pass to share the infamous, mythical Christmas lights that lit up the area.

As he watched the awe on Caroline's face, he knew he had succeeded in both surprising and wowing her. If these lights couldn't help inspire her to decorate, he wasn't sure anything could.

He took the food and a blanket from the back seat and met Caroline at the picnic table. Once he spread the blanket out, she took the potato wedges from the bag and the pizza box and set them on the table. The smell wafted to Luke's nose and his stomach rumbled again.

"Was that your stomach?" She giggled.

His cheeks prickled with heat as he sat on the bench across from her. "I might be a little hungry."

"Let's eat, then. I'm starving." She took a piece of pizza, and without even placing it on her plate, she took a big bite, a string of cheese threatening to fall in her lap. Her eyes rolled.

"This is delicious."

Luke pointed at her. "The best pizza in town. Us cops know where all the good food is."

He held the pizza in his hands, watching her, how her jaw moved gracefully as she chewed, how she kept her focus on the slice in front of her, as if she were afraid she might lose it if she took her eyes away for a moment.

A warmness radiated through his body. Finally, when his stomach was about to growl again, he took his first bite.

When they were done eating, he put the bag, pizza box, and blanket back in the car so as not to leave a trace that they had been there. Then he took her hand and led her down the sidewalk.

Luke was in awe as they strolled through the neighborhood, their feet crunching on the newly fallen snow. He had never seen the lights himself. He had only been there during the day and heard about the Christmas decorations from a fellow officer that had responded to a call at night.

Each house was decorated uniquely. One had light icicles hanging from the trim of the roof, and wooden reindeer that moved on the lawn. Another had large snowflakes hanging from the trees that lined its drive, and a Santa about to make his way down the chimney.

"How's the home-tour decorating going?" Luke had been hesitant to bring it up in case it wasn't going well, but this seemed like the perfect time and place.

"It's going okay. We are going to start decorating tomorrow. We still have a few things to add to really bring out the Christmas spirit, but I'm hoping they will come to us once we see it all put together."

Her brow was pulled tight, and she was looking away as she spoke. He didn't know Caroline too well, but he had interviewed enough people in his life to know that that kind of body language indicated she was worried. He remembered what Andrea had told him. *Ask her what's bothering her.*

He cleared his throat and she looked at him, the stress temporarily gone from her expression. He scratched at the back of his neck with his free hand, trying to find the courage to ask her. "Are you worried about it?"

She let out a deep sigh. "It's a big job. I'm a little worried about how I'm going to get the decorating done and still help all my clients at the same time. I'm sure it will work out." She gave him a confessional smile.

"This is it. Peppermint Lane."

Caroline stopped and looked up. Her eyes grew wide and her

lips parted. Luke stood there watching her, the lights from the lane bouncing off her face.

"It is amazing." Her voice was soft, almost a whisper.

He looked down the lane to see what she saw. Each house was covered in tasteful decor. Wreaths hung on windows, poinsettias grew at the feet of trees, and lights hung in all directions, weaving beautiful patterns.

"Why do they do this, if no one else gets to see it?" Caroline's eyes were glassy.

"They do it for Christmas. The Christmas spirit."

23
Caroline

aroline's day had started with a disappointing update from Alexandra. Today was the day they were scheduled to start decorating. Most of the supplies hadn't come in over the weekend, so they were being pushed back by a day. That was okay, she kept telling herself. It was more time for her to brainstorm ways to share the joy of Christmas throughout the homes. Still, the chore felt more complicated and extravagant with each passing day.

To help lighten her thoughts, which were growing heavy, she stared at the mistletoe hanging in her office doorway, replaying her evening with Luke in her mind. The lights from the Christmas decorations still danced in her head, inspiring her plans for the home tour.

Sarah peeked her head in. "Everything okay?"

Caroline snapped back to reality, refocusing her eyes on Sarah instead of the mistletoe. "What? I mean yes. I was just thinking about the tour and all we have left to do."

"Well, put that thought on hold, because you have a call about a house you put an offer on."

Her heart sank to the pit of her stomach. This was it. She would find out right now if she and Luke would be together. She sat up straight in her chair and rubbed her hands together, taking deep breaths in through her nose and exhaling out through her mouth.

"You sure you're okay?" Sarah asked again.

"Yes. It's just, I know how much my client wants this house, and I'm a little nervous for him." She cast a large fake smile in Sarah's direction, hoping she would buy the false explanation.

"Okay. I'll send the call over now."

Moments later, her phone rang. She didn't pick it up on the first ring, or the second one. She only picked it up when Sarah's chair creaked and her footsteps sounded in the hall outside Caroline's door.

"This is Caroline." She used her most professional voice and braced herself for what was to come.

When the call was over, she sat numbly in her chair, one elbow resting on her desk, the other lying limply in her lap. There was a quiet knock at the door, and when Caroline turned around, Sarah was standing there in the doorway, her arms folded across her waist and her head slightly drooped.

"Didn't work out the way you had hoped? I'm sorry." She walked into Caroline's office and placed a mug brimming with hot cocoa on her desk.

Caroline half-heartedly smiled.

Completely misunderstanding the situation, Sarah put her hands on her hips. "Well, everything happens for a reason, I guess." Then she walked out of the office.

Caroline lowered her head onto the desk. What would have happened if she had never shown him the house? What if she had simply told him that the house was no longer available? What if she had made up horrible stories about the house so that he wouldn't have wanted it?

She lifted her head and her shoulders sank in defeat. She should be happy. She just landed the most amazing deal for one of her favorite clients.

Maybe that was the problem. Luke was so much more than a client. She rubbed her temples with her index fingers. If only she hadn't become so attached, then she wouldn't have a Christmas tree, or all these old memories resurfacing. But she also wouldn't have these *new* memories.

She swallowed. She wanted these new memories. In fact, she wanted *more* new memories. Now the only way she could get those new memories was by confronting all the memories from the past. The ones that, although she adored them, were too painful to think about. Her parents had been gone for ten years, and she still missed them. She missed their Christmases and she missed talking to them. If she was being totally honest, she missed her hometown, which she had managed to not think much about until Luke came into her life.

Then there was Ella. She was going to love the house. She would get to build those same memories that Caroline had built. In the same house. There was no way that Caroline was going to stand in the way of that.

She glanced at the clock. It was eleven-thirty. Luke was working until eight tonight. She would call him after he got off his shift. Until then, she would need to keep herself busy and her mind occupied. Until then, she could pretend that she and Luke still had a future.

Down the hall, Chris's office door opened then closed, reminding her it was time for the meeting. As she thought about decorating the homes, a jolt of energy raced through her. After seeing how elegant and festive the homes looked last night, she was actually excited about decorating for the Tour of Homes. She couldn't wait to see how the homes would look when they were done with them—once they figured out how to bring more Christmas spirit into them. She grabbed her notebook and made her way to the conference room.

Caroline paced slowly, aimlessly. The decorating committee sat quietly, their eyes following her back and forth, back and forth.

"So, our decorating start day has been pushed back by a day. Alexandra, do you have an update from Jessica?"

Alexandra sat up straight in her chair and flipped her notebook back a few pages. "Yes. She said they were scheduled to arrive at the sleigh house at nine this morning and should be done placing the furniture by six tonight."

"Great. Victor and Rebecca. You both need to go to the house when we're done here and make sure that the furniture is in line with what we have planned."

They both nodded. Nick furrowed his brow.

"The rest of us will divide and conquer and make sure all the houses are in order tonight. That means checking all the exterior outlets, verifying with the owners that tomorrow is our start day, and doing a walk-through to make sure all clutter and personal items have been removed." Caroline tapped her pen on her notebook. "Any questions?"

Everyone shook their head then collected their things, eager to get on with their tasks.

❋

By the time Caroline got home, it was dark. A light breeze had picked up and it was colder. Snow would be falling soon. She lifted her head to the sky and inhaled, breathing in the moist air mingled with the subtle, fresh scent of the maple tree that protected her yard.

As she entered her home, she hung her coat and scarf on a hook behind the door and stopped for a moment to admire the Christmas tree. It was beautiful all aglow; but it looked lonely with its few but meaningful ornaments. Before she knew what she was doing, she found herself opening up the box of decorations and taking herself back down memory lane. This time, she was better prepared.

She found the creamy angels her grandmother had crocheted, with their small brass trumpets. She ran her fingers over their fine stitches as she hung them around the base of the tree. She found a bright-red wooden nutcracker with yellowing teeth, and a Santa made out of a sea star. There were several puppies wearing scarves, which had been hand painted by her mom, and a faded sleigh that her dad had so carefully carved out of wood. There were lace snowflakes with beaded trim, and crystal snowmen with dark-black eyes and buttons down their bellies. She took her time, carefully hanging each ornament in its own spot on the tree.

At the bottom of the box, she found an ornament she had loved as a child. It was made from little chunks of wood pieced together to create a fireplace. In the center, above the beads of coal, were two black boots dangling from the flue. Caroline's hand immediately flew to her chest. It reminded her of Ella and the fireplace she so badly wanted for Santa Claus. Instead of hanging this one on the tree, she slipped it inside a small Christmas bag she had left over from wrapping. She found a slip of wrapping paper with Santa Claus dancing, and she carefully cut him out, then glued him onto a piece of white card stock. Below Santa's chubby feet, she wrote Ella's name with a sparkly green pen. Then, she slipped it under the Christmas tree.

Just as she stepped back to admire the tree, there was a knock at the door. Caroline looked at her watch. She had lost track of time. She hurried to the door and swung it open, finding Lauren's face, in the middle of a large, green wreath as if it were framed.

"I heard someone has a Christmas tree this year and could use a wreath for her door." She winked at Caroline.

Caroline rolled her eyes. "Whoever could have told you that?"

She stepped aside to let Lauren enter. Before she stepped inside, Lauren held her other hand out. In it was a hook for the wreath.

She slipped it over the door, then propped the wreath on it. She stepped back, squinted, then turned the wreath a quarter turn to the right. She stepped back again, then wiped her hands on her jeans. "Perfect."

"Maybe you should be the one that's decorating the Tour of Homes." A sly grin spread across Caroline's face.

Lauren shrugged. "I've got my hands full with the Christmas Eve dinner at the shelter. Plus, it seems more like your thing than mine." She threw her coat and scarf onto a hook and made herself comfortable on the sofa, propping her feet on the coffee table.

Caroline set hot water to boil in the kitchen and called out to Lauren. "Have you eaten yet?"

"No, but I've already ordered Chinese, so it should be here in a few minutes."

Caroline and Lauren had become fast friends when Caroline first moved here. They met at a local networking night at the community center. They were the only two that had shown up, and they had single-handedly eaten all of the pizza the center had supplied.

Caroline poured two cups of tea and went back to the living room to sit with Lauren.

"The tree looks amazing."

"Thanks. I just finished tonight."

"You doing okay? I know how you feel about decorating for Christmas."

Caroline pursed her lips and cocked her head. "It hasn't been that bad. I mean, the memories have definitely been hitting hard, but I'm also finding some joy in it."

Lauren nodded. "I see you're done wrapping all the gifts for the family you adopted."

Her face lit up. "I can't wait to give them their gifts on Christmas Eve. That reminds me. How is the shelter dinner coming?"

"It's almost all planned. I think it's going to be great this year." She told Caroline all about her plans for the dinner. It was one of

Lauren's favorite parts of her job. When she was done, she eyed Caroline suspiciously.

"You seem a little off. What's going on?"

"They accepted Luke's offer on the house."

"Oh." Lauren tucked her feet under her and twisted her dark hair in her fingers. "What did he say?"

Caroline looked down at her hands, which were folded tight in her lap. "I haven't told him yet."

Lauren whipped up her head and looked at Caroline. "How long have you known?"

She crinkled her nose. "Since this morning. I didn't want to bother him at work."

Lauren leaned forward; her eyebrows lifted. "You don't have to stop talking to him, you know. You can make new, happy memories. Just as good as the old ones."

Caroline glanced at Lauren for a moment, then looked back down again. "I don't know. I don't think I can." She could barely put it into words when talking to Lauren. How would she ever explain it to Luke?

They sat quietly for a few moments. The doorbell rang and Lauren hopped up to answer it. Before opening the door, she looked at Caroline and quieted her voice. "You're going to tell him tonight?"

"As soon as you leave." She managed to squeeze out a smile.

Caroline sat on the sofa, her stomach full from dinner, her heart happy from an evening with her best friend. She took a moment to work up her courage, then picked up the phone. It rang three times. As she was preparing herself to leave a message, he picked up.

24

Luke

"Hey, I was just thinking about you," Luke said into his phone. He had been thinking of Caroline all day. It was near impossible for him to get her off his mind these days. "I was wondering if you were available this week for dinner, maybe?"

There was silence on the other end of the phone. He waited for a moment; maybe he had misread the name on his phone. He glanced at it again, then cleared his throat. "Hello?"

"Hey," she said. Luke thought she sounded more chipper than usual. "This week is kind of busy for me with all the tour decorating."

His heart sank a little.

"I do have some good news for you, though."

He tried to bring his focus back to her and away from the

disappointment that he wouldn't be seeing her this week. "What good news do you have?"

"Are you sitting down? Because you got the house."

A sudden rush of adrenaline shot through his body. His heart raced and he was full of energy. "We got the house?" He was only able to whisper it, for fear that saying it louder would make it not true.

"You did. It's all yours. They can close as soon as next week." He could hear the smile in her voice.

"I can't believe it." He was filled with so many emotions. Ella would finally have a home to call her own. At the same time, it was a sign that they were moving on. He swallowed hard. "Thank you, Caroline. Thank you for finding our home."

He hadn't intended to call it *our* home, but when he said it, he knew exactly what he meant. He did want it to be *their* home. He wanted Caroline to be involved in every part of it. He wanted Ella, Caroline, and himself to be there, together.

"You did most of the work, really. You're the one who found the home, after all."

He thought he detected something in her voice, but he wasn't sure what it was. She was probably just stressed about the home tour.

"What's next?"

"I need you to come by the office tomorrow and sign some papers. I've scheduled the inspection for the afternoon as well. You don't need to be there for that."

"All right." He was thrilled at the thought of seeing her the next day. "I'm off tomorrow morning so I should be able to make both."

There was silence on both ends of the line. Luke leaned on the counter with his elbows, the phone propped up against his ear with one hand, while the other tapped the counter.

"How about we meet at the office at eleven?" She was very

businesslike. He was sure that she just wanted to make sure everything got done and they were able to move in on time.

"See you then." He put the phone down, his smile lingering.

They got the house.

He debated waking Ella to tell her the fantastic news, but he
knew it wasn't a good idea. She would be too excited to go back
to sleep. He opened the refrigerator and took out a can of beer
then relaxed on the sofa. It was then that it occurred to him that
he would need to buy new furniture. He had enough for his room
and for Ella's, maybe part of the living room. Every other room
would need furniture, too.

Maybe Caroline could help him pick out some furniture.

There was so much Luke had to be thankful for this Christmas.
Not only were he and Ella moving into their own home, but they
had Caroline now. He could feel his heart opening up to her, in
ways he had been sure it never would again. When he thought of
the future, Caroline was in it. She was there the first day, when
they would get their keys and open the front door; she would
walk in with them. She was there helping them set up the house.
She was there choosing the furniture and helping them figure out
where it should go. She was there when they were eating dinner
and decorating the tree. And she was there long after the tree had
been taken down and the snow was starting to melt.

He thought about all the ways he could decorate their new
home for Christmas. It felt different this time. Not like he was
doing it all for Ella. He wanted the house to feel Christmassy. He
wanted it to exude the love that spread through everyone at this
time of year. For the first time in a very long time, he wasn't simply
going through the motions. He wasn't just doing it for Ella. He
was doing it for the spirit of Christmas.

He felt it in his bones. Caroline was opening him up to feelings he didn't think were possible anymore.

An indescribable excitement spread through him, and he took another drink of his beer.

This was shaping up to be one of the best Christmases yet.

❊

Luke was nervous. He didn't know if it was because of Caroline or because he was about to sign the papers for the house or because of the upcoming inspection. When he had placed his hand on the steering wheel, it was shaking. When he got out of the car, he felt the sweat trickle down his back even though it was threatening to snow again. He found himself looking around everywhere he went, a habit many police officers picked up, but Luke had managed to keep to only when he was on the job, or nervous.

He pushed open the door to Caroline's building with his hip, then headed toward her office. Sarah smiled and waved, then jumped out of her seat.

"Are you here to see Caroline?"

"I am." Luke looked down at the two cups he held in his hands.

"I'll see if she's available."

Luke nodded, and kept from laughing when he saw Caroline through a break in the decorations. She was sitting at her desk, a magazine propped on her lap, one hand gently tapping her upper lip as she read.

Sarah disappeared behind the door. He sort of missed the obnoxious bell that played "Santa Claus Is Coming to Town." He had to admit, though, he liked the mistletoe that had replaced it. Well, as long as he was the only one she was standing with underneath it.

Sarah popped back out and waved her hands in Caroline's direction. "She's all yours. Congratulations on the house." Her bright smile beamed, kindness flying from her eyes.

"Thank you." Luke stepped into the doorway, and stopped squarely under the mistletoe. He held his arms out. "We did it."

Caroline turned her chair so that it was facing him, but she didn't get up. "We sure did."

He waited for her to stand and give him a kiss, but she stayed in her chair.

"Come, sit down." She pointed to the chair on the other side of her desk.

He slid the drink across the table. "For you."

She rubbed her hands together, then picked it up and took a sip. Her eyes closed in pleasure. "Peppermint tea. Just what I needed. How did you know?"

Luke shrugged. He had stood in line debating between the peppermint tea, hot chocolate, and a cappuccino for at least fifteen minutes. He had finally decided that she would want something soothing but warm on a day like today, filled with appointments and decorating for the Tour of Homes.

When it was clear she wasn't going to stand and give him a hug, or humor him under the mistletoe, he took his seat across from her. She placed a few sheets of paper in front of him and set a pen down next to them.

His hands were no longer shaking. When she was around, he was calm. He knew it would all be okay. He longed to pick her up and hug her and feel her lips against his, just as when they had been sitting in front of the fire. This was her place of work, he had to remind himself. Any displays of affection would be inappropriate.

He watched her as she explained what the papers he would be signing were. He had a hard time focusing on her words, as he was distracted with the way her eyes bounced from the papers to his eyes. When she was done, he sat looking at her.

"Did you hear anything I said?" A smirk crawled across her lips.

"I did. I heard every word."

"Did you want to pick up the pen and sign the papers?"

Luke chuckled. He was going to, but he liked to take his time with things like this. He leaned back in the chair, rubbing his chin. Caroline tilted her head to the side.

Finally, he leaned forward and signed the papers. She shook her head in teasing disbelief, then collected the papers, tapped them on the desk to straighten them, and put them into a folder.

"Let's go see your house."

The drive to the house went by quickly. It was even more beautiful than he had remembered. The trees had a thin layer of snow on them, making them appear almost fake. The smell, however—it was magnificent. It was as if the season had magnified the smell of the Christmas trees. It filled Luke's lungs and made him smile. If he wasn't mistaken, Caroline also appeared more relaxed.

They turned up the driveway, and Luke leaned back in the seat and closed his eyes.

"You okay?" Caroline slowed the car.

"I can't believe all this is happening."

"Well, we do still have the inspection. Something may come up."

He shook his head. "There is nothing that can possibly convince me to not buy this house. Everything is fixable."

Caroline continued up the drive until they reached the house. It took Luke's breath away to see it all covered in snow. The sun reflected off the windows, causing streaks of light to dance on the ground.

Luke stepped out of the car and stood looking at the home before him. Caroline came around the car and stood near him. He turned and pulled her into his arms, holding her so close he could feel her breath on his neck. Her eyes were wide with surprise. After a moment, he felt her relax as she wrapped her arms around him. He found it hard to put the right words together to tell her how he felt, without saying too much.

"I'm really excited about what this house can be."

Her eyes were locked with his. He swallowed, trying to slow his breathing and collect his emotions. There was something about the way she looked at him, something different.

The crunch of gravel behind them made Caroline step back. She folded her arms in front of her, her face stoic. Luke watched her for signs of *something*. He wished he knew what she was thinking.

The inspector parked and greeted both Caroline and Luke. "Are you two the happy couple that are buying this home?"

Luke placed a balled hand over his mouth to hide his laughter while Caroline blushed.

"I'm Caroline, the agent." She put her hand out to shake his. "This is Luke, the home buyer."

"Oh, sorry about that. You two just look so comfortable together."

Caroline looked to the ground. Luke reached his hand out to shake the inspector's. "Should we take a look at the home?"

They walked up the stairs to the front door, and she handed Luke the keys to open it. "It's your home," she said, her eyes fixed on his.

He took the keys from her and felt the cold of the metal against his palm. This was *his* home. He took a deep breath, slid the key into the keyhole, and pushed open the door. Then he stepped aside, holding the door open for Caroline to enter first.

She looked at him, then hesitantly stepped over the threshold. As she turned around and waited for the two men to enter, Luke was almost sure he saw her wipe away a tear.

25
Caroline

Memories overtook Caroline as she entered the living room. She thought she could handle it, but it was too much. Any thoughts that she might have been able to make it work with Luke vanished, as she could see her dad standing in the corner, his cup of coffee in hand and a Santa hat on his head. She smelled the scent of cookies from the kitchen as if her mom were baking. She looked out the window and could see all her childhood friends running around the yard playing hide-and-seek.

She inhaled deeply, trying to ground herself. As she turned around, she caught Luke watching her, his smile momentarily gone. She forced a smile back to him. Regardless of what this house was to her, it was his big day. He was getting the house of his dreams, and she didn't want to ruin it for him.

"I'm going to hang out here while you guys take care of

everything." She walked over to the window and looked out as they went about their business.

Their voices carried through the house, and she could hear the inspector telling Luke about the repairs that would need to be done. He mentioned a door that stuck on the floorboards and was difficult to close. He pointed out some shingles on the roof that needed to be replaced, and he mentioned a leaky faucet in the kitchen. Caroline tried not to giggle when she heard about the kitchen, as her father had tried to fix that faucet for years, but it always leaked no matter what. "Enough to be annoying, but not enough to worry about."

She did her best to keep distracted, but their voices kept bringing her back to the house, and then to her past.

Some time passed before the two returned to the living room. The inspector shook both their hands and promised to have the report back to them by the next day. He didn't see any problems big enough to worry about. Once the inspector was gone, Luke stood in front of Caroline, leaving no way for her to avoid him.

"Are you okay?"

Her chest tightened. She wanted to tell him that, no, she wasn't okay. She missed her parents terribly and Christmas was always the hardest for her. She wanted to tell him about all the little idiosyncrasies of the house—how the fourth step up creaked when you stepped on it, how there was always a draft in the dining room, that the best views were out of the master bedroom looking to the north.

She couldn't, though, because then she'd have to tell him that it used to be *her* house. She would have to tell him that she didn't want to remember all the happy things because they just made her sad to not have her parents around.

She also didn't want to tell him that, as soon as the house closed escrow, she planned to make her exit. Because she didn't *want* to make her exit. A small part of her was hoping, guiltily, that he somehow would back out of buying the house.

She straightened her back and lifted her chin. "I'm fine. Why do you ask?"

He watched her for a moment, as if he was trying to decipher what she was *really* saying. His eyes held her steady gaze; perhaps he was trying to wait out her silence.

"You seem different. I want to make sure you're okay."

Her shoulders relaxed. Here they were, having an inspection done on his new home, and he was asking about *her*. She thought about what it would feel like to fall into his arms and tell him everything. After a moment, she erased it from her mind.

"I'm okay." She led him to the front door and absentmindedly switched the lights off, without even looking at them.

"You in a hurry to get out of here?" His voice was high, as if he was surprised.

"I'm sorry. I have a lot of decorating to do."

He followed her out. She took the key from him as he held it out, then she locked the door. They walked in silence down to the car. When they reached it, he turned around to look at the house again.

"I still can't believe it's ours."

A chill went down her spine when he said *ours*. He certainly meant his and Ella's, but there was a part of her that thought he might have meant hers, too.

As they both looked at the home, one envisioning the future, one remembering the past, he put his arm around her shoulder. She was silent.

He turned her so that they were face to face. She clenched her teeth in hopes that it would help control her emotions. He lifted a hand and brushed it across her jaw, releasing all the tension.

"I know there's a lot going on right now, with the house and the tour. I want you to know that I'm here for you. If you want to talk about anything, I'm here to listen."

Her breath caught in her throat. Luke pulled her in close and engulfed her in his arms, holding her tight.

She let herself go. Tears streamed down her cheeks in silence as she held on tightly around his waist.

She wanted to hold on to this moment, to this feeling, though she knew it was wrong. How could she make it work with Luke when she couldn't ever set foot in his house without bursting into tears? It was only fair that they be allowed to make their own memories. She shouldn't impose all her old ones on them.

Her breath bounced in her chest as she tried to calm herself. Luke held her, rubbing his hand down her hair, his chin tilted to rest on the crown of her head. She took a moment to steady her breathing before taking one last deep breath. She pulled away from him and wiped under her eyes carefully with her fingertips.

"We should probably get back."

As she got in the car and he walked around behind it, she saw him run his hand through his hair in the rearview mirror. She knew she wasn't being fair to him. What else could she do? Once the escrow on the house closed, she would let him go. Until then, she would just have to try to keep a friendly distance. An emptiness filled her as she realized that meant no more tree decorating with Ella, no more marshmallows by the fire, or horseback rides in the snow with Luke.

She shook the thought out of her head before she began crying again. She had to hold it together. Not only for Luke's sake, but because she still had the enormous task of decorating all four homes for the tour looming over her.

He quietly opened the door and sat beside her; his eyes focused on the home. This December was proving to be much more trying than she had anticipated.

❄

Sarah and Nick were rolling out a string of white Christmas lights as she pulled up to the Winter Wonderland home. They had already strung lights across most of the front of the house. There was a copy of Alexandra's rendition of what the house should look like when it was done. Luke's sketches had been instrumental in coming to an agreement on where to hang the lights and place the decorations.

"How is it going? Is everything on schedule?"

Sarah perked up immediately. "Right on track. The trees are due to arrive any minute. Rebecca, Alexandra, and Victor are working on the interior. Chris is at the office coordinating the popcorn stringing supplies and figuring out how we are going to pop such a large amount of popcorn in such a short amount of time."

Caroline nodded her head as she observed the lights. Luke was right—hanging them in a straight line across the gutters gave a much sharper appearance. "It's looking good."

She went inside and found the rest of the day's team in the living room.

"I think the sofa needs to go to the right about four feet." Alexandra tilted her head to the side and placed a hand on her hip.

Victor pushed the large sofa to the right.

Rebecca shook her head. "It's off-center now."

Alexandra nodded. "Maybe two feet to the left."

Victor pulled the sofa back to the left.

Rebecca shook her head again. "That doesn't look right."

Victor started pushing the sofa again.

"I have an idea," Caroline interrupted. "Why don't we put the tree in front of the large window, and move the sofa closer to the fireplace to create a comfortable, cozy environment."

They all looked at each other and nodded. Alexandra and

Rebecca each grabbed an end of the sofa and helped Victor move it forward.

"That looks perfect." Rebecca brushed her hair off her shoulder.

"You really do have an eye for this. I see why Mary put you in charge." Alexandra gave the room a once-over. "Let's take the decorations out of the boxes and start placing them."

Caroline continued through the house, checking that each room was on its way to being fully decorated. She went up the stairs that had been adorned with a mini wooden Santa on each step. Greenery wound its way up the railing. Upstairs were the bedrooms. She looked each room over carefully, then went back to the hallway, where the boxes of bedding had been left. She slid the lids open and pulled out a comforter with red trim and a woodsy theme. She shook it out and placed it over the master bedroom bed. It instantly lit up the room and made it feel Christmassy. *If only Luke could see me now,* she thought. Next she fluffed the pillows and added them to the bed, doing a karate chop on the top of each to give it that signature-designer look.

Once she was done with the master bedroom, she moved on to the other three bedrooms, each with their own unique woodsy quilt and pillows. As she was finishing, Rebecca came up the stairs with two boxes in her arms.

"These are for the bedrooms." She placed them on the ground in front of Caroline, then went back downstairs.

Caroline opened the boxes and found them filled with Christmas toys. There was a wooden toy soldier that she put in the room she assumed to be a boy's, and a stuffed ballerina in a red tutu wearing a crown of holly. She placed it in the room painted pink. She considered each item, carefully placing it where she would if it were her own home. She wanted it to look decorated, but lived in. It was quite the feat since most of the homeowners had removed their personal items to help sell the home.

At the bottom of the last box, she found a stuffed teddy bear wearing a Christmas sweater and holding an open book in his lap. The title read *The Night Before Christmas*. A shallow sigh escaped as she slowly placed a hand over her heart and sat down. She had a bear very similar to this when she was a child. She could clearly remember sitting on the sofa, cuddling up with her dad. Her mom would place a plate of cookies on the table in front of them as he read the famous Christmas tale to her, by the light of the Christmas tree. They could eat all the cookies they wanted, as long as they left enough for Santa.

A loud crash downstairs brought Caroline back to the present. She tried to stand, but her leg had fallen asleep, so she crawled over to the stair railing.

"Everyone okay down there?"

"Yes," Victor called back up. "Just trying to get the tree in the right place. It's huge!"

She giggled as she moved her leg back and forth trying to wake it. After a few moments, she took the bear to the room painted in a light green and placed it carefully on the bed.

Memories were everywhere it seemed. Not just at Luke's house.

26

Luke

Ella came barreling down the hall toward Luke, her arms full of stuffed toys. "Can I bring all of these with us?" Her innocent eyes pleaded with him.

He dropped down to one knee so he was her height. "You can bring everything with you. All your toys, all our furniture, it's all coming with us."

"Even the Christmas tree?" Excitement lit up her eyes.

Luke hadn't thought as far as the Christmas tree. Sure, they would need one in their new house, especially since they were due to move in the next week. The inspector's report had come through, and both Luke and the sellers had signed off on it. He was happy to do any of the minor repair himself. The house had clearly been well taken care of by all the owners, so there were no large repairs needed.

"What do you think? Should we bring this one with us? Or

should we get a new one? I'll bet we can fit a bigger one in the new house."

Ella seemed to think about it for a moment. Then she looked at Luke, and shook her head. "No. I like this one. We'll probably have to decorate it again, but I like it. It reminds me of Caroline." She smiled at her dad, then ran back to her room to continue packing.

She was right. It reminded him of Caroline, too. Would she help them redecorate the same tree? Of course, she would. He planned to make her a bigger part of their life, if she would allow it.

Things had changed so much for him. Two months ago, he had no idea that he would be in a new home this Christmas. He never dreamed that he would be opening up his heart to love again. The future held so many possibilities for him and Ella, and he couldn't wait to get it all started. He looked around the room, his weightless gaze landing on the lamp on the side table, then one of Ella's books on the sofa. There was a lot of packing left to be done. He wasn't stressed. He planned to embrace every minute of this new stage of life they were entering.

He moved through the hallway and placed a box on the floor in front of the closet. He opened the door and put all the blankets and sheets in the box. To think that the next time they would use all of these things would be in their new home sent a tingle up his spine.

Ella walked into the hallway and stopped in front of him.

"Why are you smiling, Daddy?" This time she was holding an art kit in her arms. It was one of her favorite things.

He hadn't realized he was smiling. "I'm just thinking about all the new memories we are going to make at our new home."

She smiled back at him. "Me, too." She paused a moment, then held up the art kit higher. "Can I bring this with us, too?"

Luke laughed. "Yes. Everything. You can bring everything."

"Everything?" She puckered her lips as she often did when she was thinking.

"Everything," he repeated.

"What about the trash in the trashcan?" She giggled, covering her mouth with the art kit.

"I said everything. So, if you really want to?" Luke shrugged.

Ella giggled hysterically and ran off.

Luke shook his head and laughed. As he turned to fill another box, the doorbell rang. He wasn't expecting anyone. It was probably a solicitor.

He swung open the door, prepared to send the solicitor on his way, but stopped short. There in the cold, bundled up and holding a tray of drinks with steam flowing out of them, stood Caroline.

"What a pleasant surprise." A rush of adrenaline surged through his body. "We are just packing."

"I thought you might be. I brought treats." She held up a brown paper bag.

He took the tray from her and stepped aside so she could enter.

Caroline looked around the room littered with half-filled boxes and open boxes waiting to be packed.

"It's not pretty, but it is exciting."

Ella came running into the room, a small stack of board games balanced precariously in her arms. She opened her mouth to speak, but when she saw Caroline, her eyes lit up. "Caroline! I didn't know you were coming over today!" She put the boxes on the sofa and ran over, throwing her arms around Caroline's waist.

There was a flutter in Luke's stomach as he watched his little girl embrace the woman he was falling in love with.

"It was a surprise. I brought some treats as I thought you might be busy packing and could use a little break."

Ella pulled away from her and nodded her head quickly. They both looked to Luke, catching him with a silly grin that he was sure gave away his thoughts.

"Can we have a treat, Daddy?" Ella's little hands were folded in front of her, squeezed together as if praying.

Caroline's head tilted to the side, her smile wide. "What do you say? Is it time for a break?"

He quietly cleared his throat, trying to regain his composure. "I think that would be all right."

The two girls looked at each other, and Ella's tongue swept across her lips in anticipation of whatever Caroline might have brought. Caroline held up the brown bag and wiggled her eyebrows. "He said yes," she whispered.

Ella grabbed Caroline's hand and pulled her to the kitchen. As they passed Luke, Caroline tucked the bag under her elbow and reached out for Luke as if she was going to take his hand. Then, at the last minute, she pulled it back in, holding the bag close to her.

She was such a mystery to Luke. Maybe that was part of the draw—the fact that he didn't know what was coming, the fact that he didn't know how it would all turn out. All that he did know was that he wanted to be with her, and his daughter seemed pretty fond of her as well.

He followed them into the kitchen, where he placed the tray on the counter as Caroline carefully opened the brown bag. She hesitated, then peered around the room as if she was looking for something.

"Plates?" he asked her.

She nodded and he took three small ones from a cabinet above the microwave.

"Are you ready?" Her voice was serious, as if they were about to discover a hidden mystery of the world.

Ella looked up at Caroline from her seat at the counter, her eyes growing with anticipation. She wobbled on her knees on the chair, unable to stay seated with all the excitement in the room.

Very slowly, Caroline put her hand in the bag and pulled out a small, pink pastry box. Ella rubbed her hands together as her eyes focused on the box. Once it was out, Caroline placed it on the counter. She slowly slit the tape holding the box shut and popped the lid open.

Ella leaned over, peering inside, then let out a quiet, "Wow."

The anticipation got to Luke and he leaned over, peeking into the box as well. There sat three tiny, perfectly crafted nutcrackers, lying side by side in the box. His eyebrows shot up.

Caroline reached in, and carefully tugging on the parchment paper, she pulled out a nutcracker, placing him on a plate. Ella leaned down until her nose was nearly touching it. She took an audible breath.

"It smells delicious. Can we eat them?" Her little nose crinkled as she questioned Caroline.

Caroline nodded. "You sure can. He's made of marzipan. One of my favorite Christmas desserts." She slid the plate in front of Ella. "Just pick him up with your fingers."

Caroline took the other two nutcrackers out and situated them on the other two plates, holding one up for Luke. When their eyes met, she averted her gaze.

He took the little soldier and, lifting him to his mouth, bit his head off. It was the most delicious thing he had ever eaten. Ella sat at the end of the counter, happily munching away. Caroline looked down at her plate and lifted her own nutcracker. She gently bit off his feet first, Luke noticed. As she chewed, her eyes slowly closed in enjoyment, causing Luke's heart to pound.

They ate in silence until nothing was left.

"Oh, I almost forgot." Caroline took the three drinks from the tray and handed them out. "Peppermint hot chocolate, with a healthy pile of whipped cream and sprinkles on top."

Ella tried to remove the lid from her drink, but failed. Caroline reached across the table and helped her. Ella lifted the drink to her mouth and took a long sip. "This is the best hot chocolate I've ever had." She had a streak of whipped cream across her top lip. They all laughed together.

Luke was so caught up in what felt like a family moment, he subconsciously reached over and placed his hand on the small of Caroline's back. She stiffened just slightly, but enough for Luke to notice. He was about to pull his hand away when Caroline stepped closer to him, leaning into his show of affection. At that moment, with Caroline by his side, he felt weightless. He had nothing to worry about, nothing to be concerned with. All he wanted was there, in the room with him.

Ella took another sip then stared into her cup for a moment before looking to her dad. "Can I finish this in my room? I still have a lot of packing to do." Her voice was cheery but determined.

Luke reached over and ruffled her hair. "Of course you can."

She ran off to her room, leaving Luke and Caroline together in silence.

He reached for her with his other arm and tilted her body toward him. "This was really thoughtful of you. Thank you."

Caroline held his gaze for a moment, smiling. Then she shrugged. "I figured you might be overloaded trying to pack and probably needed a break."

"I've got a couple weeks off, since we were planning to visit my sister. Now that they are coming to our new place right after Christmas, I can use the time to pack and unpack. Spend some time with Ella before we begin a new chapter of our lives." He loved to look at her, and how the shade of blue in her eyes seemed to change with her mood. He noticed how flawless her skin was, with small freckles dotting her cheeks, as if little kisses had been left there in her childhood.

"That's great." She stepped back, breaking their embrace, and walked into the living room.

Luke took his drink from the counter and followed her.

He found her staring at the tree, her forehead scrunched together as if she was deep in thought.

"I think we're taking the tree with us, and redecorating it there." He said it more to fill the silence than as an explanation.

"Can I help with anything?"

He held his arms wide. "You can help with anything you like. I'm leaving the kitchen for last."

She picked up a folded box that was lying flat on the floor and squeezed its sides until it popped open. She saw the stack of clumsily tucked blankets dangling out of a box with sheets in it. "Maybe I can help you tackle that linen closet you were working on."

As they folded and stacked sheets in the hallway, they talked about Ella and school, Lauren and the homeless shelter, and every other nonconsequential subject they could come up with.

"Have you thought about how you're going to decorate the new house for Christmas?"

He stopped what he was doing and held out his hands, palms forward as if he were framing a scene for a photo. "It's just about the only thing I've thought about. I can't wait to get out there and put up some Christmas cheer. That wraparound porch will look amazing with a string of colorful lights trailing around the columns and along the handrail."

Caroline nodded.

"I still need to figure out where I'm going to put the tree." He rubbed the back of his neck. "I can't decide if it will look better in the family room, where the television will be, or maybe in the formal living room, up front."

"You could put it in the kitchen, in front of the large bay window next to the eating nook. Then you could have a meal by the tree every day. You know, instead of putting it in a room where you won't get to see it very much."

Luke stopped what he was doing and stepped back, placing his hands on his hips.

Caroline held a blanket in her hands, half-folded. "What?"

"Well, look at you, Caroline. Coming up with your own Christmas decorating ideas."

He stepped toward the closet, but instead of taking another sheet to pack, he kissed Caroline on the cheek, sending his heart into an uncontrollable flurry.

At that moment, he knew there was no turning back. He was lost.

27

Caroline

aroline had no idea why she said it. She hadn't even begun to realize the repercussions of what she was saying until she had finished saying it. What was she thinking? If she had any chance at all of surviving Luke moving into her old house, she had ruined it.

Every year her parents put the Christmas tree in the kitchen. People always commented on how wrong it was, and that it made no sense. It made perfect sense to *her* family. They had spent so much time in the kitchen cooking and baking during the holidays that it was really the only place that made any sense. When they got up in the morning to have breakfast, the tree was there, shining in all its glory. When Caroline got home from school and did her homework at the kitchen table, it was there, reminding her of the season to come. When they gathered at night for dinner, whether it was just them or neighbors they had invited, the Christmas tree stood there, beautifully decorated with all their family ornaments, reminding them that however busy the season got, the heart of it was Christmas and family.

It really was the perfect place to put a Christmas tree.

Her arms felt heavy as she held the small blanket. She tried to cover her tracks.

"Or as you said, it would look amazing in the living room."

He shook his head. "No. I think you're right. The kitchen is the perfect place to put the tree."

She focused her attention on folding the blanket in her hands and packing the few remaining items in the closet. She didn't even know why she was there, to be honest. She had been adamant that she needed to end what she and Luke had going. Allowing it to go any further would only be torturing them both. Yet when she was driving back from decorating the homes tonight, she found herself stopping at her favorite bakery and bringing treats over.

She had tried to convince herself that she was only there to see Ella, and to give her the ornament. She had promised to go to the Christmas tea with her, and she was going to keep her word. It was only a few days away. All along, the plan had been to keep her distance with Luke, send him a message that their relationship was platonic, nothing else. But when he had put his arm around her in the kitchen, she felt all her resolve melt away into her hot chocolate. She didn't stand a chance. Now she was giving him decorating advice on his new home, so it was not only Caroline's childhood home but it would also look exactly as it had when she had lived there.

She had to find a way to get it together.

Caroline taped the box closed as Luke looked for a marker to label it. As she pressed down the last bit of tape to ensure the box didn't open in transit, Luke knelt beside her. She took the marker from him and wrote on it. He was so close his breath hit her arm. Her mouth went dry.

She turned to rise as Luke looked at her, and she found herself just inches from him. Memories of the kiss they shared the other night flashed through her mind. He was leaning in to kiss her again, she was sure. She had to make it stop.

Only, she didn't want to.

His lips brushed against hers and she was about to let him kiss her. Then that voice in her head that told her repeatedly that this was a bad idea took over, and she jumped to her feet.

"I have something for Ella," she blurted out, a pained look on her face.

"You have something for Ella?" he rubbed his neck and came to a standing position.

She was unable to form words at that moment. The feeling that something had slipped away from her was overwhelming, and she wasn't sure if she should try to save it or celebrate that she had escaped. She swallowed then nodded, ever so slightly.

"I'll go get her, I guess." He walked down the hall to find Ella.

Caroline's shoulders fell as soon as he left the room. She shook her head. *What was she doing?*

Ella came bouncing into the room. Caroline followed and sat on the sofa by her purse and pulled the small Christmas bag from it. Ella stood in front of her.

"It was so nice of you to think of me, giving me that ornament for my Christmas tree, that I thought you might like one from my tree, too."

Ella's hands flew up and covered her mouth. A dimple peeped out from behind one hand. Caroline gave her the bag.

She took it in her hands and plopped onto the sofa next to her. First, she carefully pulled a piece of red tissue out of the bag and tossed it aside. Next she tugged on the green piece, and after she saw it was heavier, she dug her other hand into the bag. She scooped the tissue-wrapped ornament out and placed it in her lap. Then, she carefully peeled the layers of tissue away until the ornament was exposed.

She gasped, then her lips stretched into a smile, the gap where she had lost a tooth visible between her parted lips. "It's the most amazing ornament I've ever seen."

"It was mine when I was a child. It was one of my favorites."

"If it's one of your favorites, then you should keep it." Her voice was tight with concern. Luke had done such a wonderful job raising her. She was so full of compassion and concern for others. She was a lot like Luke.

"It would bring me more joy for you to have it and enjoy it. I know how much Santa Claus having a chimney means to you."

Ella squeezed the ornament to her chest gently. "Thank you. I love it."

She placed it on the table, then lunged toward Caroline and hugged her, using all her strength to squeeze her as tight as she could. "I'm so glad you're going to the Christmas tea with me."

Caroline's heart warmed and heat radiated throughout her entire body. The love she felt from this man and his little girl was unlike any she had ever felt before.

Ella let go and took the ornament to the tree. "I know we're about to take it down, but I want to see it every day until we move." She placed the ornament in the middle of the tree.

Luke watched Ella. If she wasn't mistaken, it looked like his eyes were a little glassy. Her heart pounded.

How did she let this happen? How did she come to care so much about someone that she couldn't be with? She had never felt for anyone the way she did for Luke. The thought of walking away from them and not being a part of their lives felt wrong to her. Maybe she could hang on a little bit longer. She did have to make sure the closing went smoothly. She could bow out when it came time for them to move in. That would give her a whole week to spend with them and get it out of her system before she said goodbye.

"How is that a good plan?" Lauren's eyebrows lifted as she questioned Caroline's thinking before taking another sip of her tea.

"It will give me a chance to get it all out of my system and enjoy their company while I can." The hot coffee set in front of her smelled delicious, and it would hopefully help keep her awake through the day. She had only slept a few hours after staying late to help Luke pack. Once she got home, there was an excitement that buzzed through her body, keeping her from closing her eyes.

Lauren placed her tea on the table and stared at Caroline straight faced. "To be clear, you are saying that spending more time with a man you're falling in love with will help you be okay with not being with the same man you've fallen in love with?"

Caroline squinted at her. It really made no sense when Lauren said it like that. She pinched her lips together.

"So maybe it's not a foolproof plan, but—"

"It's a foolish plan."

Caroline let out a deep sigh. "Then what do I do? I care about them. When I'm around Luke, I feel like everything is going to be okay. It's like I'm where I'm supposed to be."

"Then why are you fighting it?" She ran one finger through the curls draping over her shoulder.

"Because it hurts too much. I have such wonderful memories in that house. Every time I'm there, I can't help but be sucked back to that time."

"Why is that bad if they are such happy memories?"

"They were happy times. Thinking that they will never happen again makes me really sad."

"If your parents were still alive, you would still be a grown-up. You wouldn't be living with them anymore. The memories you'd be making now would be a different, but equally happy, kind of memory."

Caroline sat with that thought for a moment. She had never envisioned what it would be like if they were still around *now*. She had thought about how it would be to have them there when she got promotions, or a new boyfriend she wanted them to meet. She had thought about how it would be with them celebrating all the big parts of life with her. She had never thought about what the day-to-day would have looked like had they still been there.

"What do you think I should do?"

She shrugged. "I can't tell you what to do. I can tell you that going this far and then not giving them a chance isn't fair. To them or to you. How do you know you won't love being in your old house? Maybe you're still grieving the loss of that part of your life. This would give you a chance to let it all go."

"I don't want to let those memories go. I love them."

"Yet you don't want to think about them."

It felt as though something had hit Caroline in the heart. Maybe she wasn't being fair. Maybe she should give them a chance.

She gave Lauren a hug goodbye and left.

❈

As she was driving to the Winter Wonderland home to check on the progress, a wave of Christmas spirit washed over her. They should *make* the ornaments they were going to put on the tree. Then they would donate the ornaments to the shelter. That was it. She pulled up to the curb and ran to the house. It looked amazing. The tree was large enough to take everyone's breath away, but it didn't take over the room. Chris was standing in the corner jotting something down. There were three large bags of popcorn kernels on the table by the kitchen.

"I have an idea."

Chris looked up at her. "I hope so. Because we have a lot of decorating to do and a winter storm is coming in a few days."

"Do you have a source for small log discs?"

Chris looked at her as if she'd gone mad. "Log discs?"

"Yes. The guests are going to make ornaments out of log discs and glue. We can have little Santa hats and greenery for miniature wreaths. They are going to love it. The station will be right out there." She pointed to a covered space next to an outdoor fireplace. "Then while they tour the home, the ornaments will be drying by the fire. When they're done, they can hang them on the tree, while the kids do the popcorn stringing."

Chris nodded his head. "I like it. It feels very Christmassy and family oriented. It will help them envision what it would be like to live here."

"Let's get going, then. We only have a few more days before, as you said, the storm hits."

28

Luke

Luke loaded the last of the boxes into the moving truck and waved to Ryan, a friend that had offered to help out. As Ella stood on the sidewalk watching, he slid the back door down then knocked on it, signaling that it was safe for Ryan to drive away. He turned to her, his hand on his hip. She was holding her favorite teddy bear.

"Should we go in and say goodbye?"

She shook her head. "I already did."

He nodded slowly, always in wonder about how mature his six-year-old daughter was. She seemed to have an understanding of the world that many adults didn't.

"I guess I'll lock up, then." He went up the stairs and stood in the doorway for a moment, Ella waiting patiently at the bottom. He thought he'd be sad to leave this place; it had so many memories in it. Instead, he felt a sense of fulfillment. He was ready to move on and make new memories, while holding on to the old.

Ella was only three when they had moved in, and she had missed her mommy terribly. He had been relatively clueless about how to go on living life without his wife. So much had changed in the past three years. Both he and Ella had grown to love their new life. This had been a home for growing and preparing. It wasn't where they were meant to stay. He knew that now. It seemed Ella had known that all along.

He rubbed the back of his neck as he took one last look around the room, then he shut the door and raced down the steps. "Are you ready to go to our new home?"

The excitement in her eyes reflected Luke's. "I've never been more ready. I can't wait to put up the Christmas tree again."

He took her hand and they made their way to the Jeep, Ella skipping by Luke, standing tall, ready for the next chapter in their lives.

The drive to their new home was a quiet one. Ella seemed enthralled by the views as they drove. This was, after all, the first time she knew this was the road to her new home. She insisted on having the window rolled down so she could see better. She had always told Luke that looking out the window was a lot like watching the world and not taking part in it. So he tended to allow her to keep the window down. Even if it was twenty degrees outside.

They turned up their new drive as he looked out the windshield and through the canopy of trees. The clouds were dark and the air flowing in through the open window was crisp. Ella's cheeks were turning red. Snow was coming. They would need to unpack the truck quickly.

He came to a slow stop in the drive next to the truck. There, standing on the steps to their new home, stood Caroline. His throat grew thick as he watched her wrap her arms around her shoulders and rub. She was smiling, waiting for them. It felt like home.

Luke's train of thought ended when Ryan knocked on the window of the car. "We'd better get unloading, man. Looks like it's going to snow." Ryan looked up, then back down to Luke as he ran the back of his hand across his nose.

"Of course. Let's get started."

As Ella slid out of the car, sure to take her teddy bear with her, he hopped out and headed for the back of the truck. Before he slid the door open, he stopped and watched Ella as she ran to the house, momentarily forgetting where he was and what he was doing. As she climbed the steps, Caroline wrapped an arm around her and led her into the home, petting the teddy bear on the head.

"Hey, Lover boy. The truck?"

Luke shook his head and refocused his attention on unloading the truck.

As they took the large pieces of furniture, one by one, up the stairs and into the appropriate rooms, Luke tried to sneak a glance at Ella and Caroline. They were busy in the kitchen doing something. Each time he would pause to see, Ryan would slap him on the back and jerk his head toward the door, reminding him of the little time they had left.

Once the truck was empty, Ryan shook Luke's hand and congratulated him on the new home, then hurried to return the truck and get back to his own family.

Luke stood back and took a deep breath. *This was it.*

He slowly made his way up the steps, the cold air biting at his ears. He moved a few of the boxes on the porch aside to create a path, then cradled one in his arms to take inside. He pushed the door open and a warm gush of air hit him. Caroline had lit a fire in the fireplace. The warmth that radiated through him was from more than the fire, though. There was banging going on in the kitchen, a sign that the girls were still busy with whatever task

Caroline had put them to. Luke brought more boxes in, lining them up along the wall. As he brought in the last one, Caroline and Ella stormed into the living room, each of them wearing an apron and a silly grin.

"What have you ladies been up to?"

They looked to each other and giggled. "It's a surprise." Ella rested her hands on her knees and burst into uncontrollable laughter. Then she ran and grabbed Luke's hand, pulling him into the kitchen. Caroline followed.

The most delicious smell of melted cheese filled the room. The table by the bay window was set with a red tablecloth and green napkins. There was a small wreath with candles in the center. "Dinner!" Ella cheered as she held her arms out to display two funny-shaped pizzas. "We made Christmas tree and stocking pizzas."

"They look delicious." Luke rubbed his hands together. He was amazed by what he was taking in. The beautiful woman standing there before him and his daughter, happy and smiling, were part of his life now. The room around them had a warm glow to it. Just then, he remembered. He held a finger up. "I'll be right back."

He ran into the living room and searched between the shoulder high piles of boxes until he found the Christmas tree. It was leaning against a wall, still bundled from the ride over. He picked it up and gently placed it over his shoulder. He squeezed his way back out of the maze of boxes and used his toe to carefully swing open the door.

Caroline's hands shot to her chest, where she held them. Ella jumped up and down squealing, "The tree! The tree!"

Luke placed it in front of the large bay window where the little light that was seeping through the clouds shone in. He unwrapped the string looped around the tree, and they all watched as the branches sprung back in place.

"Now we can have dinner." He clapped his hands together and pine needles went flying.

Caroline cleared her throat. Her cheeks were red, Luke assumed with delight. "I'm going to wash up." Her voice was calm and quiet.

Ella ran and leaped into Luke's arms, distracting him from Caroline as she left the room.

"What do you think so far?"

"I love it. It's the best house ever." She wrapped her arms around his neck and squeezed. "What do you think of the pizza? Caroline taught me how to make it from itch."

"You mean 'scratch'?" He poked her in the belly. She giggled furiously.

He took Ella to the table and sat her on the bench. They both turned and looked out the window, watching as the sun slowly set behind the trees. A flock of birds frolicked in the wind, squawking as they did. Ella placed her pointer finger against the glass and drew a heart. "It's really cold out there."

Caroline came back into the room looking refreshed. She placed the pizzas on the table and cut them into her best attempt at slices. Then she took a lemonade out of the refrigerator and poured each of them a glass.

Luke held up his glass to get their attention. "I want to say thank you for making all of this possible. Without you, Ella, asking for a new home, I don't know if this ever would have happened. Without you, Caroline, I wouldn't know the true beauty of the area. Not to mention, this fabulous dinner. This is amazing."

They clinked their glasses together and drank and ate until they were full and tired. Then Luke found Ella's boxes and took the ones with her necessities to her bedroom. As he helped her brush her teeth, Caroline made up her bed. When they walked back into Ella's room, they found Caroline at the window with her arms folded in front of her.

"It's snowing. I should probably get going." She turned back to face them. She looked more serious than Luke had ever seen her.

He held up his phone. "I just got an alert from the station. A snowstorm is already hitting Sweet River and is headed this way. I think you'd better stay here."

"Are we having a slumber party?" Ella's eyes lit up like lights on a Christmas tree.

"I guess we are." Luke rubbed her back. "Why don't you let Caroline have your room tonight and you can sleep with me?"

Caroline's hands were clasped tightly at her waist. Her brow furrowed and her fingers were twisting in knots.

"I don't know. I'm sure I can make it home."

"No way. I couldn't in good conscience have you leave. If something happened to you—" His chest tightened.

She let out a sigh. "I can't take Ella's bed, then. It's her first night in this room. That's kind of a big deal."

Ella nodded in agreement. "You could sleep in here with me?" She jumped on her bed and snuggled under the blankets.

Caroline's eyes moved around the room as she shifted her weight from one foot to the other. The idea of sleeping in Ella's room clearly made her uncomfortable.

"You could take my room. I can sleep with Ella."

"It's kind of a big deal that you sleep in your room tonight, too. How about I sleep on the sofa downstairs?"

Luke rubbed his chin. That could work. He could refresh the fire and pull blankets from the boxes downstairs. Her eyes followed him closely, looking for his approval. He nodded. "You've got a deal."

"It's settled, then." She sat at the edge of Ella's bed and placed her hand on Ella's knee through the covers. "Enjoy this room. I happen to know that the little girl that lived here long ago had many sweet dreams in this very room."

Ella smiled, the gap from her lost tooth showing. "Good night."

"Good night." Caroline rubbed Ella's hair away from her forehead.

She rose from the bed and left the room.

Luke watched her as she went, then sat on the bed with Ella. "I'll be right next door all night. I'll leave the hall light on. Okay?"

Ella nodded. "I love this room already. It feels like home should, warm and cozy."

Luke bent down and kissed her on the forehead. "Want me to read to you tonight? I'm sure we can find a book in here somewhere."

She shook her head. "It's okay. I'm really tired." She yawned.

"All right. Good night, then."

Luke stopped at the doorway and looked back at Ella, tucked tightly into the bed. She looked so happy there, in her own room. He couldn't believe how quickly time had passed. It seemed like just yesterday that she was in pigtails and pull-ups and they were moving into the apartment. Now here they were, in a home of their own.

When Luke reached the bottom of the stairs, Caroline was coming in from outside. She had small piles of snow on her shoulders and head. "You're not trying to go home, are you?"

She shook her head and snow went flying around her. "I could barely find my car." She held up a black duffle bag. "I was getting my gym bag. I have a few things I could use in it."

He couldn't take his eyes off her as she removed her jacket and hung it on the coatrack by the door. Funny, he hadn't even noticed there was a coatrack there. He liked how she felt so at home. Maybe it meant she would be spending a lot of time there. His heart raced at the thought.

She held up her bag and pointed to the restroom. As she passed near him, he could smell her. It made him weaken. He ran his hand through his hair, and when she shut the door, he began looking through boxes for blankets.

The boxes were easy to find, as they were the only ones that had her writing on them. When she came back out, he held up one of the blankets. "Remember these?" He was sure that she did by the red that briefly appeared on her cheeks.

She took the blanket and disappeared behind the pile of boxes hiding the sofa, then came back to get two more. As Luke handed them to her, their fingers touched, sending a shockwave through his body. They both stopped, caught in the moment, their eyes locked. Luke moved closer until they were inches apart. He leaned in and kissed her. The shockwaves returned, sending electricity shooting through his entire body. He thought his heart might leap from his chest.

When she pulled away, he saw something different in her eyes that sent one heavy beat to his heart. She took the blankets from him and held them up. "Thanks for the blankets. Good night." Then she disappeared to the sofa behind the stack of boxes where he heard her take a deep, deep breath.

29
Caroline

The yard was covered in a thick blanket of snow when Caroline woke. She hadn't slept much, being back in the home again. She had hoped that being boxed in would help her forget where she was, but no matter how hard she tried to convince herself that she was somewhere else, that familiar smell of the wood in the fireplace and the same old creaks that had once comforted her kept her awake. The sounds and smells of her childhood had been so potent she had dreamed that she was living in the house again, with her parents. They had decorated it for Christmas, and she was sitting by the fire wrapping presents with her mom. They wrapped box after box after box, but Caroline had no idea what was in them. Every time she asked her mom what the boxes contained, she would smile and say, *You'll know soon enough.*

The dream had been so real, she woke with her mom's words echoing in her ears. She rubbed her temples. It was too much.

Her heart ached at the resistance that was tugging at her. When she thought of Luke, she wanted to be with him. She had a hard time imagining what it would be like to be without him, even though they had just met. He had an effect on her. But this house had an effect on her, too.

She wished her mom was here for her to confide in. She would have known what to do. A lump grew in Caroline's throat as she thought about her mom. What would she look like now? Would her hair have gone gray? Would she spend most of her days in the kitchen cooking for neighbors in need and baking for the community center like she had before? And her dad. He had loved the snow so much. Would his old age have begun to slow him down yet? Or would he still be out there, running around with the new batch of neighborhood kids?

Ella would be one of those kids now.

The third step from the bottom creaked and Caroline looked up to see who was there. She found Ella standing on the bottom step, still in her nightgown, snuggling with her teddy bear.

Just like that, she forgot about the night she had.

"Good morning." Ella was very cheerful for it being so early.

"Good morning. How did you sleep in your new room?"

"Good. I think there was an owl outside my window." She rubbed her eyes.

"Ah. Yes, there are a lot of owls in these parts. There used to be one that liked to perch in the big tree in the backyard."

Ella made her way between the boxes and sat next to Caroline on the sofa. She was very quiet. Caroline wasn't sure if something was bothering her or if this was just what she was like in the morning.

"Look, out there, by the little tree." Caroline pointed out the window behind the sofa. There were two small birds dancing around each other, fluttering up and down from the lowest branch to the ground.

"What are they?"

"Those are Brewer's sparrows. You don't see too many of them in the winter. If we are really quiet, we might get lucky and hear them sing."

They sat perched together on the sofa, watching and waiting patiently. After a few moments, the birds started to sing. It was a beating sound, almost like a frog's croak that segued into a beautiful trilling whistle.

"Wow," Ella whispered. "I've never heard anything like that before."

"You are going to hear some amazing things out here."

She looked at Ella. She was going to miss her. She had grown quite attached to her, and it surprised Caroline how strong her feelings for this child were. She pushed the thought out of her head.

"What are you ladies doing?" They both jumped, Luke's voice surprising them.

"Daddy, you have to come see these birds. They are amazing." Ella scooted over, leaving a space for Luke to sit between her and Caroline. He squeezed in.

"Brewer's sparrows," he said quietly.

Caroline was surprised he knew what they were. He was sitting so close she could feel his warmth against the side of her body.

"You should hear them sing. It's so beautiful." Ella smiled up at her dad, her dimples more pronounced today.

He rubbed Ella's back, then placed another arm around Caroline. It felt like family.

She looked around her, at her old home that should feel like home but only felt like sadness, and her heart started to pound. She had to get out of here.

"Who wants pancakes?" She leaped to her feet.

"Me!" Ella's hand shot into the air.

"Why don't you go get dressed while I help with the pancakes," Luke said. He helped Ella to her feet and she scrambled up the stairs.

Caroline grabbed her bag and headed for the bathroom. "I'm going to freshen up. I'll be there in a minute." She wound her way around the boxes and into the bathroom, where she closed the door behind her. Around the top of the small powder room a faded ivy-and-flower pattern was painted. She remembered clearly when her mom had painted it. There had been a storm that weekend and they were bored. The roads were flooded, so they couldn't go anywhere or play outside. So her mom found some old paints and decided to paint the bathroom. They had created the stencils together, drawing the details with care. Then her mom had cut them out and carefully taped them along the top of the wall. She had even let Caroline help with the painting.

Her mom had been like that. If you were going to do something, you should get to do all of it. She was always encouraging her to try new things, even things that she thought Caroline might be too young to do. Her mom was always there, offering encouragement and praise, no matter how the project turned out.

It struck her how much she still missed her mom even though it had been so long since they had passed. Everyone had said time will heal, which was true. She just didn't expect the void to still feel so large this many years later.

She splashed water on her face and quickly got herself ready. She only had to make it through pancakes and then she could head home.

Luke was in the kitchen, moving boxes around, no doubt trying to find the utensils. When Caroline walked in, he triumphantly held up a bowl and a fork, apparently all he had managed to come up with.

"That's all we need, really." She wiggled her eyebrows at him as she passed. His eyes followed her, sending a warmth throughout her. It felt so right to be with him.

How could she walk away from all of this? She looked around

the room and her heart sank. She had to. It was too much for her to stay.

She opened the cabinets and gathered the few ingredients needed for the pancakes.

"Where did those come from?"

She shrugged. "I bought you a few groceries to help you make it through the first few days. I thought you might need them with the storm coming."

Smoothly, he walked across the kitchen and put his arms around her, placing them on the small of her back. He leaned in, resting his forehead against hers.

Caroline's pulse raced as she broke out in a cold sweat. How could one person be so strongly torn in two different directions?

"I'm glad you're here. You make it feel even more like home."

She swallowed. A shuffling came from the living room. Caroline took it as her chance to get away. Did she really want to, though? She would happily stay in Luke's arms for hours, anywhere but here.

Against her longing, she pulled away. "Sounds like Ella is looking for something."

He kissed her promptly and went to help Ella.

The morning passed quickly. Caroline moved swiftly through the kitchen, her body returning to old habits. She made the pancakes and helped with the dishes before turning to them both. "I think I'm going to leave you to make your new house a home. I have to get back to decorating some houses."

"Do you have to go so soon? Can't you help us decorate the tree?"

Caroline reached out for Ella and brushed her hair behind her ears. "That sounds like a lot of fun, but I do really need to get going."

Ella pouted. "Okay."

"I will still be at your school on Tuesday for the tea." She bent to Ella's height and hugged her.

"I can't wait!" She skipped out of the room and up the stairs.

Luke rose from his chair and made for Caroline. Before he reached her, she turned and walked to the living room, where she gathered her things. She wanted to stay, but knew she couldn't. There was a pulling at her heart telling her that she should talk to Luke about all of it. But what would that fix? There was nothing he could say that would change the situation.

She fought back a tear as she realized this would probably be the last time she would ever be in this home. Possibly the last time she would see Luke.

He stood in the doorway to the kitchen watching her. "Is everything okay?"

She turned to adjust her belongings in her bag so that he couldn't see her face. "Yeah. I just have a lot to do today. I'm sure they've plowed the roads by now. They're usually pretty quick about it."

She looked at him. His hands were tucked into his front pockets; he was leaning against the doorway. Why did he have to look so handsome today? Her resolve was fading. Maybe there was a way she could make it work.

The birds outside sang their song, breaking the silence, and reminding Caroline of all the mornings she and her mom had sat on the patio watching those birds, listening to them. She threw her bag over her shoulder and walked around the boxes toward the front door.

Luke stood in her way. He stepped forward until his chest was nearly against her. He smelled like fresh soap and aftershave. She wrung her hands in front of her, and repeated the words over and over in her mind: *time to let go, time to let go.*

He pulled her close and pressed his lips against hers. At first she didn't respond, but soon she found she had no control over herself. She pressed her lips against his and let herself enjoy the kiss. When they parted, he was smiling.

She walked to the door, and as she placed her hand on the doorknob, he called to her.

"Caroline—"

"Yes?" She wasn't sure how long she could keep her composure.

He paused, as if he wanted to say something, but wasn't sure how to. He shook his head slightly. "Drive safe."

"Of course." She stepped out into the cold and closed the door behind her, her heart pounding.

Once she was in her car and down the driveway far enough that he could no longer see her, she stopped the car. Her chest was heaving and the tears were fighting to slip down her cheeks. She turned the radio up and let herself cry.

Her phone rang. It was Luke. She gathered herself as best she could, then answered.

"I was wondering if you'd like to go out tomorrow night? Just you and me." His voice was tentative.

She should say no. She should walk away now, before it was too late. Yet, his voice was kind and hopeful.

"I'd love to."

"Great. I'll see you then."

She took a tissue from the center console and wiped her eyes. When the weight of what she had done hit her, she expected the tears to fall again. Instead, she found herself smiling and justifying her decision.

She would just avoid the house. It was as simple as that.

30

Luke

Luke sat in the living room, surrounded by boxes. There was so much to do, yet he was sitting here thinking about Caroline.

"Did you find them yet, Daddy?" Ella called from the kitchen.

He snapped back to the present, and on the ground next to him was a box that had the word *ornaments* scrawled on the side in Ella's writing. "I've got them," he called back to her.

He carried the box to the kitchen and set it on the table. Ella hovered over it clapping her hands together in excitement. He slowly flipped back the flaps and tore away the tissue paper.

"There it is!" she squealed as she took the wooden ornament Caroline had given her and placed it on the tree.

Luke's heart skipped a beat as he watched the joy on his daughter's face. She had always been a cheerful child, even when most children would have been an emotional mess. Lately, though, there was something about her happiness that he couldn't put into words. She seemed to be more settled.

They decorated the tree again, Ella giggling as she went through all the ornaments, trying her hardest to remember where they had been on the tree at the apartment.

When they were done, it was bedtime. Luke walked Ella to her room and waited as she got ready for bed. He looked around her room, which had been full of boxes that morning. They had worked hard all day unpacking the two bedrooms, making themselves at home as soon as they could. The soft curtains framing the windows and the way the moonlight hit the floor gave Ella's room a whimsical look, as if fairies used it as a playground. Every time she entered her room, she was so overcome with happiness that she spun around in circles across it.

He kissed her good night and went back downstairs to unpack a few more boxes. He sat on the sofa where Caroline had slept and found himself lost in thought again. He rested his head back on the sofa, and her scent lifted off the pillows. He would never finish unpacking this house if he kept daydreaming about her. He lifted himself up and opened another box, anxious to make a dent in the pile.

Andrea had offered to babysit Ella that night, as she was itching to see their new home. She had brought them a tin with a cheery snowman on it, full of chocolate chip cookies, and promises that Ella would be in bed on time. Luke had a hard time believing it.

On his way to Caroline's, he stopped at a small flower shop in Brambling Falls. He wandered through the store looking at the colorful stems lined up in buckets waiting to be included in a bouquet. What would Caroline want? She certainly wasn't a rose kind of girl. Those would be much too formal for her. Daisies, maybe? No, too immature. He had to find something that conveyed beauty and sophistication, with a strong side of playful. He ran his fingers over the petals of a lily, then a peony. He was about to ask for help when a small arrangement caught his eye. It was a combination of exotic red and white flowers. Large green leaves surrounded the cluster of colors, with small sprays of light green popping out in between. It was perfect for her.

By the time he arrived at her house, his hands were shaking and he had a funny feeling in the pit of his stomach. She still had that effect on him. He slipped on his jacket and straightened his collar before walking up the path and ringing her doorbell. He was happy to see the Christmas tree was still shining bright in her window.

When she opened the door, his breath escaped him. She was beautiful. Her hair was swept to the side and she was wearing a black dress that looked as though it was made specifically for her. She was smiling, and he noticed for the first time that she had a dimple in her left cheek.

"You look amazing." He tried to keep cool, but his voice cracked, giving him away. He held the flowers out to her.

"Thank you. These are beautiful." She held the flowers in the vase to her nose, her chest lifting as she inhaled. She placed them on the table beside the Christmas tree and picked up her coat. Luke took it, holding it out for her to slip on. She smiled in thanks.

Luke held his arm out and linked her elbow into his as they walked to the car. He opened the car door and she entered. When he opened the driver's side door, he found a small box sitting on his seat.

"What's this?" He held it on his lap, but was unable to look away from her gaze.

"It's a little thank-you for all your help with the Tour of Homes." She folded her hands in her lap. "Aren't you going to open it?"

He rubbed behind his neck and shifted his focus to the box in his lap. He pulled at the red ribbon that was dangling from the bow and it unraveled. Slowly, he lifted the lid and looked inside. Sitting on a bed of cotton was a keychain.

His throat grew thick as he held it up to the light. Swinging from the keyring was a small, metallic tree with two birds sitting in it, one large, one smaller. His chest grew heavy. When Ella's mom passed, he had referred to himself and Ella as two birds floating through the world looking for their nest. There was no way Caroline could have known that. She must have sensed his affection for birds came from somewhere deeper. He was amazed at how someone that had known him for such a short time could know him so well.

He shook his head, at a loss for words. "Thank you." He watched her sitting there, watching him. She rubbed her hands along her arms and shivered.

"Maybe we should go." He let out a small chuckle.

Caroline nodded.

When they pulled into the parking lot next to the subdued sign that read *Darion's Steakhouse*, Caroline's hand shot to her mouth.

"Is this okay?" he asked, afraid he had made a mistake.

"It's fabulous. I've always wanted to try it but didn't ever have the occasion. I hear they have a fantastic chocolate soufflé."

"I guess we'll have to try it for ourselves and see."

Her eyes stayed focused on the entrance to the restaurant, happiness emanating through them.

As they approached, the maître d' opened the door for them. He quietly asked for the name on the reservation and seated them at a table by a window.

As he handed her the menu, Caroline smiled then went back to gazing out the window. Luke followed her sight line and was amazed at what he found. There was a lake that started directly below their table and stretched out in every direction. Across the lake was a thick line of trees. There was a light layer of snow from the weekend storm still clinging to the branches, making the vista look as if it were taken from a painting.

He shifted his view back to Caroline. He wanted to get to know her better. He was beginning to learn her mannerisms and her way of thinking, but he wanted to really know about her and her past. Had she ever been in love? Had her heart ever been broken? He wanted to know all the little things that made her the person she was.

"The ribeye for two looks good."

"Sold." Luke winked at her, and they both put their menus down. When the waiter came by, Caroline ordered a small salad to start and Luke ordered a soup and the ribeye for them both, with the chocolate soufflé and a scoop of house-made ice cream for dessert.

As the waiter poured them each a glass of red wine, Luke built up the courage to ask her about her past. He leaned forward in his chair, resting his forearms on the edge of the table and clasping his hands together.

"Tell me about you, Caroline." He felt the heat rise to his cheeks. That hadn't been quite as subtle as he had hoped for.

She adjusted her position in her seat, resting one elbow on the table and bringing her hand up to her chin. "What would you like to know?"

He instantly felt at ease. She did that to him. Anytime he thought he was going to lose it, he took one look at her or heard her voice, and all was right in the world.

"Have you ever been in love?" He threw it out there as if it were a leaf blowing in the wind.

She paused, her eyes settling on him, making him wonder if he had been too forward. Then she tilted her head to the side.

"I suppose I have."

His muscles tensed. She was going to make him draw it out

of her. "Did he break your heart?" He lowered his voice, trying to be sensitive to whatever the situation might have been.

She shook her head slowly. "I think I may have been the one doing the heart breaking." She crinkled her nose as she said it. It was almost a whisper.

He didn't know what to do with this information. Caroline? A heartbreaker? He had a hard time seeing it. She had always shown so much concern for him and Ella. She gave Christmas to a family she didn't even know. How could she possibly ever have broken anyone's heart?

"Should I be worried?" He cocked an eyebrow.

She giggled. "It wasn't like that."

"Tell me about it." He grinned at her like a schoolboy with a crush on his teacher.

"We met in college in Eugene. He had lived there his whole life and his family was there and everything he ever wanted was there. Except I didn't want to stay there. I wanted to go back to Brambling Falls."

"You couldn't agree over thirty miles?"

She shrugged. "Twenty-three miles, actually. It seems silly now, neither of us willing to budge. I felt like if he wasn't willing to move to Brambling Falls for me, then maybe there was something more missing. I guess you could say the same thing for me. If I couldn't do that for him, then he wasn't the right person for me."

Luke nodded.

"My parents passed a year or so later, and I ended up leaving Brambling Falls anyway. I suppose everything happens for a reason."

He thought back to that day they first met in the toy store, fighting over the last Fluffy the Dog. They had been brought together for a reason. He didn't think so at the time, but he felt it now. He felt it every time he saw her. In fact, he felt it even more on the days he didn't see her.

"How about since then? Has there been anyone special?"

She shook her head. "It took me a while to get back on my feet after my parents. I pretty much threw myself into my career and didn't give myself time for anything else. Then I met Lauren and she brought me back into the real world. She used to drag me out for Taco Tuesday or trivia night. Anything to get me out of the house. I'm so thankful for it now."

"But you haven't met anyone special?"

"I've dated here and there. Nothing has turned into anything special. How about you? Have you dated much since Ella's mom passed?"

He rubbed the back of his neck as he gathered his thoughts, trying to put them into words that would make sense and not give away how strongly he felt for her, and how he hadn't felt anything for anyone since his wife.

"I guess you could say I've been putting all my energy into being the world's best dad. Ella deserves it."

Caroline's face softened at the mention of Ella. He could see how much she meant to Caroline.

They fell into a comfortable silence as their dinner arrived. They ate quietly, enjoying the view.

He was mesmerized by Caroline. He had let himself fall for her and knew in his heart that it was the right thing. It was exactly where he was supposed to be.

31

Caroline

Luke was the type of man that Caroline had always dreamed about meeting. He was kind, caring, and always put others first. She had been pouring her heart out to him, sharing things she hadn't shared with anyone before. It felt right to her.

"I've been thinking about something." He rested his wrists on the edge of the table, fork and knife still gripped tightly. "Ella and I finished setting up the two bedrooms. The rest of the house is still a mess of boxes."

Caroline stiffened when he mentioned the house. She had been enjoying their date so much that she had forgotten about the house entirely until he brought it up. She tried to mask her feelings by smiling, but it felt stiff, inauthentic.

"I'm not really good at making places feel… feminine. I think Ella would really appreciate it if it didn't look like a man cave."

Caroline wasn't sure what he was trying to say, but she was already beginning to feel queasy. She had to avoid the house. It was the only way this would work.

"I was hoping you could help us set up the house so it looks more like a family lives there."

She swallowed, then moved her head up and down slowly, tentatively. Her brain scrambled for something to say. Anything that would get her out of it. Anywhere else, she would have been thrilled at the prospect. But there? At her old home? She couldn't do it. It wasn't even an option.

"You have a good eye for where things go in the house. You seemed like you felt at home over the weekend."

That was the problem. She had felt *too* at home.

She squirmed in her seat, trying to come up with the right thing to say.

"I don't know. It's not really my thing. I'm sure you could find someone that would do a much better job."

She tried to keep it light. He watched her, his face still, unreadable. After a moment, he let it go and went back to his dinner.

She exhaled quietly and took another bite, although she found her appetite had gone.

Caroline decided the safest route was to change the subject, so she brought up how much progress had been made on the houses for the tour. The snowstorm had slowed down the exterior decorating, but they were still able to make a lot of headway on the interior.

When she thought she was safe and that there might be a chance to make this work, he brought it up again.

"I was thinking of having a party at the house. Inviting a few friends to see our new place and the neighbors so they can come out and meet us. What do you think?"

She stopped chewing her food as that feeling of dread returned. Her mother had loved entertaining in that home. Memories of every birthday party, Christmas gathering, and Valentine's Day party she had ever thrown came flooding to her mind.

Aside from getting past all the memories, what if her old neighbors still lived there? She was sure the Johnsons would never leave their home. It had been in the family for generations. How would she explain how she knew them to Luke?

It was suddenly very hot in the restaurant.

In that moment, she knew what she had to do. She only had to make it through tonight, then she would make a clean break.

Not from Ella of course. She didn't deserve to be abandoned that way. Caroline knew in her heart, though, that she and Luke could never be together. The house and their feelings were too intertwined for it ever to work.

She mentally pulled herself together and smiled at Luke as if there was nothing wrong.

"I think that sounds like a great idea."

He seemed to perk up at Caroline's agreement. His eyebrows shot up and his eyes smiled.

"Great. I was thinking the week after Christmas. We could have finger foods and maybe even grill—"

Luke went on about his plans for the party, but Caroline had tuned him out. She poked at the soufflé that had been placed in front of them and nodded her head every few words to make as though she was listening. The whole time in her head, she was going over her escape plan.

It was perfect timing, really. She would be busy with the Tour of Homes—the ultimate distraction. It was also the perfect excuse to not be able to see Luke. After the tour, she would quietly taper off the calls, slowly take her time in returning his. Then she would only talk about Ella when they did talk. In no time, he would get the message and move on.

As the waiter brought the check, Caroline offered to pay, at least for her half, but she knew it was useless. Luke would never let her.

When it was time to leave, Luke suggested going for a walk to get a coffee down the street. Caroline declined, telling him that she was tired and had to get up early the next day as she still had to decorate the rest of the houses for the tour.

Luke's shoulders drooped, and he looked at the ground for a moment before resting a hand on her shoulder.

"Is everything okay?" His deep eyes looked right into her. She wanted to scream *no* and fall into his arms, but she couldn't. She wanted to pour her heart out to him and explain how everything had gone so wrong and how she tried to keep him from buying the house, but she couldn't.

What if she did tell him? Sure, he would understand, but that wouldn't change the circumstances. They would still be in the same bind. The house was Luke's now. She couldn't bear to be flooded by the memories that came with it. There was really no way out aside from cutting ties and moving on. Telling him everything would only burden him, and that wouldn't be fair to him.

So instead, she smiled even harder and faked a yawn. Then she repeated that she was just tired and would be much better after a good night's sleep.

He left his hand lingering on her shoulder, as if he was trying to read more into her words than she had actually said.

She looked away and wrapped her arms around herself to let him know it was getting cold. He leaned in and kissed her on the forehead. It took every bit of strength she had to keep from bursting into tears.

"I'd better get you home, then." He put his arm around her and they walked back to the car. When he pulled up in front of her home, he walked her to the door. The light from the Christmas tree was shining on the ground by their feet as they stood on the porch.

"I had a really good time tonight." He stepped in closer.

"I did, too." She took a deep breath and tried to avoid looking into his eyes, but she was so drawn to them, still, even after she had made up her mind.

He leaned down and kissed her good night. Her heart raced and mind spun. After a moment, she pulled away and he stood watching her, smiling a boyish grin.

"I'll be at Ella's school tomorrow at noon for the tea."

He nodded, brushing a strand of hair behind her ear. Finally, he slid his hands into his pockets and made his way back to his car.

Caroline fumbled with her keys, trying to unlock the door as fast as she could. She wanted to get inside, away from where he could see her. She wanted to get away from any feelings she had for him that she couldn't get rid of.

She pushed the door open and stumbled inside, locking it behind her. She leaned against it and slid to the floor, where she let the silent tears fall.

She was moving on with her life. She was leaving her old home and the pain behind her. That was the last time she would see Luke.

Somehow, though, she wasn't sure this new pain was any more bearable than the one she was running from.

When Caroline arrived at the school office to sign in, the woman behind the desk smiled at her, as if she was extra excited that some-one was there for Ella. The school was clean and friendly looking. The halls were all decorated with handprint wreaths and construc-tion-paper Santas with cotton-ball beards. Caroline's heels clicked on the linoleum floor as she scanned the signs for room One-D. She found it at the end of the hall with its door festively covered in a life-sized Christmas tree made of green stars, a child's photo squarely in the center of each. At the top was a glittery gold star.

The door was propped open and scents of chocolate and vanilla wafted out. She poked her head in. The teacher waved for her to enter.

"Welcome. You are the first mom here."

"Oh, I'm not—" She began to correct the teacher, but before she could, Ella came running to her and wrapped her arms around Caroline's waist.

"Caroline! I am so happy you're here. Look, I've decorated a spot for us to sit." She pulled Caroline toward a table for two and showed her where to sit. On the place mat in front of her, someone had written *Mom for a Day: Caroline*. When she looked back, the teacher winked at her. That's when it dawned on Caroline that today was not only for Ella, but for her as well.

Within minutes, all the moms had arrived and the children began their program. They sang a Christmas song and then sat with the moms to take a photo together and decorate a frame. The kids poured tea for the moms and served them reindeer-shaped cookies and green treats made from Rice Krispies.

Ella was talking nonstop, telling Caroline about everything she had learned and her friends and how much she liked her teacher. In all the jobs and volunteering Caroline had done in her life, she had never felt so welcomed or loved.

She was enthralled with Ella and how well she expressed herself. There was so much about her that reminded Caroline of Luke. The way she wiggled her eyebrows when she laughed, the way her eyes gave it away when she was excited even if she was trying to hide it. There were parts of her that Caroline didn't recognize as well. These she must have gotten from her mom, a mom she would never know. She had adjusted to life without a mom so well. She seemed to float effortlessly through her young life without missing a beat, even though she would never know what it's like to have her mom there with her, supporting her all the time.

This was something Caroline and Ella had in common.

Although, Caroline had had the chance to know her own mom. She could remember everything about her as if she had just spoken with her that morning. Like the way she would let out a deep sigh whenever Caroline called, as if she was relieved to hear her voice. Or how easily and gracefully she moved through the house as she cleaned and swept and did laundry, as if it were her life's passion, and not her daily chores.

Ella would never know those things about her mom. Was it worse to have those memories, to remember someone exactly how they were when they were here? Or to never know those things about them at all? She suspected they were both pretty awful. She couldn't imagine what her life as a child would have been like without her mom. At least Ella had her dad.

Luke.

Her chest heaved unexpectedly, surprising her.

"Are you okay?" Ella asked.

Caroline let out a deep breath and rubbed Ella's back. "I'm fine. I'm just so happy to be here with you."

"Great." She jumped to her feet and grabbed Caroline's hand. "I want to show you the playground." She pulled Caroline along behind her, barely giving her time to slip her coat on before stepping out into the cold.

After she showed Caroline the play structure she played on when it was sunny and the garden that grew flowers in the spring, the teacher rang a bell inside the classroom. Ella's shoulders drooped and she frowned.

"I guess the tea party is over. It's time for you to go."

Ella placed her hand gently into Caroline's and let her led them back to the class. When they reached the door, she looked up at Caroline.

"Thank you for coming. It really meant a lot to me to have you here."

Caroline knelt on one knee and took both of Ella's hands

in hers. "Thank you so much for inviting me. I had a wonderful time." She was about to stand to leave, but she couldn't. She knew she wouldn't be seeing Luke again and she couldn't bear to simply walk out of Ella's life. "I am happy to spend time with you whenever you want. I may not be your mother, but I will be here for you if you ever need me."

Ella beamed at her, with the same depth in her eyes as Luke had. She leaned in, threw her arms around Caroline, and squeezed her tight. A surge of adrenaline rushed through Caroline as she stood and waved goodbye to Ella.

As she walked out of the building, visions of people decorating cookies, stringing popcorn on trees, and making ornaments ran through her mind. She imagined the looks on the kids' faces when they would meet Santa on the Tour of Homes and the peace that would sweep over the visitors' faces as they walked between the luminaries and listened to carolers singing their favorite songs.

The entire tour was coming together and felt as if it were filled with the Christmas spirit. She raced to her car, eager to get back to work, eager to share her ideas and enthusiasm with her coworkers.

Eager to fill her time before thoughts of Luke and saying goodbye could seep back in.

32

Luke

The phone rang against Luke's ear. Caroline hadn't answered when he had called earlier in the day to see how the tea went at Ella's school. She still wasn't answering. When he picked Ella up after school, she had told him what a great time she had with Caroline. He heard every detail.

It was eight in the evening and he was sure that she had gotten his message by now, even if she was incredibly busy with the Tour of Homes.

He had spent the entire day unpacking the house, trying to make it look more like a family lived there. He got the message from Caroline loud and clear, that she didn't want to help him set up their new home. It had been a lot to ask, he realized. They hadn't known each other that long and she was already stressed about the Tour of Homes. It hadn't been fair of him at all to ask her to help arrange their home. She didn't even live there.

It didn't matter that he wanted her to be there all the time.

As he had moved the boxes around and unpacked things, he had asked himself, on more than one occasion, where would Caroline put this? His house had become a big mishmash of where he thought things should go and where he thought Caroline would think things should go.

So when Ella entered the living room and asked why there was a set of kitchen towels in the bathroom, Luke wasn't surprised one bit.

"I guess I must have gotten a little distracted." He made an overly frightened face.

Ella burst into giggles as he pulled her into his lap.

"You don't think the towels with pictures of garlic and onions and tomatoes should go in the bathroom?"

She shook her head drastically from side to side, her long hair flipping across her face.

"Should we go on a hunt and look for other things I may have gotten a little wrong?"

She laughed heartily this time and nodded her head. She jumped off his lap and grabbed his hand, pulling him to his feet.

"Come on. It will be like a treasure hunt. Let's see who can find the most treasures."

For the next forty-five minutes they ran around the house looking for anything that seemed out of place. Each item they found Ella would hold up before bursting into giggles, occasionally crying, "Daddy! What were you thinking?"

Luke would shrug his shoulders and they would put the object where it belonged. When the clock struck nine, Luke put Ella to bed. It had been hard to keep her on a schedule in their new home. There was so much to explore, and they found themselves constantly getting distracted.

Not to mention Christmas was only a week away and all the excitement that surrounds it was hovering around Ella. As soon as they had gotten home, she had begged him to put up more decorations. He had reasoned with her that the tree was enough for right now.

Tomorrow while she was at school, he planned to decorate everything like she had never seen before. He secretly drew up plans in his head, deciding where he'd hang lights and snowflakes and making a mental list of things he would need to buy at the store.

As he tucked the blankets around her in her bed that night, he was sure she was glowing. He felt her life was finally getting on track to where it should have been all along. She had a home. Santa had a chimney to visit through. She even had a woman she could turn to when needed.

He found himself stalling repeatedly to keep the emotions down.

After she was fast asleep, Luke headed back downstairs to clean up. He stood in the kitchen, the lights from the Christmas tree lighting the room, and his mind drifted back to Caroline, as it often did. He should try to call her again. Surely, she would have a few minutes to talk at this hour.

He held the phone to his ear, listening to the ringing, his nerves racing in hopes of hearing her voice.

It went to voicemail again.

He left her one last message, saying good night and that he looked forward to talking to her tomorrow.

He knew decorating the houses for the Tour of Homes was a draining task for her. He had seen the emotional toll it was taking on her the other day when she broke into tears. She must be exhausted. He went upstairs and plugged in his phone, leaving it by his nightstand. Maybe she would call first thing in the morning.

❈

Luke had just dropped Ella off in her classroom when her teacher pulled him quietly aside.

"Caroline was lovely with Ella yesterday. I was a little worried that she wouldn't have anyone to bring when she told me your sister recently had a baby. She had a wonderful time. I'm not sure I've ever seen her face light up quite so bright."

"Caroline is very special to us. I'm glad it all worked out." Even the teacher loved Caroline. She had that effect on people. When she was around, people were drawn to her. They wanted to be near her. It was even more charming that she had no idea what kind of effect she had.

He said goodbye and waved to the teacher. He had an agenda today. He had to get to the store and get started on decorating. It was a big house, and if he wanted to surprise Ella, he would have to stay focused.

As he pulled into the parking lot, the sun shone off the small piles of snow, encouraging him even more to get in the Christmas mood. After nearly skipping through the front door he grabbed a cart, then made his way down the aisles until he came to the Christmas section.

There were inflatable elves and shining angels. There were plastic Christmas trees and solid snowmen. He was in Christmas heaven. There was everything he could possibly hope for. He simply had to sort through it all. He went back to the list in his mind: *lights, snowflakes, reindeer, Santa boots.* He tried to imagine what would make Ella smile, what would she find the most amusing, and he went with it. He was piling it all into his cart and wheeling his way to the register when he came across a large spool of velvety red ribbon. It made him think of Caroline and the sketches he had made for her. It would look amazing in large bows in windows or lining the pathway to Santa. It fit her vision almost exactly. The bows were cheerful, but not commercial.

He put three of the spools in his cart, then checked out.

He knew his time was limited and he had a lot to do, but he couldn't help himself. He still hadn't heard from Caroline and was itching to see her.

Before he realized what he was doing, he turned his car down the road toward the house he knew Caroline was the most concerned about. When he pulled up onto the street, he saw her car parked out front. There were several people in the yard hanging lights and adjusting wreaths.

He took a deep breath as he tried to calm himself. His heart was racing and his hands felt clammy. It was the usual effect she had on him; it was still there. He wiped his hands on his jeans, then grabbed the bag of ribbon next to him and got out of the car.

As he walked nervously up the pathway, a man standing on a ladder watched him.

"Are you the extra help they're sending?"

It sounded as though they were behind.

"I'm a friend of Caroline's."

"She's inside." He let out a sigh then jerked his head toward the front door.

When he stepped inside, there was a long line of luminaries on the floor and a woman he recognized as the assistant pouring sand into them, being very careful not to spill. When she looked up and saw him, she inhaled quickly. "Oh," she said to him. Then she turned her head toward the kitchen and called, "Caroline? You're needed."

"Coming," she called from another room. When she stepped out and her eyes fell on Luke, she went pale.

His heart fell.

She quickly smiled, but Luke had seen it. He knew there was something going on, and her not returning his calls was more than her being busy. His knees felt week.

"Luke. It's so good to see you." She stepped forward tentatively, as if she was unsure if she should hug him or not. He stepped forward and wrapped his arms around her. He could swear he felt her heart pounding in her chest. She hugged him back, but her arms were bent and weak. She was quick to release him.

He reached for the bag and held it up. "I was at the store getting some decorations for the house and I came across these. I thought you could use them for the tour."

She peeked inside and her eyes grew wide. "These are perfect." When she looked back up at him, the old Caroline was back. Her eyes were sincere and heartfelt.

"Well, I see you're busy. I'd better get going. I'm decorating the house as a surprise for Ella and I want to be done before I have to pick her up."

"Okay." She reached her hand out and left it on his elbow. He wasn't sure if she was trying to hug him again or ward him off. He bent forward to kiss her just as she turned her head to look at the luminaries that Sarah was holding up. He ended up kissing her temple.

He was glad to know his heart was still beating when it did a flip in his stomach as his lips touched her skin. He quickly turned and left the home before anything else could go wrong.

As he passed the ladder, the man on it called something down to him, pointing at a pile of lights on the ground.

Luke was so preoccupied with the awkward interaction with Caroline that he kept walking, barely registering that he had been asked for help.

His head was numb as he drove. On his way to see Caroline he could only think of ways to decorate his new home. Now, he had a hard time concentrating on the road in front of him. He came to a stop sign and clenched his hands into fists. What had happened?

He accelerated and another driver blew on their horn. He slammed on the brakes just in time to avoid hitting the car driving through the intersection.

Luke raised his hand in apology. He took a deep breath and

ran his fingers through his hair, then proceeded through the intersection when the car was gone. He had to get it together. He had a house to decorate, not to mention he had no proof that Caroline was ending things; he was basing it all on a look on her face for a split second. His head told him not to worry. There was a logical explanation for Caroline's behavior.

Nevertheless, his gut told him something wasn't right. And all those years on the job had helped him fine-tune his instincts.

He hoped with his whole heart that, this time, his instincts were wrong.

33

Caroline

The sun was starting to dip below the line of trees behind the house. They were almost done. Tomorrow they would finish the last house on the Tour of Homes. She took one last circuit of the inside of the home with Sarah close behind, her notebook in tow, jotting down any final changes.

The tour was coming together better than Caroline ever could have imagined. They had every last detail down. Once tomorrow's house was finished, the last thing that was left would be the dry run scheduled for tomorrow night. They had to have everything perfect for the opening on Friday night.

They were about to lock up when Sarah cleared her throat and crossed her arms around the front of her notebook. She seemed to be hesitating, unsure of something. Finally, she spoke. "Did things not work out with you and the handsome client?"

At first Caroline wasn't sure what Sarah was talking about.

Her mind was racing through all the little things left to do. She tilted her head to the side and furrowed her brow.

"Mr. Miller? You two seemed a little… less friendly than last time."

Caroline let out a long sigh.

"I'm sorry. It's really not my business."

"It's okay." Caroline hadn't thought about the repercussions of breaking up with Luke. She hadn't realized people had been paying attention and she would have to answer to them. "He's just a client." Her voice was flat, but inside her heart hurt.

Sarah kept her gaze steady. As Caroline turned away, she thought she saw Sarah roll her eyes, but couldn't be sure.

Outside the house, Victor was loading the ladder onto his truck while Nick was testing the lights. When they were plugged in, they gave an ethereal, unreal look to the house. It appeared as though it had been magically transported directly from the North Pole.

Luke would love this. She caught the thought too late. It didn't matter what Luke loved. She had moved on. She was pretty sure that he had figured it out, too, after showing up at her work unannounced. She had been fighting with the feeling all day that that kind of thing was exactly what made her fall in love with him. It was the exact kind of thing that made things so hard.

She shook the thought out of her head. She needed to clear her mind of all of this.

She looked back at the decorations. They were truly amazing. Even she could appreciate them.

The team gathered and they quickly went over the plans for the next day before heading out.

As everyone drove away, Caroline sat and looked at the house for a few more minutes from the warmth of her car. Her parents would have been so proud of her for putting this Christmas Tour of Homes together. They would have been overjoyed with every part of it. She missed them.

Now she missed Luke, too.

*

It was Caroline's turn to pick the restaurant for her dinner with Lauren. She had picked one of her favorite little cafes in the heart of Sweet River, overlooking a large field that was normally bathed in flowers. Today it looked like a blanket of snow would cover it until the spring. She was seated at a small table overlooking the snowy field that shone in the setting sun.

The Christmas decor was minimal, with only red and green ribbons framing the windows and small clusters of gold bells hanging from the middle. Each table had a red flower in a small clear vase, which was tied with a green bow around its center.

The bell above the door jingled and Lauren stepped inside. She had on a thick jacket, a scarf, and a knit hat. Caroline giggled when she took a seat across from her.

"Are you expecting a snowstorm?"

Lauren rolled her eyes. "It's near freezing out there." She swept her hand around them. "I see you picked the restaurant with the least amount of Christmas?"

"I needed a break. I've been spending so much time with the Tour of Homes that I'm dreaming about—"

"Sugarplums dancing in your head?"

"Exactly."

"I'll bet Luke is dancing with them, too." Lauren wiggled her eyebrows.

Caroline looked down at her arms, folded across the table.

"Oh no. Tell me you didn't."

Caroline looked out the window to avoid Lauren's accusing gaze.

"I thought things were going well. What happened?" Her

voice was soft now. She reached her hand across the table and placed it on Caroline's arm.

She had done a good job of avoiding thinking about Luke until he had shown up at her work. Now she was having a hard time getting him off her mind. She wasn't sure that she could tell Lauren about it without falling apart.

"I was there helping them unpack when the snowstorm hit." Caroline looked at Lauren, hoping she would be able to figure out the rest.

"You had to spend the night?"

She nodded. "On the sofa, in the living room, where all my childhood memories live."

The waitress approached and Lauren ordered tea for both of them.

"I'm sorry. That must have been really hard."

"I haven't been returning his calls and he showed up today at one of the houses I'm decorating."

Lauren inhaled sharply, her eyes growing wide.

"I was so surprised to see him, I don't think I responded the way I should have. I didn't have time to think."

"Did he catch on?"

"He seemed off after that. He handed me a bag of ribbons he thought I could use and then left. It was incredibly awkward."

"How did you end it with him? What did you tell him?"

Caroline sunk into her chair. She lowered her chin until it sat against her chest.

"Caroline. Please tell me you said *something* to him. Tell me you're not blowing him off."

"I thought it would be easiest to sort of drift apart." Caroline shrugged then shook her head.

"And by drifting apart you mean not returning his calls and leaving him in the dark?"

"I know. It's awful. It seemed like a good plan at the time. Now, I don't know. It feels sort of unfair."

Lauren leaned back in her chair, one eyebrow lifted. Caroline knew that look. It meant Lauren disagreed with her but didn't want to hurt her feelings.

"Are you having second thoughts?"

"I want him to be able to live his own life. Make his own memories."

"You have some amazing memories. Why wouldn't you want to share those with him?"

"Because I miss my parents too much. I want them here with me. I want them to meet Luke and Ella and be part of our lives. I want to make new memories with all of them."

Lauren sat quietly looking at Caroline. She had something to say, Caroline knew that. She was just waiting for her to say it. She and Lauren had always been honest with each other. It was why they were such good friends. They were each other's reality check.

Lauren reached a hand across the table again and placed it on Caroline's.

"Your parents aren't coming back. They would want you to live your life to the fullest and not be afraid of making new memories without them."

"That's so much easier said than done."

"I'm sure it is."

They sat quietly for a few moments. The waiter approached again and they placed their dinner orders.

"So, what's your plan?" Lauren finally asked after they had both sat watching the light fade outside.

Caroline shook her head. "I don't know."

"Are you planning to apologize?"

"I don't want to be with him."

Lauren's eyebrows shot up. Caroline twisted her hands into themselves, trying to find some answers.

She placed her hands on the table and looked at Lauren squarely. "Okay. I *do* want to be with Luke. But I don't want to hurt. So, I can't. Not now that he has the house."

"All right. Let's make a plan then on how you're going to get yourself out of this situation."

"I'm going to wait for him to call again. When he calls, *if* he calls, I will tell him that I've got a lot going on and need to step back."

"You don't want to tell him the truth?"

"If I tell him the truth, then he might not love his house as much or he may be resentful, or—"

"He might understand and make you feel worse about the whole thing?"

Caroline nodded.

Lauren shook her head in pity. "He's a great guy, Caroline. Another one like him might not come around anytime soon."

"I know. I've thought about that. Who's to say he'd stick around with a woman that turns into a crying mess every time she visits his house?"

Lauren looked down at her plate as the waiter set it in front of her. "Then maybe it's not the situation that needs to change. Maybe it's your thinking that needs to change."

❄

Caroline sat in her living room with a book in her lap. She was facing the Christmas tree, which seemed to be shining brighter than usual tonight. Her lips curled up into a smile. Having a tree turned out to be a wonderful idea. She had spent countless hours near it, enjoying it. If she was being totally honest with herself, she would have to admit that she had missed the smell of the Christmas trees that had been present throughout all of her early life.

She had even grown accustomed to the decorations that used

to hang in her parents' home. She had decided to add a box of new decorations to the old as well, to help make it more bearable. It was a sign that she was moving on with her life, while still holding on to the past.

Could she do this with her old home? Could she find a way to mix the old with the new in Luke's home?

She shook her head. No. She couldn't. It was too much. She should just be happy with the progress she had made thus far. There was a tree in her home and she had almost enjoyed decorating the houses for the Christmas Tour of Homes. Two things she never would have thought were possible a couple of months back.

The packages underneath the tree reflected the lights, making it look as if they were glowing. She looked forward to Christmas Eve, when she would meet the family she adopted to give them their gifts. The excitement and hope the kids always had in their eyes was inspiring. It gave Caroline faith in the future and in the world that there were still children that believed anything was possible.

Next to the family gifts was a box wrapped in glittery red paper with a shiny gold bow wrapped around it. After the Christmas tea at Ella's school, Caroline had bought her a dress. It was pink and frilly and would fly out and around her when she twirled. She had to find a way to see Ella again before Christmas.

She thought about seeing Luke and her heart did a flip. She hoped it was nerves, but she knew better. Her feelings for Luke were not going to go away overnight. She would have to learn to control them, keep them at bay. Otherwise, seeing Ella would be impossible, and she wasn't willing to abandon a child. Ella had dealt with enough in her life, and Caroline refused to be the one to add to her bad fortune.

Caroline put the book down and stood in front of the tree. The ugly ornament Ella had given her was there, perfectly at eye level for Caroline to see every time she walked by. Her heart hurt.

She missed them both. She missed what only a week ago she thought her life could have been.

This was going to be much harder than Caroline had anticipated, but she could do it. She'd made it through much worse in the past. She could make it through this.

34

Luke

Every time he called Caroline her phone rang three times then went to voicemail. Every time she didn't answer, his heart grew heavier and heavier.

Where had they gone wrong? They had a great time the other night on their date. But the more he thought about it, the more he found little things that could add up to one bigger thing. One thing like Caroline was not as interested in him as he was in her.

She had gone quiet about halfway through dinner. He remembered it clearly because it was right around when dessert had come. They were looking forward to it. The chocolate soufflé was supposed to be the highlight of the meal. Then she had only picked at it, and shortly after that, she had asked to go home because she was tired and had a long day ahead of her.

Had he said something that bothered her? Maybe he had been misreading her all along. Is it possible that, to her, he had just been a client? Perhaps now that he had his house, she was ready to move on.

None of this sounded anything like Caroline. There *had* been something between them. He had seen it in her eyes. He had felt it in her kiss. There was no way she hadn't felt it, too.

Had he been so wrapped up in the idea of being a family again that he was seeing things that weren't really there? He rubbed the back of his neck before picking up his phone one last time.

He dialed her number again; this time it went straight to voicemail. He hung up.

He glanced at his watch, then headed out the door to get Ella. As he reached his car he turned around and took one more look at the house. He had done a fine job. There were colorful lights strung along the eaves at the front of the house and around each window and the front door. There were large, glowing snowflakes hanging from the tree at the side of the house. Three small elves were perched next to the second-story balcony, with Santa's feet peeking out from the chimney. On the grass in front of the house were two reindeer that turned their heads every few minutes.

He tried to see it through a child's eyes. He tried to see how the shimmering lights resembled Santa's magic and how, depending on where you stood, the elves appeared to be looking in different directions, giving the impression that they were moving.

He couldn't wait for Ella to see the house, and he couldn't wait to see her reaction to it.

Ella was excited about the surprise Luke had promised her. She was trying to guess what it was and, so far, had thought that maybe Santa had come early or Luke had got them a puppy. He assured her that neither of those had happened, and she'd just have to wait patiently to find out.

For the house to have the grand effect that Luke was hoping

for, they had to wait until it was dark to return home. To pass time, Luke had a plan.

"How do you feel about going to that nice little diner in town for an early dinner tonight? I thought it would help us meet some town people. Maybe even make a new friend."

She tilted her head up to the sky and placed one finger on her chin. "Can we get pie?"

"Of course."

"Let's do it then."

They took their time driving down the highway, watching the snow-covered trees pass, taking note of signs for parks and trails they wanted to visit when the weather got warmer. As they pulled into the main part of town, Luke's body relaxed. He felt at home here. They drove along until they found a parking spot. When they got out of the car, they meandered down the street, looking in stores and noticing the details on the Christmas decorations they hadn't seen before.

The town buzzed with Christmas spirit. People were smiling everywhere, wearing red or green scarves and selling chocolate-covered treats and drinks that smelled of peppermint. Ella watched it all in amazement. Everywhere she turned, there was Christmas. Luke could see it in her eyes, how much she enjoyed it all. He wished he could see inside her mind and learn about all the wonderful, creative Christmas things she must be imagining.

"They should make a cranberry-mint pie." Ella nodded her head as she looked up at the sky in thought.

Luke tried not to wince. He liked cranberries. He liked mint. He certainly didn't like the sound of them together.

"Cranberry-mint?" he asked her.

She nodded. "The perfect Christmas colors. Red and green!"

They both laughed.

They approached the diner and a shiver went down Luke's spine, leaving him with a somewhat empty feeling. He had brought Caroline here. He sighed abruptly and shook his head. He brought her here, thinking he was sharing something special with her, when it turned out she had grown up in this town. It hit him then that there was a lot he didn't know about Caroline. Probably because he hadn't asked. He had been so preoccupied trying to get the house of his dreams and give Ella the home she deserved that he hadn't asked Caroline all the questions he should have.

Sure, she had told him about her life in the town growing up, but hadn't it all been to show him what a great place it would be for him and Ella to live? He had never even asked her where her home had been or what school she had gone to. It brought him back to that same sour feeling he had earlier—maybe he was simply a client that had gotten carried away.

"Didn't Caroline come here when she was a kid?" Ella's curious eyes looked up at him, bringing him back to the present.

"Yes. She spent a lot of time here." It hadn't been his imagination. She had cared for Ella, too. Would a real estate agent take a client's daughter to a school tea to get the sale of a house? He didn't think so.

What had gone wrong?

"What's her favorite pie?"

He took a deep breath. Not thinking about Caroline was going to be harder than he anticipated. "I'm not sure. She never told me, I guess."

"We'll just have to ask her next time we see her. I'll bet it's strawberry."

"Or we can ask someone here that would probably know." It wasn't an awful idea to ask Cathy about Caroline.

The waitress seated them in a booth for two along a wall. There were even more decorations than he had remembered from his last visit. There was a Christmas tree in the corner, brimming with ornaments. Stockings were hung along the beam above the counter, with names embroidered in them in a shimmery silver.

Bells hung over every table, and a bouquet of mistletoe hung over the cash register.

Cathy approached the table, and before she could say anything, Ella jumped in. "I love your striped apron."

"Well thank you, doll. I think it's quite fashionable myself." Cathy did a little spin then curtsied to Ella. She turned to Luke and paused, holding one finger pointed at him. "Aren't you Caroline's friend?"

Luke smiled. "I am. My name's Luke and this is my daughter, Ella."

"It's good to see you again. What brings you out here this afternoon?" Cathy placed cardboard coasters in front of both Ella and Luke.

Luke leaned back and rubbed his hands together. "We just moved into the neighborhood and decided to stop by for dinner, maybe meet some of our new neighbors."

"Isn't that great! Welcome to the neighborhood. Which parts are you living in?"

Ella said, "We're in that big house up the road past the post office. It's beautiful up there. We're surrounded by Christmas trees. I can even see the tallest tree from my bedroom window." She held her hands out, palms up, her excitement beaming from her.

"I know that area. You must be the new family that moved into the Windersons' home. Caroline's old stomping grounds. I'm sure she told you all about it."

Luke nodded. "She told us quite a bit about the neighborhood. It sounds like she loved it growing up here."

Cathy nodded slowly. "She did. It was really sad what happened to her family. Her parents were a sudden and great loss to our community. An even bigger one when Caroline left. We all understood, though. It would have been hard for her to stay in the house on her own."

Ella nodded, wise beyond her years.

"If you can see the old tree from your bedroom window, you must be in Caroline's old bedroom." Cathy looked into the distance, deep in thought.

Ella crinkled her nose.

Luke's heart felt as if it had been squeezed. *Caroline's old bedroom?*

"Wait. Are you saying our home used to be Caroline's home?"

Cathy's eyes landed on Luke's. "You didn't know?"

Luke shook his head slowly. Ella looked at him, her lips puckered up to her nose. She was thinking hard, he could tell, trying to figure this all out.

"She hadn't mentioned it."

"Oh, I'm sorry. I thought you knew. I thought maybe since she was here with you last time and the way you two—I'm sorry. I must have misread the situation."

Luke rubbed his neck.

"It is a lovely house, though. You'll be very happy in it. You'll make lots of wonderful memories, I'm sure."

Luke nodded.

Cathy pointed at the menu in his hand. "So, what can I get you today? Would you like your regular shepherd's pie?"

Luke smiled. *His regular.* "Absolutely."

"How about chicken soup for you? It's our kid's specialty and everyone loves it. It's filled with pasta shaped like stockings and Christmas trees."

Ella licked her lips as her eyes grew wide. "Can I also have a piece of pie, please?"

"Of course. What kind would you like?"

"What is Caroline's favorite?"

"Mmmmm. Great idea. I'll get you a piece of strawberry pie to go with that soup." Cathy winked at Luke and made her way back to the kitchen.

Once they had packed themselves, full and happy, back into the car, Luke drove them home and surprised Ella with all the decorations. She had been so amazed and overjoyed by it all, it had taken him almost thirty minutes to get her to go inside the house and take a bath and get ready for bed. It had been a long day, and he hadn't had a minute to digest what Cathy had told them.

When he was putting Ella to bed that night, all he could think about was that this room had once belonged to Caroline. She had lain in this same exact spot as a child, just like Ella.

He made himself a cup of coffee and sat at the breakfast table, in front of the Christmas tree. As he watched the lights dance on the tree, it all began to make sense. It had been Caroline's idea to put the tree in the kitchen. The weekend she had helped them move in, she had made herself at home so quickly, or so it seemed from the way she flitted around the kitchen making pancakes and cleaning up.

The whole time Luke had thought it was because she felt comfortable and at home with them. It hit him with the weight of a sleigh landing on his shoulders. She felt comfortable and at home there because *it had been her house.*

The same house that carried all the memories that she had moved to get away from.

35

Caroline

It was a sunny and clear Friday and Caroline had woken full of energy. Today was the start of the Tour of Homes. She enjoyed a long, warm shower and took her time doing her hair. She went to her closet and pulled the outfit off the hanger that she had set aside last night.

She slipped the warm red dress on over her head and tugged at the sleeves. The little specks of gold throughout gave it the slightest shimmer, making it the perfect Christmas dress for someone that didn't normally dress for Christmas. After smoothing her skirt down, she took one last look in the mirror, then headed off for the homes.

The sun reflected off the snow piled on the side of the road. As she drove, Caroline ran through all the tasks that had to get done before Mary and the rest of her coworkers would show up for the first official tour.

She turned onto the street and parked near the corner. As she approached the home, her breath escaped her. It was a magnificent sight. At the base of each window was a wreath wrapped in a big red bow—lively pops of color accentuating the traditional white brick of the home. What struck Caroline the most, though, was Santa's workshop. She looked inside. It had been a relatively plain, flimsy wooden structure only days before, but Chris and Alexandra had worked their magic and now it was a hearty, warm cottage, replete with luxurious velvety fabric covering benches along the walls. On the far wall, next to a faux stained-glass window depicting elves hard at work in Santa's toy shop, was a majestic wooden chair, upholstered in a deep-red velvet. It was Santa's chair. Candy canes hung from silver ribbons strung across the ceiling, dipping low enough for Santa's helpers to reach up and distribute them to the anxiously waiting children.

She pulled her coat across her chest and walked up the path lined with poinsettias and into the home. She made her way through the house, meticulously checking off each decoration in each room.

Today felt different. It felt lighter. There was something in the air that excited her. She was actually looking forward to the lines of people that would wind their way through the homes. She couldn't wait to see their reactions to each and every little decoration that her team had so carefully created and placed in the perfect position.

She finally felt that she was spreading the Christmas spirit through decorating the homes.

She locked up the house and looked at her list. She would visit the Winter Wonderland next.

Although she had been the one in charge of the team, and had been there every step of the way, each time she approached one of the homes she was blown away by the final results. The colors felt brighter to her. The wreaths felt cheerier to her. They had truly accomplished their goal.

A few weeks ago, she had no idea if she was even going to be able to pull this off. Now here she was, ready to shine.

It occurred to her then how much her life had changed in the last month. She was filled with a new confidence that she hadn't felt in a long time. This time, though, hidden somewhere in that confidence was something that didn't feel right. Something was pecking away at her.

She knew what it was and quickly shoved the thought out of her mind. She didn't have time to think about Luke today. She didn't have time to think about how much he had helped her with the decorations. She didn't have time to think about how much harder this would have been without him. She didn't have time to think about what could have been.

She stood in front of the stately home, the huddle of carolers at the curve of the driveway. The sun had just dipped behind the tree line, allowing the Christmas lights to shine bright. There was a chill in the air, but she was full of warmth. Caroline glanced at her watch. Mary and the pack of agents would be arriving any minute. Soon after, the Christmas Tour of Homes would be open for everyone.

Caroline's heart beat rapidly in her chest, sending a hum throughout her body. A shiny sedan parked in front of the home and Mary stepped out with Jeff, her assistant, and two of the top agents in the office.

Caroline took a deep breath. Sarah glanced at her out of the corner of her eye. She walked over and stood next to her, shoulder to shoulder, then subtly squeezed Caroline's hand.

"We've got this," Sarah whispered.

Caroline nodded once.

Mary approached them; her steady Realtor smile pasted to her face. "I can't wait to see what you have in store for us at this home, Caroline."

Caroline smiled and blinked.

Mary and her crew followed the trail of luminaries and disappeared into the home.

"What does that mean?" Sarah's hand shot to her mouth as she chewed a nail.

"Nothing. Everything turned out great." The confidence boomed in her.

Sarah clasped the clipboard to her chest. She had swapped out the notebook covered in Christmas stickers for a plain wooden clipboard, with a single bow on the top back corner.

They stood there, quietly, appreciating the decorations. The wreaths hanging at the base of each of the upstairs windows gave a sophisticated feel to the home. The soft red ribbon wrapped around the pillars that framed the front door gave the otherwise cold home a welcoming feel.

The spread of windows across the front of the bottom floor of the house made it easy for Caroline to see where Mary and her crew were. They stood in the living room, in front of the hearth that had a roaring fire and three large, red stockings hanging from the mantel. Mary was nodding, pointing at something beside the fireplace. Across from the hearth stood the Christmas tree, decorated in all-white lights and angels of different sizes. Traditional red, green, and silver ornaments dotted the tree. Jeff held up his phone and took a photo of the Christmas tree.

When Mary and her crew stepped out of the home, they were all smiling.

"You've all done an amazing job. I am truly impressed."

"Thank you." Caroline felt both relaxed and exhilarated at the same time.

"Let's head to the Winter Wonderland home so we can get this started. What do you say?"

"We'll see you there."

When Mary had gotten in her car and gone, Sarah squealed like a little girl and hugged Caroline. "We did it. We actually did it."

Caroline nodded, her pride beaming through her smile.

As they both made their way to their cars, Caroline stopped for a moment and looked back at the home. The luminaries made an inviting path to it. She imagined, for a moment, all the people that would walk through the home in the next few days. Hopefully, her work would bring the Christmas spirit to some of them.

When Caroline arrived at the Winter Wonderland home, there was already a crowd gathering. The tour didn't open for another twenty minutes, but people congregated on the sidewalk, taking in the twinkling lights.

She took a deep breath. The lights had turned out even more amazing than they had planned. Victor and Rebecca had hung them in such a way that they truly resembled snow glinting in the moonlight. Snowflakes of all sizes dangled from the trees, gently blinking on and off. The rain gutters were edged with icicles adding to the wintry look. Through the picture window, she could see the Christmas tree, tall and majestic, overflowing with ornaments made of wood and pine cones. There was a warm and gooey feeling deep inside her, like melted chocolate and marshmallows.

Caroline approached the front gate, which had been propped open, and a red ribbon now stretched across the walkway. Mary, holding a large pair of scissors, stood nearby alongside a woman in a black pantsuit and red fitted Santa coat, holding a basket, ready to collect admission tickets. With every passing minute, the crowd grew.

When it approached five o'clock, Mary stepped forward and

Christmas music boomed from the speakers for a few moments before dropping off to serve as a more subtle background. She held up the scissors and waved at everyone, then cut the ribbon.

The crowd made its way forward, handing their tickets one at a time to the woman in the Santa jacket. Caroline stood by the gate, welcoming everyone as they made their way in. It had been too long since she'd felt such a sense of accomplishment. It was as if she were floating.

A woman caught her attention, asking questions about the home, and how long it had been on the market. Caroline took her information down to pass on to Maggie. Anxious to see how the other three homes were doing, she decided to check them out. She waved goodbye to Mary and turned for her car.

Standing there, in the middle of the driveway, were Luke and Ella.

Caroline's back went stiff and her breath hitched.

Ella came running up to her and Caroline welcomed her into her arms.

"Caroline!" She squeezed her tight. She hugged people the same way she did everything else, with all her heart and soul.

"It's so great to see you." Caroline bent so she was eye-level with Ella. "What do you think?"

She stepped back and threw her hands out, palms up, fingers spread. "It's amazing. I've never seen anything like it."

"Well, you should definitely check out all the houses. The last one on the list has a special surprise." She winked at Ella.

Luke had kept his distance on the sidewalk at first. When he saw how friendly they were being, he approached.

"It really does look amazing."

Caroline stood up, clasping her hands in front of her. "Thank you. You were a big help. In a lot of ways."

Luke kept his hands in his front pockets, watching Caroline. She swallowed, unsure of what to say next.

She wanted to apologize for not returning his calls. She wanted to say *something* to him. She just didn't know what to say. Now that he was standing in front of her, the only thing that came to her was how much she missed him and how she wanted to go back in time.

She couldn't say any of that to him, ever. The things she *should* say to him, if she could figure out what they were, couldn't be said here, on the sidewalk, in front of her boss and all the people in line for the tour.

She smiled weakly at him. What else could she do?

There was a sadness in his eyes. Had she caused it? Had he figured it out already? Did he know that she didn't plan on being part of their lives? He must.

His gaze left Caroline's and landed on Ella, standing there, admiring the house. He softly clapped his hands together. "What do you say we check it out?"

Ella's head bounced up and down. "I can't wait."

As he passed to collect Ella, he came within inches of Caroline. She could smell him—the faint scent of Ivory soap and cinnamon. Her heart raced. He lifted a hand toward her, but then slid it into his pocket at the last minute, as if he had meant to reach for her but thought better of it.

"It was good to see you." His voice was soft, and if she wasn't mistaken, it cracked midsentence.

All she could muster was a nod, and murmur back a quiet, "Mm-hmm."

"See you later, Caroline!" Ella bounced down the path, pulling Luke by the hand behind her.

Caroline nodded and gave her a tight-lipped smile.

She watched as they made their way down the path and into the home. Once they were out of sight, she walked to her car. The sound of her feet crunching in the snow was louder than it should've been. The trees around her seemed to sway back and forth, though no wind was blowing. She pulled her keys from her purse and fumbled with them, dropping them in the street. As she bent to gather them, she forced herself to take deep breaths.

What was happening to her?

Finally, when she was safely in her car, she pulled away and around the corner, then up to a curb. Her hands rushed to her face as she gasped for air. *Keep it together,* she thought over and over.

She should have known that Luke would be there. Ella had been so excited about helping with the Tour of Homes, and she had invited them, hadn't she?

She knew it wasn't going to be easy to walk away from Luke. Since she had only known him a few weeks, though, how could it be *this* hard?

If seeing Luke hurt this much there was only one way to fix it. That was to avoid him.

She closed her eyes and balled her fists together, taking a deep breath. Once her nerves began to calm, she turned the car back on and drove toward the second house on the list.

If she was quick, she could do a swift loop, checking on all the houses, and make it home safely without seeing him again.

36

Luke

Luke walked numbly through the house, vaguely aware of the decorations around him. He watched as Ella bounced from room to room, pointing out all her favorite things. He managed to give a meager nod as she did.

What was he thinking, bringing Ella to the opening night? Of course they were going to see Caroline. It's all she's been doing the past few weeks. It had encompassed her life.

When he did see her, what exactly had he expected her to do? Fall to her knees and beg his forgiveness? Run into his arms and tell him how happy she is to have free time now? Stroke his cheek and remind him that she had just, indeed, been busy with the home tour?

Of course, he hadn't expected any of that. He also hadn't expected the dagger of pain that shot through his heart at her vague indifference to his presence. She had been happy before she saw him, beaming, actually. Then her eyes landed on him and that look appeared again. The same look she had tried to hide last time he showed up unannounced.

Man, had he been stupid.

If he wanted any chance for this to work out, he should have lain low. He should have found a way to talk to her alone. He should have found a way to tell her that he knew about the house.

What if he was wrong, though? What if the house didn't have anything to do with her leaving? What if she left because she was no longer interested in him? She was still enamored with Ella, that was clear. He could tell by the way Caroline watched Ella when she spoke. Caroline had been excited to see her. It was Luke that she hadn't wanted to see.

He tried to clear his mind of Caroline and focus on the Tour of Homes with Ella. The only problem was everything in these houses reminded him of Caroline. She had clearly been inspired by his sketches, following some almost exactly. He had hoped to be here, celebrating with Caroline. Not hiding from her.

They wound their way through the rooms. Every little detail hinted at Caroline. The way the dolls were sitting on the beds just as she had placed Ella's dolls that night they had moved in. But of course, that was probably the same way she had placed dolls on her bed when she was a child.

His hands tightened into fists, and he shook his head. If only he had paid closer attention. There had been signs. He had been up all night thinking about it and had come up with a list of them. He had been so wrapped up in making his new life, putting Caroline into a role that filled the gaps in his life, that he had never thought to see if it was what she wanted, too.

"Daddy? What's wrong?"

Luke turned his attention back to Ella. "Nothing, sweetheart. I was thinking about work, that's all."

She nodded and took his hand. The moment she touched it, he relaxed.

He hadn't told Ella about Caroline yet. He wasn't even sure what to say. He shoved that thought out of his mind. Something would come to him eventually.

Once they finished touring the home they were in, Ella turned to Luke, batting her long lashes at him. His heart melted immediately.

"Do you think we'll see Caroline again at one of the other houses?"

Luke placed his hand on top of Ella's head. He would love to see Caroline, if only things were the way they used to be. Under the current circumstances, he just wanted to go home and hide. Not that everything in his new house wouldn't remind him of her as well.

"I think she's really busy, and we should probably stay out of her way for right now."

Her smile disappeared and she looked at him as if she knew what he was thinking.

"You're right. We should give her a little time."

It felt as though the wind had been knocked out of him. If only he had been able to pick up on the cues as well as Ella could.

Maybe now that Caroline was done, she would have time to think about what she truly wanted.

And just maybe, what she truly wanted was Luke.

Luke woke the next morning with birds singing outside his window and the horrible taste of sadness in his mouth. He tried everything to cheer himself up. He poured some eggnog into his coffee, and he and Ella blasted Christmas carols as they danced around the kitchen making pancakes. He was happy, in the moment. As soon as the moment passed, he felt himself slipping back into that slump.

He couldn't go on like this. Christmas was only three days away, and he had to get it together, for Ella's sake.

When Pam pulled up their drive and came running to hug Ella, Luke promised he'd only be gone a few hours, trying to wrap up all his Christmas errands.

He drove through the town and back to Sweet River, where he hoped to find a Fluffy the Dog.

There was one store left that hadn't been answering their phone but were rumored to get the occasional Fluffy in from time to time. He crossed his fingers. He just needed a little bit of luck.

He thought back to the first time he tried to get the stuffed dog and had let it go to Caroline instead. He swallowed his emotions, taking a deep breath. Then it came to him.

The homeless shelter.

If anyone knew what was going on, it would be Lauren.

An hour later, and still empty handed, he pulled up in front of the homeless shelter. The Christmas Eve dinner was two days away, and Lauren had to be working out all the details. He skipped half the steps as he ran up the stairs and pulled the door open. From the entrance he could see it—the third door on the left was open and a light was on.

His feet thudded across the floor as he ran down the hall and swung into the office.

Lauren jumped.

"Luke. You scared me. I had no idea what all that noise was."

"I'm sorry. I need your help."

She leaped to her feet and was about to follow him out the door. "What is it? Is someone hurt?"

He reached a reassuring hand out to calm her. "No. Nothing like that. I mean *I* need your help."

Her shoulders slouched and she plopped back into her chair.

"Oh. You mean Caroline."

He nodded.

Lauren motioned to the chair across from her as she inhaled and shrugged. "Have a seat."

He told her everything, not holding back any details. He told her how he had fallen in love with Caroline and how badly he regretted not paying closer attention. He told her how, when he bought the house, he imagined she would be there, sharing their lives together. He told her how he knew it was her home. He told her how he had to do something, anything, to give them another shot.

"I know she felt something. She had to have. It wasn't all in my head, was it?"

Lauren listened with her elbows rested on the desk, her chin leaning on her joined hands. Her eyes sat on his for a moment before answering.

"She cares a lot about you and Ella both, but I think this is bigger than that. At least to her it is."

"I know that. Trust me. I know how tricky memories can be. You don't want to lose them. You want to keep them right here." He placed his hand on his heart. "But you also don't want them staring firmly at you all day, every day. Or when you're not expecting them. I get it."

"Then what do you want me to tell you?"

"There's got to be something I can do. I don't want to do this simply because I miss her. I want to help her. I want her to enjoy the memories she has, and to not be afraid of building new memories."

Lauren nodded. "She has to be ready for that."

"Do you think she is?" He held his breath, waiting for her to answer.

"I think she's more ready now than she was before. She didn't want to do the Christmas Tour of Homes at first, but she came around. Last time I saw her, she was even excited. That was in large part because of you."

His left eyebrow lifted. "So, you think there's a chance?"

She reached out to the miniature Christmas tree on her desk and straightened a tiny chain of tinsel. "I think there's probably a chance."

"What do I do?"

"You've been able to get to her much faster than anyone else. I'm sure you can come up with something."

His pulse raced at the thought that maybe, just maybe, Caroline would even hear him out. He let out a sigh. "Will you help me?" He leaned toward Lauren.

"On one condition."

He raised his eyebrows.

"I need help with the Christmas Eve dinner. You can bring Ella. She'll have a good time."

"Deal."

She laughed, shaking her head slowly. "Okay. You come up with a plan, and I will help get her to talk to you. Other than that, I'm not getting involved. She is a grown woman and can make her own decisions."

"Thank you. I'll come up with something."

The world felt lighter as he walked out the door. The biggest obstacle had been removed. Lauren was going to take care of that. He only had to come up with how exactly he was going to win her back.

Before he did that, though, he had to get Fluffy the Dog. He raced to the toy store, and as he pulled into the parking lot, his heart sank. In the front window hung a sign that read, in large red letters, No Fluffy the Dog. Sorry.

He sighed. He knew Ella would be okay without the dog. He had gotten a house for them to live in, and that was way more than either of them had expected. As her father, he had always felt the need to try and get her exactly what she asked for. Especially when she rarely asked for anything at all.

He took the long way to get to the highway since it passed one of Ella's favorite candy stores. He wanted to get her a few treats for Christmas morning. It had always been an adventure visiting this candy store. He and Ella loved wandering the aisles filled with candy from all generations and eras.

The bell overhead jingled as he pushed the door open. The scents of cotton candy, vanilla, and caramel mingled in the air. Memories of Halloweens and birthday parties from his childhood came racing back. His heart filled with the joy of an innocent child.

That was it. That was what Caroline needed.

She didn't need to let go of her old memories. She needed to be reminded of how precious and important they are to who she is today. She needed to remember that memories can still be happy even when we've lost the people in them. She needed to remember that memories are the best way to keep people we've lost alive in our hearts.

Luke knew just how to help her, too.

37

Caroline

Christmas Eve was finally here. Caroline sat in front of the Christmas tree sipping a hot chocolate covered in whipped cream. Cinnamon was scattered over the top, a last-minute addition inspired by her mother. When she was young, her mom and dad and whoever was visiting that Christmas would gather around the tree and drink a cinnamon hot chocolate together, sharing their happiest moments of the year that had just passed.

Last week when she had come across the framed photo of her parents sitting in front of their own Christmas tree before she was born, she couldn't help but place the photo on the mantel. It was huge for Caroline to be sitting here. Her hands shook. She had accomplished decorating for Christmas, even if the majority wasn't at her house. Something was missing, though. As soon as she glanced at the photo, she knew what it was.

She sipped the hot chocolate as it warmed her hands, memories of the past year flitting through her mind: the hike she and Lauren had gone on that summer, the camping trip they had survived in the fall, the horseback riding with Luke, the picnic with Luke and Ella, the evening Luke had taken her to see the lights in the Verdant Gardens neighborhood.

Her eyes watered.

Everything came back to Luke.

She turned to the photo on the mantel. Her parents were so happy. They had been more in love than anyone she had ever known.

Didn't she deserve that?

Could she have that with Luke?

Sitting with the memories of her parents was hard. Was it possible it would get easier with time? She shook her head as a tear threatened to fall. Swiping her hand carefully across her cheek, she caught the tear.

It was time to pack up the gifts for the family she adopted. As she carefully placed them, one at a time, in a large red bag of silky fabric, her body tingled. This family was getting the Christmas they had hoped for. She had filled one bag and prepared another when she noticed a light snow had started to fall. It was almost the perfect Christmas.

She placed the last package into the second bag and tied the drawstring into a large bow, smoothing the ends down. One at a time, she moved the bags to the front door, then looked back at the Christmas tree. There were two packages left. One for Lauren, one for Ella. She slipped on her coat and placed Lauren's gift under her arm and carried the bags to the car.

The drive was a pleasant one, with Christmas lights reflecting off the snowflakes as they fell. The world seemed to be full of the Christmas spirit this evening.

❅

The homeless shelter was lit up like Caroline had never seen. There were lights around the main doorway and a wreath hanging high above it. A long red carpet had been laid along the main hall, leading everyone to the cafeteria. Voices trailed down the hall, a pleasant accompaniment to the Christmas music gently playing through the speakers. She stopped at Lauren's office, empty of course, and left her gift on her desk. When she reached the cafeteria, she gasped.

The tables were draped with green cloths, each with a poinsettia placed in its center. There were bowls of red and green candies at each table, along with baskets of snacks and fruits for each family.

Along the left side of the room was a taut, red rope, leading to a majestic gold chair. A Santa cap hung from the top right corner of the cresting rail. There were buckets of candy canes and bags of crayons and coloring books for the kids. There were clusters of families congregating together throughout the room.

Christmas Eve dinner was always special for both the families in need and the families that adopted them, but Caroline had never seen it decorated with such an eye to detail. She was amazed at the time and effort that Lauren had put into it this year.

Lauren was at the front of the room, next to an enormous Christmas tree decorated with large red, green, and white ornaments shaped like teardrops. A smooth, golden ribbon wrapped its way around the tree. Next to the tree was a table with a group of children stringing popcorn. There were two smaller trees nearby, the ornaments from the Tour of Homes strung all around them.

Lauren waved her over.

Caroline put the bags of presents along a wall with all the others and joined Lauren by the tree.

That's when she noticed the large fireplace. Her jaw dropped. How had she missed it? It was a magnificent piece of work. Large enough for Santa himself to come through. Ella would love it here.

Lauren smiled at her. "You like the decorations?" Her arms were stretched out, Vanna White–style.

"This is amazing. Did you do all this on your own?"

There was a glint in Lauren's eyes as she held back laughter. "One of Santa's assistants and his little elf may have helped me out."

A jolt of energy flew threw her. *Luke?* She narrowed her eyes and tilted her head. "Lauren—"

"Calm down. Not everything is about you." As Lauren turned her attention back to the children, Caroline was sure she saw her giggle.

The evening went by quickly. The kids all sat on Santa's lap, everyone's bellies were full, and each family had a bag of gifts to take home for the morning. A warmness spread through Caroline's body. It was a feeling she hadn't felt in years, and she was suddenly excited about everything around her. The Christmas tree was brighter than it had been. The presents gleamed in the candlelight from the centerpieces. Everything looked promising.

As the last of the families made their way out the door, Lauren pulled out a chair next to Caroline and sat down.

"They are such a nice family," Caroline remarked.

"They were thrilled with the bags you brought. I can only imagine the looks on their faces tomorrow morning when they open their gifts."

"They're lucky to have you."

Lauren tilted her head. "You made their Christmas. Not me."

Caroline shook her head. "No. *All* of this made their Christmas. The gifts are the icing on the cake. The real gift is tonight. How many families get to gather together, surrounded by people that care enough to do all this?" She waved her hands in the air around her.

"It conveys a beautiful thing. The community coming together and helping each other out. I just provide the space."

Caroline looked at her through the corner of her eye. Lauren would never agree that without her none of this would have happened.

"Did I mention I had quite a bit of help?" Her voice was confident, as if she was trying to make a point.

"Luke helped you?"

Lauren nodded slowly.

Caroline's heart flipped in her chest. He was all she could think about. She had been trying lately to embrace her past, to remember all the good memories without thinking about how hard it was now without her parents around.

Maybe she *had* been too quick to let things go.

"In fact, he left something for you." She held up her index finger and got to her feet, then disappeared down the hall. When she returned, she was carrying a small white box, with brown twine tied into a bow around it. A miniature glass bird dangled from the center of the bow. It was a Brewer's sparrow.

Lauren pointed at the bird. "You know, sparrows are known to symbolize joy and protection."

Caroline ran her finger along the bird's back. "There were sparrows the morning I was snowed in." Her voice was quiet, almost inaudible.

"Well, are you going to open it?"

Caroline smiled at Lauren, her eyes growing wide. "I'm afraid to."

"What are you so afraid of? He's a great guy. Sure, you have a lot of memories in that old house. Are you so set on forgetting them that you would risk not making any amazing new memories? I never met your parents, but from what you've told me about them, I'm pretty sure that's not what they would want for you."

The lump in Caroline's throat grew. She'd thought a lot about how she wished she could ask her parents what to do. Never, not once, did she ask herself what her own parents would have done in her exact situation.

She pulled on the end of the twine and watched the bow fall open, catching the bird in her free hand. She slowly lifted the lid of the box. Inside, she found a red piece of paper folded in half. When she pulled it out, it fell open. There was a note from Luke inside.

Come make new Christmas memories in your old house. No strings attached.

—Luke & Ella

Energy pulsed through her body. Was it excitement? Fear?

"He knows about the house?"

Lauren shrugged. "He figured it out somehow."

Caroline stared at the paper in her shaking hand.

"You knew about this?"

"I had to get him to help me decorate somehow." She winked. "So, are you going to go?"

Would she go? She didn't know. She wanted to. This was the first time she felt in her heart that she needed to be in that house with Luke.

She wasn't sure what had come over her, but she finally felt that, maybe, she could find a way to make it work. Maybe he could help her through it.

The energy grew stronger. She had to try, didn't she? She opened her mouth, the energy eager to escape. "I think so."

❈

Christmas morning brought with it a beautiful fresh blanket of snow. Caroline had gotten out of bed early and spent some time watching the Christmas tree glow in the early morning sun. When she had finished her cup of tea and eaten a scone she had bought the day before, it was time for her to go to Luke's.

The drive to her old home was a peaceful one. There was barely anyone on the road and birds were flitting around from tree to tree. There was a silence in the air that only came on snow-clad Christmas mornings. As she drove, her mind wandered to the night before and the joy that everyone had shared in together. It reminded her of the parties her parents had thrown when she was a child. Everyone was so happy to be in each other's presence. Songs were sung, sweets were eaten, and hugs were exchanged. The gifts were more of an afterthought. They weren't what brought everyone together, but more of an extra surprise.

She drove through the town; all the business lights were off, as everyone was home celebrating. Green garland were strung from one lamppost to another, their brilliant lights leading the way, hinting at the coming evening. Tonight, the town would be buzzing with townsfolk handing out cookies and hot chocolate. At the tree, everyone would gather to sing carols and then head to the community center together where a potluck dinner was held.

On the seat next to her, the peppermint brownies gave off the most heavenly scent. They would be a big hit at the potluck tonight. She had used her mother's recipe that everyone had loved. She couldn't wait to see the look on Cathy's face when she would taste them. She had always said she would be able to recognize those brownies anywhere.

When Caroline finally came to the driveway of her old home, she stopped herself. It was Luke's home now. As she turned off the road, she noticed something new. He had planted two poinsettias, one on either side of the driveway. A gold ribbon wrapped around the bars of the gate that now stood open; a large wreath made of dried branches, holly, and pine cones hung in the middle.

A tinge of excitement ran through her body.

The drive was slick with snow and there was some ice under the trees that hung over, creating shade that would be much appreciated in the summer. As she pulled up to the clearing, she drew a breath. He had decorated the home perfectly, with elves and reindeer and lights. She hadn't seen the house look this beautiful in years.

As she drew closer, she saw that along the strings of lights there were little figurines of different birds, each of them wearing tiny scarves.

She put the car in park, took Ella's gift in her hand, and made for the stairs. Hanging from the eaves was a new sign that read

Welcome to Sparrow's Haven

Her jaw dropped. It was perfect. In the distance, the Brewer's sparrows sang their trilling song. It was pronounced in the quiet that stood around the house. The smell of the Christmas trees, heavy and potent in the cold, calm air seemed to encourage their singing.

She reached the top of the stairs and took a deep breath. Her pulse was racing. Today, she wasn't feeling any sorrow or loss. In the moment, all she felt was excitement for what was to come.

38

Luke

The knock on the door startled Luke and Ella. They were sitting at the table, eating breakfast—pancakes baked with red and green confetti sprinkles, doused in a strawberry sauce, and covered in whipped cream. Next to Ella on the bench sat a beautiful doll she had received that morning. Luke lifted his eyebrows at Ella.

"Who could that be?" Her eyes were wide and there was a smear of strawberries on her cheek.

Luke shrugged. He hadn't mentioned Caroline to Ella in case she didn't show up. He wasn't even sure it was her. It could be anyone. "I'll go check. Finish your breakfast." He reached over and rumpled her hair.

He walked slowly, trying to channel the calm he hoped to portray if it was Caroline at the door. When he placed his hand on the knob, he was sure his heart was about to leap from his throat. He took a deep breath and opened the door.

She was more beautiful than he had ever seen her. There was a warmth that was radiating from her. The joy in her eyes was unlike any he had seen before.

Every worry that was in his body vanished. She was here.

"Merry Christmas." Her voice was quiet. She looked unsure of what to do or say.

He couldn't keep from smiling. "Merry Christmas."

Ella came running in from the kitchen and poked her head out the door. "Caroline!" she cried and threw her arms around her.

Caroline kneeled and hugged her back. When Ella pulled away, she held out her doll. "Look what Santa brought me."

"She's beautiful. She looks just like you."

Ella beamed, then grabbed Caroline's hand and pulled her through the doorway.

"Whoa, hold on there, Ella. Let's let Caroline take her time." Luke turned to Caroline, making sure she was still okay. He knew coming back to her old home was difficult for her.

Caroline stepped in far enough for Luke to close the door behind her. He waited to see her reaction to what they had done to the house. He watched as her eyes tracked around the room and took in all the changes that had been made.

Her jaw went slack and Luke held his breath. Had he gone too far? Was the house too different?

Her hand reached up to cover her mouth. Her eyes were glassing over. Luke stepped forward and placed a hand on her elbow. "I'm sorry. I thought that if we—"

She shook her head. "It's so different." Slowly, her lips curled into a smile. "It's amazing. The tree looks perfect in front of that window. I never would have thought of that." She pointed to the tree in what used to be the dining room. Two arm chairs and a sofa along with a bookcase filled the space now.

"Can I show you around?" He led her across the hall to what used to be the living room. A fire glowed in the fireplace that opened onto a dining room table set with red linens, green place mats, and silver snowman napkin rings. Plush curtains framed the picture window overlooking the tree where the sparrows liked to sing and play. "Our dining room. Or what Ella likes to call the 'bird observation room.'" Sitting on the bench by the window was a stack of papers and a box of crayons. There was a colorful sketch of a bird on the top.

While she took it all in, he let his hand fall next to hers. When she didn't pull it away, he slipped his hand around hers and led her to what used to be the library with the dark wooden walls.

A television hung on the wall across from the L-shaped sofa. Bins of toys were sprawled about the room. Ella sat on the floor changing her doll's clothes. Luke held out his free hand. "The family room."

Caroline didn't say much, but her eyes told him everything. This is what she had needed. A little help in the right direction. He looked around the room, trying to see things the way she might. He looked at the framed pictures and the birds he had painted on the wall to look like they were flying around the room.

Throughout the house, he and Ella had placed bird figurines. Ella liked them because they made her feel like her mom was watching over them. Luke thought they would help change the look of the house, and maybe help Caroline feel like she could move forward.

"We just had pancakes. Would you like some?" He led her into the kitchen. Ella followed, doll in tow.

"I'm going to get dressed, Daddy." Ella ran up the stairs as Luke nodded to her.

There wasn't much he could do to change the kitchen, so he and Ella had creatively determined where everything should go. They put utensils in drawers they normally wouldn't be in and placed the mixing bowls in the open shelves where the daily dishes are typically kept. "We are going to paint the cupboards. We just didn't have time."

Caroline whipped around so that she was facing him. "You did this all for me?"

He rubbed the back of his neck, landing his hands in his front pockets. "Cathy told us this used to be your home."

"Ah. Cathy." She nodded.

Luke reached for her hand, squeezed it, then whispered, "Why didn't you tell me?"

She looked away, out the window for a moment, then looked back at him. "I saw how much you loved the house. I didn't want to stand in the way of your and Ella's future."

He wished he could go back in time and fix all of it. He wanted to take away all the heart-ache and loneliness she must have felt over the past few weeks while he obliviously, selfishly planned his future.

"I want you to be in our future." His voice was hoarse. "I'm sorry I was so wrapped up in everything going on in my life that I didn't notice you were struggling."

Caroline shook her head. "I should have found a way to tell you. You were so kind in trying to help me through the Tour of Homes. I never could have done it without you. I never thought I'd be able to enjoy myself while decorating again."

"You enjoyed decorating?"

Caroline tucked her hair behind her ear. "I really did. Not at the start, but as time went on, you showed me that you can decorate to inspire people to feel the Christmas spirit. That's what drove me through the whole project. I wanted people to feel the happiness that my parents provided me when I was growing up."

A warmth spread through him. Knowing that he had brought her joy and helped her through some of those memories made his heart grow. It meant there was a chance that this could still turn into something.

"Memories are tough." He looked at Caroline. "I want to help you build new memories, while honoring the old ones. I had no idea being here brought you so much pain. I can't imagine how it must have felt to be here after all that time, and listen to us go on and on about this town and how great the house is."

She sniffled. "I want to keep those memories close. I don't want to forget them. I also want to make new ones."

He waited for her to say *with you,* but she didn't. He was starting to think that maybe helping her get through this was enough. Maybe that was his role in her life. Knowing that he helped her move forward would have to be enough for him to go on. Even if it wasn't.

He tried to swallow his feelings.

"I understand."

"If it's okay, I'd like to start making those new memories today. With you and Ella."

He lunged forward and threw his arms around Caroline's waist, lifting her into the air and spinning her around. When he put her down, they were face to face. She was so close he could smell the sweet scent of her.

He leaned in until their lips were lingering barely an inch apart, and he kissed her. His heart raced as fireworks exploded in his mind.

The thud of Ella's feet sounded on the stairs. He pulled away from Caroline to find her smiling, with a starry gaze in her eyes.

She cleared her throat and turned to Ella. "I brought you a present. I left it under the tree."

"There's some under the tree for you, too." Ella raced into the other room, then called down the hall, "Come on, let's open them."

Luke and Caroline walked hand in hand to the tree and Caroline sat on the sofa. Luke reached under the tree and went through the presents, handing Caroline hers one at a time, and then passing a box to Ella.

"Daddy, you missed one." Ella pointed to the bottom of the tree. It was a big green box with an even bigger red bow.

Luke took it from under the tree. The tag simply read

To Ella, Merry Christmas

He placed it next to Ella.

"I'm saving that one for last," she said. Ella tore the bow off the present from Caroline and pulled the lid open. Her mouth gaped as she pulled the dress out by its shoulders and held it up. "It's beautiful."

Caroline smiled at her.

"Open yours." Ella hopped onto the sofa next to her.

Caroline opened the boxes and found a new scarf, a pair of mittens, and a winter hat.

"Daddy let me pick them out for you."

"I love them. Thank you."

Ella bounded back to the floor and placed the green box in front of her. She picked it up and held the weight of it in one hand, then the other. Then she shook it and pressed her ear against it. Finally, she placed it in front of her and kneeled beside it. "I wonder what it is," she whispered.

Caroline leaned back into the sofa to watch as Luke put his arm around her.

Ella rubbed her hands together and very slowly untied the ribbon. She rocked back on her toes, took a deep breath, then very carefully popped the lid off the box. She peered inside and froze.

"No way!" she squealed while diving her hands into the box and pulling out a Fluffy the Dog. She held it up triumphantly. "I knew Santa wouldn't forget." She grabbed her doll and Fluffy the Dog and ran into the family room to play.

Luke and Caroline sat there in silence, taking in the feeling of Christmas spirit that was heavy in the air.

"That was really sweet of you, to give Ella the Fluffy the Dog. I don't know what to say. Thank you." He wanted to express his gratitude to her for thinking of Ella, but didn't know how.

Caroline's lips squeezed together. She looked at the tree, then back to Luke. She shook her head. "I didn't. That wasn't me. I brought her the dress." Her eyes darted back to the tree, searching the base of it for clues.

"Then where did the dog come from?"

"It wasn't you?"

"I looked everywhere. I couldn't find a Fluffy anywhere. You got the last one."

They locked eyes again, searching each other for the answer, checking to see if one of them wasn't telling the whole truth.

Luke thought back to when she had arrived. She only had one package with her, and she put it down by the tree as soon as she saw it. Had the other gift been there then?

Caroline turned her attention back to the gift, then slid off the sofa and onto her knees.

"Luke." She motioned for him to join her. He did.

She pointed to one of the corners of the box that had a small dent in it. Luke looked closer. There, next to the dent, was a smudge. He ran his index finger across it then rubbed it with his thumb and smelled.

He jolted his head back, confused. "It's soot."

Caroline looked at him, wide eyed. Luke looked back at her. They both giggled.

"Santa never lets anyone down." Caroline's voice was calm.

"He sure doesn't." Luke leaned in and kissed her again, this time knowing that it was the beginning of the rest of their lives.

39

Caroline

A warmth like no other wrapped around Caroline as she spent the day with Luke and Ella. For lunch they ate biscuits stuffed with chicken and cranberry sauce while they sat at the dining room table watching the birds outside. Ella occasionally let out a chirp that led into her version of the sparrows' trilling song. Caroline and Luke laughed as she would flap her arms and bounce around the room.

The day felt easy to Caroline. She didn't know if it was that the house looked different, allowing her to envision it as a new part of her life, or if it was that she knew she had Luke's support. Every now and then, she would catch him watching her, checking for any signs that she may be feeling stressed or that the memories may be overwhelming her. Each time she would smile back, letting him know that she was fine, then he would softly rub his thumb across the top of her hand.

It was the best Christmas she had had in many years. She was able to take it all in without the worry of it triggering any unexpected memories that would dampen the spirit of the day.

When it was time to head to the town for dinner, Caroline took a deep breath. She was excited and nervous, and anxious to share her hometown with Luke and Ella. This was when the town was at its best. They had already fallen in love with Brambling Falls, and they hadn't even experienced the best part yet.

As they walked to the car, there was a lightness in Caroline's chest as she told them about the tree and the singing and the hot chocolate and the dinner and all the wonderful things they were about to experience. She knew she was rambling on, but she couldn't stop herself. Now that she was there and embracing this new chapter of her life, she had so much of her old life that she wanted to share with them that she couldn't hold it back.

When a memory she wasn't expecting caught up to her, she would stop and give it a moment. She would allow herself to recall how it had been. Then she would grab Ella lightly by the hand and share the memory with her and Luke. She knew it wouldn't always be this easy, and the sadness was sure to come again, but it was much lighter now that she had Luke and Ella rooting for her.

They parked a few blocks from Main Street. Caroline knew it was going to be crowded and parking would be difficult. As they made their way down the small road lit by the colorful Christmas lights draped from street signs to trees and back again, she suddenly recalled a Christmas that her dad had been sick. He had come down with the flu a few days before, and while he had been able to join them for presents in the morning, it had been a particularly cold winter, and her mom had decided he should stay home.

Like tonight, they had parked a distance from the tree where the festivities would start. As they had walked together, her mom had been very quiet. She remembered asking her what was wrong, and she had replied, "It's hard to celebrate and get on with life when those we love are not with us. But we need to do our best to hold them in our hearts and continue to live life to the fullest."

At the time, Caroline had just nodded. She missed her dad that night, but she knew she would see him again in a few hours. Tonight, as she was there with Luke and Ella, and trying her hardest to carry her parents in her heart, she understood the true meaning of what her mother had said.

Just then, Ella looked up at her and took her hand. Luke matched their pace and took Ella's other hand.

"I hope they like our food." Ella looked down at the ground, seemingly worried.

"I think they're going to love it." Caroline squeezed Ella's hand and gave her a reassuring smile.

"Who wouldn't love marshmallow gooey pie with graham cracker crust and cherry pie filling?" Luke sounded like he couldn't wait to try it himself. He raised the bag that held their pie and Caroline's dessert and inhaled deeply.

"You're right." Ella perked up and skipped ahead of them as they turned onto Main Street. It was a sight to behold. It had been impressive before, and cheery. Now, there were no words to describe this tiny town. As she took it all in for the first time in many years, she wasn't sure how she had ever left Brambling Falls.

The lights shone brightly as the snow gently fell to the ground. It was warmer than it had been in the past few days, so Caroline was sure that the snow wouldn't stick. It was as if it were a Christmas gift from above to the town, just for that evening.

"I can't wait for my sister to see this when she arrives tomorrow." Luke caressed Caroline's hand as he spoke. She looked to him and smiled.

The jingle of bells and children's laughter flowed down the street, luring everyone to the center of the activities. Once they passed the only two-story building on Main Street, Caroline stopped and lowered herself to Ella's level. Ella paused beside her, anxious to hear what Caroline had to say.

Caroline only pointed past the buildings ahead of them and to the right, where they could now see the top of the Christmas tree, its golden star shining brightly high above everything else.

"Wow," Ella whispered. In the quiet, carols poured through the air from a distance, causing Ella to bounce up and down. "Can we go faster? I don't want to miss anything."

"Don't worry. It's not going anywhere." Caroline got back to her feet and pointed to Cathy's Diner. "Let's stop by and see if she needs help with anything."

The diner's lights were on, and they could see Cathy preparing for the evening festivities. They knocked on the door and pushed it open. When Cathy saw Caroline standing there, holding hands with Ella, she stopped what she was doing.

"Caroline? You're back again?" She came running over to them and hugged her tightly. Caroline hugged her back. In the middle of their embrace, Ella joined in and threw her arms around the two women. When Cathy pulled away, there were tears forming in her eyes. "It's not Christmas without you in this town."

Caroline playfully swatted at Cathy. "Christmas just isn't the same anywhere else."

Then Cathy turned to Luke, a finger pointed directly at him. "And you, you had me believing you and Caroline were nothing more than business." She hit his shoulder with the back of her hand. "You're a sneaky one, aren't you?"

Luke shrugged. "Well, I'm glad I was wrong." He reached an arm across to Caroline and rubbed her back.

Suddenly, Cathy stopped what she was doing and held her nose high in the air. "Wait a second. Do I smell…? Caroline? Did you bring your mother's famous brownies?" Her eyes were wide in disbelief.

Caroline nodded.

"Have you tried these brownies? I have long been dreaming about these tasty treats. I can't wait to get my mitts on one." She rested her hand on Ella's shoulder as she spoke.

"Well, then I guess I can't, either." Luke laughed with them all.

They helped Cathy carry her bags to the community center for the potluck. She had brought a large dish of the shepherd's pie as well as some pastrami sandwiches and a large bowl of creamy chicken soup.

They made it to the Christmas tree right as everyone was gathering. It began as a soft murmur in the crowd, but soon, everyone was singing along to "We Wish You a Merry Christmas" as they stood around the tree. An old man was handing out candy canes to all the children, and there was a table nearby with cups of hot chocolate for the kids.

As she stood watching everyone around her, and familiar faces began to materialize, a flood of happy memories hit her. These were the people she had spent her childhood with. They had helped shape her into the person she had become. They were the ones that had been there and helped take care of her when her parents suddenly passed. And they were here now, welcoming her back with open arms.

Luke stood beside her. She could feel his eyes on her as she took it all in. He stepped closer and whispered in her ear, "Are you okay?"

She looked at him with tears forming in her eyes and nodded. For the first time in a very long time, they were tears of joy. "I'm great. This is the most wonderful Christmas."

She watched the people around her come together as a community and welcome Luke and Ella as if they had always been there.

In that moment, she realized that there was no other place that she would rather be than in Brambling Falls with Luke and Ella.

THE END

Author's Note

Thank you for purchasing *Selling Christmas*. I know there are so many books to choose from, but you chose this one, and for that I am very grateful.

I hope you enjoyed it. If so, it would be really nice if you could share this book with your friends and family on Facebook and Twitter.

I would also love to hear from you and hope that you could take some time to review it on the platform where you purchased it. Your feedback and support is an invaluable resource that helps me to improve my writing craft and will make future books even better.

If you would like to keep up to date with me, you can subscribe to my newsletter at www.Angelinagoode.com, and I'll send you a bonus chapter for one of my other books, *The Average Girl*.

Acknowledgments

This book started one Thanksgiving when I announced to my family that I was going to write a Christmas novel… and have it done before Christmas. I would like to thank my family for cheering me along every step of the way, even though it took much longer than through Christmas.

Thank you to my parents for taking us to Oregon every summer. The days spent breathing in the fresh air and experiencing life outside of the big city helped mold me as a person. My imagination wouldn't be what it is without those trips. Your never-ending support and feedback (eh-hem, praise) of my writing is what keeps me going.

Thank you to Christine, for reading my first, second, third, etc. drafts and always giving your honest opinion. Also, thank you for helping me name my characters, and remembering what I've named them when I've forgotten.

My beta readers are truly what makes my writing make sense. Tish Kato, Erin Pieronek, and Katie Demick, you are amazing people. Your feedback is invaluable. I am forever grateful for your keen eyes and kind hearts, guiding me to inconsistencies and suggesting necessary details.

Thank you to Damonza for creating the book cover of my dreams.

And a huge thank you to my copy editor, Michael Schuler, for making *Selling Christmas* perfect.

Finally, my husband and children are forever patient with me disappearing with my computer to write, while still managing to check in on me every few minutes. I would be so lonely without you. I hope I make you proud.

The Average Girl

1

J sit quietly at the Starbucks on the corner of Wilshire and Santa Monica Boulevard, pretending to work on my laptop. Two tables away from me and next to the condiment counter sits my client, Sarah, drinking coffee and pretending to read a book. This is our second day at this Starbucks and we have already been here for forty minutes. I am beginning to wonder if we should re-evaluate our plan.

Suddenly a wave of hushed excitement spreads through the store. Everyone's eyes are glued to the swinging front doors as Ryan Scott strides through with his shoulders back and chin up. Everyone's eyes, that is, but Sarah's. She looks at me without turning her head, and I give her the tiniest of nods before spinning back around to stare. She responds to my nod by feigning interest in her Jane Austen novel.

Great Sarah! Keep calm. I know you want to burst inside, but play it cool.

Ryan's eyes quickly scan the room. Before they return to the menu board, they briefly linger on Sarah, the only person who appears *not* to notice him. He orders his grande latte with a double shot of espresso and leans smugly against the counter with his arms folded across his chest. He appears to be staring into space, yet every few moments his eyes fall back to Sarah, who has still *not* looked up from her book.

The barista calls his name, and he pauses to make sure every-one hears it before he reaches for the drink. When he turns around, Sarah is beginning to pack her things, leaving the Austen novel on the table. He heads toward the condiment counter for his regular three sugars. Just as we had rehearsed, Sarah stands up, still focused on packing up, and he tries to pass her. He stops for a moment, Sarah blocking his way.

Thank goodness these celebrities are creatures of habit. It makes my job so much easier.

"Oh, I'm sorry, I didn't see you there." She breathes calmly as she speaks to him. She slings her navy-blue Coach bag over her shoulder and smiles, her head leaning to the side, her eyes soft.

"That's all right," Ryan responds. He stands waiting for her to move but blocks her exit. He half smiles at her.

"Okay then." Sarah glances toward the door behind him, still smiling.

"Oh, now I'm in your way," he declares as he steps aside and watches Sarah move toward the door. "Wait, hey, your book!"

I exhale. The one contingency worked as planned. Should be easy from here on out, as long as she sticks to the script.

She stops and turns back, hiding her smile. Ryan stands there, holding her book in his hands. "Jane Austen, huh." He smirks. "I'm shooting a movie based on one of her books next month."

"Oh, you're an actor. What book?" she asks, pretending not to know.

"*Pride and Prejudice*." He seems intrigued by Sarah's indiffer-ence. "Well, here you go—" He ends his sentence by fishing for her name.

"Sarah," she finishes for him.

"Sarah," he repeats, revealing a slow, sexy smile, "maybe we can have a cup of coffee next time." He holds out the book but is not loosening his grip.

"Yes, maybe." She takes the book from him, and he lets her.

"Thanks." Then she is out the door. Ryan turns and grabs his three sugars, looking around the room again to make sure everyone is still watching. Before he finishes stirring them in, I am out on the street and dialing Sarah's cell number.

"Wow! That was unbelievable! I can't believe it worked!" she cries.

"You were awesome! Did you see the way he looked at you?" I ask.

"Yes! I did!" She pauses. "Thank you so much, Olivia. You really made my dream come true. I mean, I never could have done this without you. I'm going to recommend you to all my friends," she rattles on.

Thrilled that all went as planned, I head back down Santa Monica Boulevard toward my office.

A tall, gawky girl in her late teens stands in the waiting room. She has a goofy smile and frizzy brown hair. She shyly stares back at me through her outdated glasses, waiting for an invitation into my office as she taps her arm softly, rattling her bracelet.

"You must be Becky." I gesture for her to enter.

She is young, just out of high school and reminds me a lot of myself when I was a teenager and hanging around outside Brad Griffin's hotel, waiting for my moment.

"So I hear you can work miracles." She sits down softly in the big purple armchair and looks at me, her face filled with hope.

Her innocence brings to mind just how far I've come. Five years ago when I started this business, meeting clients at coffee shops and working out of my apartment, I had no idea what a demand there would be for my services. I always knew people wanted to meet celebrities, but I quickly learned they were willing to *pay* quite a bit for that privilege, especially if they could meet them in a way that didn't make them look foolish. And when it comes to fans, the saying "birds of a feather flock together" has never been more true. Almost all my clients, like Becky, find me through past clients.

I sit behind my desk, folding my hands and smiling. "That's what they say. I help my clients realize a plan that will manifest their greatest dreams. I help everyday people, like you, meet big-time celebrities in a situation that's comfortable for everyone. You get to be yourself, and the celebrity doesn't even know you're a fan."

Becky nods, encouraging me to continue.

"I do all of the research and planning, everything from facilitating a makeover to word-feeding into earpieces, if necessary. The perfect scenario? I arrange for you to 'accidentally' meet your idol in an unremarkable but cute way. If the meeting goes extremely well, I can help arrange another 'accidental' meeting. Many of my clients, though, are happy with a simple encounter. Just knowing that, for a few moments, their idol's attention was focused exclusively on them in some normal, average way is enough."

"Well," Becky says, "I'll need a miracle because even if I do run into Robert Collins, I don't think he'd so much as glance in my direction." Her expression momentarily shows defeat, and then she looks down briefly and smiles again. "I grew up with my dad, and his sense of style is, well," she points to her dark purple and black-striped turtleneck and brown plaid pants, "I guess you could say style was low on the priority list."

"I wouldn't worry too much about style; that's fixable," I assure her. *I must look intimidating to her in my high heels, fitted blouse, and tailored pants.*

"So you can help me?"

"As long as you're eighteen or over, I can help you."

She nods encouragingly.

I slide my welcome packet across the desk. "First we have to get through some paperwork. You know, stuff my lawyer makes you sign." We go through the document page by page. First she must acknowledge that I will help her meet her idol and nothing more, and that there are no guarantees. Then we go through the confidentiality clause: She is not ever to mention my services to anyone (unless it's a referral), especially not to her idol. I am always cautious when I first meet a client. Since a large part of my success depends on anonymity, I can't risk working with anyone who might publicize what I do to celebrities.

Next is the "no stalking" policy. I don't provide home addresses or phone numbers, and if my clients demonstrate any stalker qualities, I immediately cancel our agreement with no refunds. Finally, if the idol is mean or rude, I am not responsible. This section of the contract is particularly important when meeting the celebrity who Becky is interested in.

"How much is this going to cost me?" she asks.

"Well, it all depends what path we take. We can do the—"

"I don't just want to bump into him: I want Robert to notice and remember me; I want to be beautiful. Whatever it costs. I've finally received my mom's inheritance, and she died fifteen years ago. What do you recommend we start with?"

I hesitate. I don't want to insult Becky, but there is a lot of work to do. Robert Collins is notorious for being, well, a prick, to put it nicely. The last client who I helped "accidentally" meet him was abruptly knocked over by his dog. And he didn't so much as offer to help her up. He just looked at her nursing her twisted ankle and walked on by. Luckily that particular client was satisfied with the honor of being able to tell everyone about "the time she got run over by Robert Collins' dog." The only upside of Becky choosing to meet Robert Collins is that he's the star of *Little Town, Big People*, his own sit-com, which means he is often out and about and seems to stick to a regular schedule.

"Well, I should warn you, Robert is pretty well known for—"

"He's a jerk. I know. I'm a huge fan. I've read it all. He punches photographers, flips off journalists, and refuses autographs. That's why I need to be spectacular, not…this. I get that. I just need you to help facilitate it."

I can't help but wonder what a sweet girl like Becky sees in a celebrity with such a bad—and accurate—reputation. Part of me wants to take her under my wing and help build her confidence. Help her find a *real* guy, a real *nice* guy. Or help her realize she doesn't need a guy at all. But that's not my job. So I push all the helpful thoughts out of my head and focus on the task at hand.

"Right." I look Becky over again. She may not be winning any awards for style, but she is smart. "Okay, then the best way to do this is for you to forget you like him."

"What?"

"For you to be spectacular, as you put it, in his eyes, you can't be a fan. You need to be just some average girl." I get up and walk around my desk. I sit in the lavender armchair next to her. "Unless you want to have sex with him just once and never hear from him again. In which case, please, fall all over him. But that's not the kind of service that I provide."

She leans forward in the chair, intrigued.

I continue. "You need to be the kind of girl who doesn't appear to care that he's in front of her. Act like he's in your way. *That* will get his attention."

"You want me to be rude?" She looks at me with a wrinkled brow.

"No, not rude. Just nonchalant," I correct her.

Becky wrinkles her lips and nose, deep in thought. "Hmmm. I never looked at it that way."

"And that's why you've come to me." I give her a reassuring smile as I rest my hand on her arm.

"Okay," she starts, "this could work." Hope is growing in her eyes.

"Let's get started then." I reach out my hand, and she shakes it.

I finish making all of Becky's appointments and set another date to meet with her. "Your homework is to get every bit of information you can on Robert Collins. Legally, of course. I have a lot, but who knows, you may come up with something I haven't come across."

"Great!" Becky yelps as she grabs her pleather bag and stands up. "I can't wait!"

My file on Robert Collins is pretty thick with information and previous clients' results. In my five years facilitating accidental meetings, not one that involved Robert Collins ended how I had hoped. At least Becky is going into this with realistic expectations. I start looking through my notes.

"Walks his German shepherd every morning," *not trying that ploy again.* "Gets Mercedes-Benz washed every Tuesday," *unless Becky has a very expensive car, probably not a good idea to meet there.* "Visits (allegedly) psychologist every Wednesday," *not useful… unless, nah, forget it.* "Gets manicure every Thursday morning," *this is a possibility.*

After drawing out a loose plan for Becky, I flip through a tabloid, looking for more information on Collins; then I stop short on page twenty-three. Right there, midway down, is a picture of the happy couple—the woman starting to show her "baby bump," as the writer puts it. This isn't just any couple, though; this is Brad Griffin and his noncelebrity wife, essentially the couple that, unknowingly, started me in this business. His bright blue eyes jump off the page as much as they did on his posters, which adorned the walls of my teenage bedroom. He has definitely aged but is still as sexy as he was when I, along with millions of other teenage girls, screamed our hearts out as he belted out his pop ballads on the stage.

I can clearly remember claiming my spot with the throngs of fans outside his hotel, hoping he would make an appearance, at which time he would, of course, take one look at me, see what a big fan I was and fall instantly in love, and we would live happily ever after.

Clearly none of that happened, and I know now, it rarely if ever does. Instead, he waited until his popularity died down and found a cute young lawyer who probably never even thought of driving by his hotel. They got married two years later, and that's when it dawned on me: Celebrities don't want to marry, or even date, a "fan." They don't care how many concerts you've been to or how many times you've seen their movies. They want a normal, average girl and a normal, average relationship—they want a normal, average life.

The day of Brad Griffin's wedding, I decided to do for other women what I wish someone had done for me.

I can still feel the blood rushing to my cheeks when I think about how naïve I was, waiting outside a hotel in a tour T-shirt. Not to say he didn't appreciate my (and everyone else's) fandom. It was just not going to get me where I so badly wanted to be—by Brad's side.

Sillier still, as I linger over Brad Griffin's photograph, I feel my heart starting to race.

In order for my business to work, I have to be calm and collected around celebrities. Otherwise I could never be successful at my job. But Brad Griffin is one celebrity who, even to this day, I couldn't keep it together if I saw him.

This, however, I've decided to think of as an asset since it feeds my passion for my work. Remembering how strongly I once felt about a celebrity helps me relate to my clients and sell my service. Balancing empathy with the fact that I would *never* fall for a celebrity keeps me levelheaded so I can get the job done.

The phone starts ringing and brings me back to reality. I take a gulp of soda and turn the page.

"Olivia Fowler speaking," I chirp into the phone.

It's Maria, my best friend. We have plans tonight to go to

James Beach, a popular but mellow bar by the beach. My brother, Preston, and his friend Charlie are joining us, as usual. "We still on for tonight?" she asks.

"Yeah, I'm gonna head home in a bit. Want to grab dinner before?" Maria only lives two blocks from me, so impromptu dinners are common.

"Wish I could. I need to stay a little longer and help my boss with some stuff. Something wrong? You don't sound quite as chipper as usual." There is no point in hiding anything from Maria. "Oh, I know. You read the tabloid, didn't you?"

"Yep. The happy couple is pregnant." I sigh.

"Just remember, Liv. If it wasn't for that very lucky baby mama, you would still be fetching coffee and punching numbers into a calculator for a boring, old accounting executive, instead of running your own business." An accountant herself, she is practical by nature and often provides a reality check. Maria comes from the *everything happens for a reason* school of thinking.

"I know, but give me some credit. I'd like to think that after five years, I wouldn't *still* be fetching coffee." I giggle into the phone.

"We hope," she giggles back. "I'll see you at nine."

2

can hear the music playing across the street as I get out of my car. I feed dollar bills into the parking lot pay machine and glance around, searching for a familiar car, though don't find it.

Apparently, I'm the first one here. James Beach is in an inconspicuous building on a dark street in the residential area of Venice. If not for the music pouring out of the open door, you'd never know there's a bar there. Every month, Preston, Charlie, Maria, and I get together at one of our favorite hangouts. This one happens to be Charlie's. Even though he lives on the other side of town, he still comes here whenever possible. Maria and I occasionally join him.

When I get to the door, I smile at the bouncer, and he winks back, moving aside to let me in. It's not too crowded for a Friday night. I make my way to an empty stool at the bar. I'm about to order a drink when I'm interrupted.

"She'll have a Tom Collins, and I'll take a Jack and Coke," he says to the bartender, and then faces me. "That's still your drink, right?"

I turn to see a tall curly-headed blond smiling at me. "Charlie! I thought I was the first one here! I didn't see your car outside." I've known Charlie, or maybe I should say Charlie has known me, my entire life. He and my brother met in preschool and have been best friends ever since. He likes to tease me by reminding me that I used to run around the house singing Barry Manilow songs, wearing my mom's nighties. There are videos to prove it. Thanks, mom.

"I got a new car when I got promoted. Has it really been that long since we've hung out?" He leans over and gives me a big hug. "Let's go find a table." I open my purse to pay for my drink, but he motions for me not to. He grabs both our drinks and leads us to an empty table on a ledge above the main floor.

"You got promoted? That's great! Preston didn't tell me!" I hold up my glass toward his and yell "cheers."

After he takes a swig, he leans over. "I'm an actual publicist. No more administrative work. It's pretty cool. Instead of running copies and putting together gift bags for the big boss, I have people putting gift bags together and running copies for me. I'll even get to plan some big events in a few months."

"That's amazing." I smile at Charlie, and he smiles back.

He opens his mouth to say something.

"Hey, friends!" I look up to see Maria waving her arms at us; Preston's a few feet behind her. "What's up?" She slides in between Charlie and me and gives us each a hug, her gold and silver bangles jingling on her wrist.

"Hey, big bro!" I say as I lean over to half hug Preston.

"Hey, Liv. Where's the waitress?" he asks, as he raises his head and tries to flag one down. "I need a drink. What do you want, Maria?"

"I would like that one, right over there." She smirks and discreetly points to a tan man in jeans and a polo.

"And she hasn't even started drinking yet!" Preston says, as he rolls his eyes. "How about a martini?"

"Yeah, I guess that'll do too." She shrugs and sits down. "It's pretty happening here. There are quite a few hotties tonight." This last part is directed at me, but I can see that Charlie overhears it and leans toward Preston to say something. Preston shakes his head.

I'm not one for meeting men at bars, but Maria's fine with it. In fact Maria doesn't mind meeting men at libraries, coffee shops, gas stations, salons—She seems to meet men everywhere she goes. Petite, blond, and with a smile that lights up an entire room, she's hard not to notice. In fact, it's not uncommon for drinks to regularly show up at our table throughout the evening. Tonight she looks spectacular in her skintight jeans, semisheer tank top, and adorable strappy heels with a zipper down the front.

"Check that one out," she whispers and nods toward the pool table. "He's a cutie. And look, his friend is even hotter."

I see the man she's checking out who is about to hit the cue ball. He is handsome, in a Maria sort of way. He has a shaved head, and his clothes are rather nondescript. Standing directly across from him is his friend. Not very tall and with dark and thinning hair, he is unconventionally attractive. The way he holds the cue, supporting it while gently guiding it in the right direction, makes me wonder how it would feel if he were holding me instead. He is wearing jeans that hug him in all the right places, held up by a silver-studded black belt. His white T-shirt is tucked in the front, not in the back. This friend, though, catches my eye for another reason. He is a celebrity.

"Maria! Do you know who that is?" I breathe. "It's Daniel Walker!" By now, Preston and Charlie notice who we're looking at. "I need to write this down." I yank my phone out of my purse and start to type.

"What are you doing, Liv?" Preston asks.

"It's Daniel Walker," Maria explains. "She needs to take notes in case one of her clients requests him," she says matter-of-factly and flashes him a big *duh* smile.

"You're really writing down what he's doing?" Preston squints his eyes and shakes his head at me. "Isn't that a little intrusive?"

Here we go again. When I left my steady, boring accounting job at William-Nelson to start my own business, Preston had a fit. He went on for literally forty-five minutes, without stopping for a breath, as to why it was a bad idea for me to start my own business and, of all things, to help people meet celebrities. I wasn't surprised by this. He's always been very by-the-book. He graduated valedictorian from our high school, with honors as an undergraduate from Harvard, and from Wharton business school. He now works for Platinum Equity as an analyst. It's a wonder we've been so close all these years.

"No, Preston, it's not. He's in a public place, playing pool. It's not like I'm spying on him while he's taking a shower."

"But it's his private life, Liv," Preston argues. "If he wanted everyone to know about where he was, he would've called a press conference."

"If he doesn't want anyone to see him, he should remain in the privacy of his own home," I fight back. Maria is still watching Daniel Walker, and I can tell she's scheming.

"He comes here every week," Charlie interrupts. "He's a regular."

I look at Charlie and so does Preston. Why is he telling me this? He knows what I do for a living, and he's my brother's best friend. I would think, of all people, Charlie would loathe my career choice since he's a publicist and is all but friends with some of the same celebrities that I track. But he's never chided me about what I do. He's actually never said anything at all. So why he's suddenly offering his help, I'm not sure. Preston gives him a dirty look and then shakes his head. Charlie mouths *what?* back to him.

"Would you like me to follow him into the bathroom and ask him his underwear size? Would that help your clients?" Preston mocks me.

"I help them *meet* famous people, Pres, not buy them underwear."

"I just don't understand why you can't support yourself in another way. This is beneath you, Liv." Preston gives me a pitying look. "You're so smart. You should be doing something meaningful with your life. Something the whole world can know about."

"What she does makes people happy, Preston. There's nothing wrong with that. And the celebrities don't even know what's happening," Maria explains. She has always been supportive of my business. While working at an accounting firm she isn't able to gather much celebrity information, but she is helpful in another way. She is my human guinea pig.

Five years ago when I started my business, I had a lot of ideas as to how to meet celebrities, though no proof that they would work. It would have been foolish for me to test them out on my clients, so Maria cheerfully offered herself as a subject. Thanks to me, I think she's met more celebrities than all of the hosts of *Access Hollywood*, combined.

The first celebrity we tried to meet was Kyle Evans. He is more of a B-list celebrity, always playing the best friend in movies. I eagerly searched every tabloid and read hundreds of blogs looking for information about him, setting up resources for future searches. I had found online—on his fan club webpage, of all places—that he plays soccer every Sunday evening. By looking in the *Hollywood Hitlist*, a database that lists all Hollywood heavy-hitters agents, publicists, and home addresses, I discovered that he lives in Santa Monica (I now consider *Hitlist* my best friend. It costs a small fortune to gain access to but is well worth it). A few phone calls to some soccer-playing friends in Santa Monica informed me that there is a co-ed league that plays at one of the local private school soccer fields on Sunday nights, and Kyle Evans does indeed play on one of the teams.

So I had Maria join a team in that very same league. She started playing soccer every Sunday night, me on the bleachers loyally watching. *Loyally watching* Kyle play, that is. I studied his game technique and personality, calculating ways for Maria to get his attention when their two teams played each other. Five weeks later, the two teams were finally set for a match, and I had a plan formulated.

I had Maria wear a small amount of makeup and play with her hair down (which she fought me on, even though all women know men like girls with their hair down). The first half of the game she acted as if he wasn't there, playing her hardest as she had the previous weeks. But shortly after halftime, things changed. It was time for her to take control. She stuck near him, waiting for him to go for the ball. As soon as he did, as planned, she went in for the steal, the steal that was meant to fail, and it did. Right as she was about to kick the ball, she "tripped" falling flat on her back by his feet. In the process of tripping "accidentally," she got her feet caught up in his.

Once she was down, the referee blew his whistle and everyone stopped. Kyle squatted beside her, sincerely concerned for her well-being, apologizing repeatedly. I was sitting on the bleachers secretly cheering. He then put his arm around her, scooped her up, and walked her off the field to the benches. My plan had worked. But it didn't stop there. As the two teams continued their game, he ran off to find her some ice. When he returned with it, Maria insisted that she was fine and that he should go back and play. Not only had my plan worked, but it had succeeded beyond expectations.

At the time, it seemed odd to me that it could be so easy to meet a celebrity and control the outcome. Maria has always said it's fate, that I'm meant to do what I do. I think I might agree.

"I'm skeptical," Preston says. "Your clients are so obsessed that they're happy when you get them in the same room as their idols."

"Wanna bet?" Maria seems to have taken over arguing for me. "We'll prove the power of what your sis does, right here, right now." *Oh, no. What does she have in mind,* I wonder. She turns to me and smiles. "Liv is going to make it so that Daniel Walker notices me." She pats me on the arm.

"You're on!" Preston takes his wallet out. "I'll bet you one hundred dollars that it doesn't work. You willing to take that bet, Liv?"

"Yes she is!" Maria answers for me, again.

I'm getting nervous about this experiment. "But guys, I don't have any information on him, other than that he plays pool at this bar." I'm not sure I can orchestrate an 'accidental' meeting without researching his background. I usually have at least a month to collect information and come up with a plan.

"I've got some information; I'll help you. Take the bet," Charlie says. Again, Preston shoots him a dirty look. "Sorry, man. But I think she's got a good thing going."

"Okay then," I smile, "you're on!"

Charlie starts to tell me everything he knows about Daniel. "He comes in every Friday to play pool. That guy with him? He's always here, almost nightly from what I hear. I think his name is Jamie. He's pretty popular with the girls, but Daniel seems to be a little reserved. I've only seen him leave with a girl once."

"Does he seem friendly? Have you ever seen him sign an autograph or allow a fan to take a picture with him?" I ask. What I'm asking is very important. A friendly celebrity requires a different type of plan than a surly one. They are harder to get to since they are nice to everyone; they assume everyone likes them. Great for a fan, but not so great for a fan who wants to appear not to be a fan.

"Yeah, he always signs autographs. Look, someone is getting one now." Charlie nods his head toward the poolroom area. Sure enough, two women in short skirts, low-cut tops, and smiles that stretch from ear to ear are giggling as Daniel enthusiastically scribbles something on some pieces of paper. He hands the two pieces of paper to the girls, and they almost knock him over as they lunge forward to give him a hug. Recovering quickly, he kindly puts his arms around their waists and smiles as though he greets everyone that way, even his housekeeper, giving them a big bear hug. The girls euphorically prance down the stairs, and Daniel casually turns back to finish his pool shot.

"I've never worked with him personally, but he has a reputation for being up for any charity event. Publicists love working with him. I don't think he has a girlfriend. He was last dating Kristen Landers, you know, from the TV show *Dark Dreams*. But she left him for some rocker." Charlie swirls his drink in his glass as he talks. "Ummm, that's all I can think of, unless you want to know what movies he's been in." He lifts his eyebrows at me.

"No, that's perfect. I think I can come up with something. I just need a minute." I try to drown out the thumping of AC/DC's "You Shook Me All Night Long" and come up with a plan.

Maria is bobbing her head and lightly shaking her shoulders to the music when I interrupt her. After I give her the details, she smiles and pulls out her compact to make sure she looks pretty.

"Okay, I'm ready." She beams.

Per my directions, she walks up to the pool table area and approaches the table. Daniel and his friend stop playing and look at her. She smiles and starts taking something out of her pocket. Daniel chuckles and, before Maria can say anything, grabs a napkin, signs it, and says something to her as he hands her the napkin.

"Ha! See! I told you it wouldn't work!" Preston stands up and does the touchdown dance. "Hand over the money, sis!"

"Wait," I insist. He stops dancing and watches.

Maria, now frowning, shakes her head and says something. She pulls a dollar out of her pocket, holds it up, and then puts it on the table. We see her mouth, "Next game," and she begins to walk back to us.

Daniel holds up his hand and speaks loud enough for Maria to hear him over the music. "Hey, we're just finishing this game. Why don't you play the next one with us?" he shouts, as he crumbles the napkin and throws it away. His friend chuckles and whispers something into a nearby girl's ear. She scoots closer to him, and he puts his arm around her.

Charlie looks at me and starts chuckling. Smiling at Preston, I shrug my shoulders and say, "See, I told you it would work." Preston mumbles inaudibly and takes out two fifty-dollar bills and throws them on the table. Now I jump up and do the touchdown dance.

"Dance all you want. I still think it's wrong." He takes a gulp of his drink.

Maria winks at me and heads back to play pool with her new friend. He welcomes her by giving her a cue stick and putting out his hand for her to shake.

The rest of the evening passes as Preston and Charlie debate over which sport requires more muscle: baseball or golf. I sit there waiting for Maria to return and save me from my brother and Charlie's male-centric discussion. I occasionally glance over at Maria and see that she's getting along well with Daniel. Really well. So well that what started as him helping her with her pool technique—standing beside her and guiding the cue stick—has evolved into his standing beside her with one arm around her waist and the other holding her drink.

I have to hand it to Maria. I may have the know-how when it comes to arranging "accidental" meetings, but she has the know-how when it comes to producing instant adoration. Finally, after an hour and a half, she stops by our table. She has a huge smile on her face.

"Wow! You just had to play one game to prove the point, Maria. You didn't need to spend all night with him," I tease.

"Yeah, about that," she giggles, "I'm going to head out with Dan. I'll call you tomorrow, and I'll see you all next week for my birthday." She gives me a big hug and heads back to Daniel who's waiting and watching nearby. Preston rolls his eyes and looks away, disappointed in me.

"I didn't plan for that," I sigh. "Poor guy. He's gonna fall in love with Maria, and she's never gonna call him again."

Charlie starts laughing. "Yeah, Liv, because I'm sure he's never done that to any girl."

Preston chuckles. "All right, I'm heading out. It's been fun. Next month let's meet up in my neck of the woods." He man hugs Charlie before leaning in to give me a hug. "I'm proud of how successful you've made your business, Liv. I just wish it were something a little less…gray."

"Thanks, Pres. I'm taking off too, as soon as I finish my drink." I smile, assuming Charlie will leave with Preston. Charlie turns to me. "It's okay, I'll be fine by myself," I assure him.

"I'll wait with you. Wouldn't want you to walk out by your-self." Charlie sits back down. Preston gives him a weird glance.

"See you, man." He pushes his way through the crowd and disappears.

"You really don't have to stay on my account. I'm sure I'll be fine. I'm parked just across the street," I insist.

"I don't mind at all." He smiles as he sets down his drink. "I figure I may have information you might be able to use for your business."

I look at him quizzically. I'm not sure why he is so willing to help when my brother has made it blatantly clear that he doesn't approve of my career choice. I think about Charlie's behavior throughout the night and how my brother kept looking at him. I don't know what's going on; regardless, I figure I can always use good information. Especially from a reliable source like Charlie.

"Well, if you really want to help." We finish our drinks as I ask a multitude of questions and Charlie answers them all as best he can. Once I've exhausted all questions, I put down my empty glass and start playing with the straw.

"Thanks, Charlie. This is exactly the kind of information I need to help me figure out the perfect circumstances for a meeting. You're the best!" I give Charlie a big hug and notice that he's blushing before he turns to push a chair out of our way. "Should we go?"

"After you." He smiles at me. "And here, call me when you're looking for any information about any other celebrities. I'll help however I can." He hands me his card with his new title, even though I have his number programmed in my phone, and then he steps aside to follow behind as I walk out of the bar.

www.ingramcontent.com/pod-product-compliance
Lightning Source LLC
Chambersburg PA
CBHW021811110726
47902CB00006B/1747